LOVING TAYLOR

REGAN URE

Cover Design: © L.J. Anderson, Mayhem Cover Creations

Formatting by Mayhem Cover Creations

ISBN: 978-1-911213-23-9

I dedicate this book to my niece Jade.

Table of Contents

Chapter One

I lay on my back. My head hurt, and my hand touched my forehead gently. It felt like an army of elephants marching through my head. I recalled the memories of the night before. It wasn't like I'd gotten drunk enough to make a mistake I would regret, I knew exactly what I'd been doing.

Movement beside me brought me back to the present as I opened an eye and took in the sight of a beautiful naked girl, barely covered with the sheet, curled up by my side. Remembering our night together made me feel empty inside. The fleeting closeness of sex was over and the hollowness in my chest tightened, reminding me of what I was still trying to outrun.

Girls in my life were like everything else: temporary, fleeting and disposable.

I stared at her for a few seconds, trying to recall her name, but all I could remember was that it started with a T. Was it Tracy or Tiffany? It didn't matter. The initial attraction and reprieve she'd held were gone. After this we would be strangers in the hall, barely acknowledging each other, which suited me just fine.

My attraction to the opposite sex didn't usually last long. One night was all I could offer. I'd dealt with enough situations to know I couldn't give more. If I wasn't up front it would lead to tears and hopes I couldn't live up to.

I swung my legs over and sat up. I needed space.

I'd been clear and up front when I had promised her sex with no strings attached. Most guys my age were shallow and sex-crazed but my issues went deeper than that. This wasn't something I was going to outgrow.

The girl in my bed sighed slightly in her sleep. I grabbed my jeans from beside the bed and pulled them on, wanting to escape before she woke up.

I needed coffee. My stomach grumbled slightly. And food.

Without a backward glance to my overnight guest, I left my room. The party we had thrown the night before had been wild. The living room downstairs was a mess. Discarded cups —some empty, some not—littered most of the surface area.

"You look like crap," Slater, my best friend, said as I walked to where he was casually leaning against the doorway to the kitchen.

He was tall and similarly built to me. I had dark blue eyes with short black hair and he had light blue eyes with light brown hair that was slightly longer. If we had similar hair coloring, we could probably pass for brothers.

We even shared a love for tattoos and piercings. He had an eyebrow ring. I had both ears pierced as well as my lip. He sported a tattoo sleeve like mine. Some tattoos were markings from our past to remind us of what we had overcome.

"So do you," I replied bluntly. He looked tired but I knew it wasn't the result of our party. He never got enough sleep. Demons from his past kept him awake at night. Mine kept me from finding solace in anything in my life.

He shrugged. "At least one of us got laid." He straightened up when I passed him into the kitchen.

"You had a girl ready to tear your clothes off last night," I reminded him as I got a mug and poured some coffee into it. "What happened?"

"She was too clingy," he admitted, running a hand through his hair.

He shivered like it was something to be afraid of. And the truth was we were. We avoided girls who wanted more than one-night stands like the plague.

And virgins. It didn't matter if they understood and agreed with the rules of what a one-night stand entailed, I believed it was just in their genetic make-up to get emotionally attached to their first lover. It was just easier and less of a hassle to avoid them altogether.

We had enough to deal with without adding girls who had dreamy ideas of love and commitment to the mix. I knew I had issues about getting involved but I had nothing on Slater. He took it to a whole other level.

"You want coffee?" I asked.

"Nope. I've already had three."

"I don't know how you can function with such little sleep."

He shrugged. "I just do."

There was that familiar sadness in his eyes. It had been there for the last few years. I knew the reason why and it wasn't something that could be fixed. It was difficult to watch him wrestle with it and not be able to do anything about it. He only managed a few hours of sleep a night. It was his conscience that kept him awake in the middle of the night when he was alone with his thoughts.

I couldn't choose my family but I could pick my friends.

Slater, I had picked. I trusted him more than I trusted anyone. He was more family to me than the people who shared my DNA. In our world trust didn't come easily. We had fought hard to get this far, getting a chance at a normal life with opportunities we hadn't had before.

Even if all of this came from him, I thought with some distaste, refusing to think of the man who hadn't wanted me. It opened the wound to the little boy inside of me who had desperately wanted a father. I shoved it aside, refusing to allow it to play on my mind. I tried to always live in the moment, refusing to remember the past or look to the future.

Footsteps and the arrival of our other roommate stopped any further talk of Slater's weird sleeping habits.

"Hi, guys," Eric said in greeting. I gave a brief nod in acknowledgement. I wasn't close to Eric at all. He was just another person who lived in the house with us. He was pretty quiet and kept to himself, which was fine with me. There was something about him that put me on edge, but I couldn't explain why.

He was the type of person who tended to blend into the background. He wasn't a hit with the girls, if anything he usually gave them the creeps. He had short blond hair with light green eyes. It wasn't like he was unattractive. I figured it was his inability to socialize well that hampered his luck with girls.

"Hey," Slater said to him, friendlier than I had been.

I don't know why I had posted an ad for another roommate but I had. It wasn't like I needed the money. I owned the house. Maybe it was because I didn't like the quiet. The silence brought thoughts and memories I didn't want to deal with. I rubbed the back of my neck but it did nothing to soothe my slight hangover.

"Next time I'm staying away from the tequila." I was convinced the last two shots of the lethal alcohol on top of what I already had drunk was the reason I was feeling like this.

Slater shook his head with a slight smile. "Famous last words."

Eric poured some coffee as Slater and I talked. Eric wasn't a big talker but even with the few conversations we'd had there was something about him that nagged at me. I just put it down to the fact that the friendship I had with Slater was deeper because of our similar backgrounds and the years we'd spent watching each other's backs.

We only had to share a look to know what the other was thinking. He was the brother I had never had.

"Sin." The sound of my name from feminine lips brought our attention to my overnight guest, who was dressed in one of my shirts. I noticed she had touched up her makeup.

Slater raised an eyebrow in my direction. I knew exactly what he was thinking. Clingy. He left the kitchen so I could take care of our unwanted visitor. Eric followed, leaving me alone with the hot blonde who'd shared my bed.

She walked to me seductively like the fact that we had shared a night together made us something more. I felt the irritation vibrate up my spine when she slung her long blond peroxided hair over her shoulder. I'd been clear but I could tell she was already working up to more.

"I woke up alone," she whined slightly, which made me frown. The sound of it was like nails scratching against a blackboard.

"I needed coffee." I gave a one-shoulder shrug, hoping I wouldn't have to be too abrupt to drive my message home.

I didn't want to hurt her, that's why I had been brutally honest about what was on offer. One night. Nothing more.

Her hands went to my waist and she leaned closer. The sweet scent of her perfume intensified my headache. It was enough. I put my mug down on the counter before I eased her unwanted hands from me.

"Don't make this more complicated than it needs to be."

She looked slightly taken aback when I removed her hands.

"We were so good together," she whispered, looking a little surprised I was giving her the brush-off.

It annoyed me. Even though I had been clear and up front, she was still trying to make more out of this than there was.

"It was sex." My voice was firm. I couldn't allow her to get any ideas about me. My only consolation for my guilt was the fact that it would hurt her more if we dragged this out.

"Why stop when it was so good?" The hoarse voice and fluttering eyelids only annoyed me more.

"It's over." My tone was cold.

She frowned when she realized I was sticking to the rules we had originally agreed upon.

"Your loss," she said, throwing me one last lingering glare and pouting before she left in a hurry.

I didn't sleep with the same girl twice. The temporary solace I found with the physical closeness of being with a girl didn't allow me to emotionally connect with them. I knew there was something wrong with me but I didn't know how to fix it.

Girls were geared to get emotional during sex and I had learned if I kept it to one night it decreased the odds of girls wanting more. Shaking my head, I picked up my mug again.

A few minutes later Slater walked in with a grin on his face. "She was not happy."

I shrugged. "She knew the rules."

It wasn't my fault she changed her mind. I drank some of my coffee and began to feel better.

"You want some cereal?" Slater offered me.

"That cardboard crap will kill you," I said, walking over to the fridge. I needed a real breakfast.

I got the eggs and put them on the table, when I heard the distinct sound of high heels on the steps before the front door opened and slammed closed.

"Not a happy customer," Slater commented with a growing smile.

"I am," I countered with a confident smile that hid the emptiness I felt inside.

Girls were complicated and I didn't do complicated. It led to emotions and that usually led to heartache. It only took one look at my mother's life to see how emotions clouded your judgment and led to mistakes.

Girls viewed me as a challenge. They wanted to tame the bad boy, but I would never change.

Later that night a couple of friends had come over, joined by a few more. It had grown into a party that was still in full swing.

The music was blaring but I loved the noise. It kept me from thinking too much. The hot girl who was trying to flirt with me was also a welcome distraction. Her toffee-brown eyes sparkled when she smiled at me suggestively. From her seducing eyes to the way she trailed her tongue across her bottom lip, I could read the signs. She was making sure I knew she was available.

I leaned closer and she whispered in my ear, "I really like you."

She didn't know me, I hadn't revealed anything about myself. It was lust, pure and simple.

Girls, I knew well. Within the first five minutes I could tell if they were too clingy or not geared to one-night stands.

Some girls couldn't keep physical and emotional separate, and those were the ones I had to keep far away from.

I was barely managing with my past, I couldn't deal with more. The temporary peace I achieved from being with a girl dictated my actions. To the outside world I was a player with an appetite for women, but that was a lie.

I had issues about letting people get too close. I didn't need a shrink with degrees to link it back to my childhood. Maybe it wouldn't have been so bad if my mom had been loving, but I'd spent my childhood craving the love most children took for granted.

For the most part it was something I didn't concentrate on. There was nothing I could do to change my past. Some bad choices mixed with a hard upbringing had molded me into the person I was today even if some of those mistakes echoed in the nightmares that plagued me from time to time. There were lots of kids who grew up with less than stellar childhoods so I wasn't unique.

Slater was also a prime example of a messed-up childhood that made it difficult for him to let people close. We were two scarred people who knew how hard life could be. It had helped us understand each other and it had bonded us together, closer than our families.

Pulling myself back to the present, I gave the girl who was still trying to flirt with me a slight smile that I knew made girls weak, while I debated taking her upstairs to my room. She was beautiful but I bet she looked even better naked. My eyes trailed over the swell of her breasts as I imagined what she would look like with nothing on.

I never bedded drunk girls. It was a rule I lived by. It ensured there were no misunderstandings the next morning. I felt the familiar pull in my veins at the thought of running my hands over her body and making her moan with contentment.

"I've seen you around campus," she said, her hand on my arm covering part of my tattoo sleeve. I nodded distractedly.

I allowed my eyes to wander around the party to see if I could find Slater in the throng of people. He'd been talking to some girl and I wondered how it was going.

Slater didn't have any problems picking up girls and they usually gravitated to him but he was pickier with his choices than I was. I was emotionally scarred and Slater was worse but, knowing his childhood had been a lot harder than mine, I understood why. I was the only one who knew about his past.

I was still scanning the crowd, looking for Slater, when my eyes meshed with a pair of blue eyes attached to one of the most beautiful girls I had ever seen. Any thought of Slater or the girl who was still talking disappeared out of my mind.

The girl with the striking, large blue eyes with shoulder-length platinum-blond hair looked at me tentatively as I continued to stare at her. She was breathtaking. Her figure was incredible in a short mini skirt and top.

I continued to hold her stare, wondering how long it would take her to look away. My look was direct and suggestive. The side of my mouth tipped in a half-smile. I'd used it on so many girls and knew it was lethal. Her eyes were fixed on me. The warning bells were already going off but I ignored them. I could tell by the way she pulled the red mini skirt down that she wasn't comfortable in what she was wearing. She lacked the confidence I was used to in the opposite sex.

It either meant she was innocent or she hadn't had a lot of experience. My blood heated at the thought of her. A quick sweep of her long legs quickened my pulse.

"Are you listening?" the girl beside me said and I brought my attention back to her, suppressing the automatic frown at being interrupted.

"Sorry, I was looking for my friend," I explained without missing a beat.

My eyes drifted back to the girl with the blue eyes but she was talking to a girl I recognized.

Jordan. She was not a fan. I would bet she was probably warning the girl from getting involved with me. I experienced a moment of disappointment that I wouldn't get a chance to get to know the blue-eyed girl better. Just as well, I reminded myself. There was a vulnerability about her that had tugged at something inside of me. It was unsettling.

"Do you want to go somewhere quiet?" the girl said, continuing to flirt with me.

The attraction I'd felt only moments before had dwindled and I knew it had something to do with the blue-eyed girl across the room.

"Maybe next time," I told her. She looked disappointed but I brushed it off. "I'll talk to you later."

I escaped to look for Slater, and I found him in the kitchen talking to a girl. With a look he could tell I was agitated. He made an excuse to the girl and headed to me.

"Everything okay?" he asked. I nodded as I found a beer and opened it.

"Everything's fine," I insisted before I took a gulp from the bottle.

He never said anything more but he gave me a knowing look. I refused to open up about the reason I was feeling a little unsteady.

Two drinks later, I felt more collected so I left the kitchen. I couldn't stop myself from looking for the blue-eyed girl who had piqued my interest before, but I couldn't find her.

I pushed my way through the crowd dancing in the living room as I made my way across the room.

Chapter Two

Just as I broke through the crowd, I spotted her standing with her hand on the wall like she was struggling to stand upright. She swayed and I stepped forward to catch her. My arm wrapped around her and I held her up against me.

"Sorry," she mumbled, slightly slurred as she looked up at me. Her eyes were glazed over. I frowned when I tried to figure out how long it had been since I had last seen her. It hadn't been that long ago.

"You okay?" I asked, searching her eyes.

"Nope...I...," she said before she closed her eyes briefly. "The room...won't stop."

"I think you need to sit," I suggested, steering her to the stairs.

She stumbled on the first step and I tightened my arm around her to hold her steady. Three steps up she was struggling so I lifted her into my arms effortlessly and carried her up the remaining stairs. Inside my bedroom I kicked the door closed and set her down to sit on my bed.

"I'm sorry," she mumbled again, pushing the hair out of her face.

"It's okay," I told her. "We've all been there."

She put her hand to her head. "I can't...didn't drink...that much."

Her words echoed my previous thought.

"I'll get you some water," I said, heading to my bathroom. I got a glass and filled it halfway with some tap water.

When I returned I handed her the glass. She took a couple of sips but struggled to stop some water from tilting over the rim. I took it from her and set it down on the table beside the bed.

"You're hot," she said, looking at me dreamily as I turned to face her. Her statement took me by surprise.

"So are you." I allowed myself to openly appreciate her. I had rules I didn't break but I was tempted to throw them out the window to find out if her lips were as soft as they looked.

"You have a reputation," she revealed. Her tongue swept across her bottom lip and I felt a rush of excitement at the small action. I hadn't been so affected by a girl since I was a young boy. The years of experience had taught me control, which was swiftly evaporating with every second I spent in her company.

Jordan had told her about me. I wasn't surprised. The reputation I had did well to hide my inner turmoil and emotional inability to make a deeper connection with a girl.

"What did you hear?" I asked out of curiosity. I folded my arms.

"That you're kinda a manwhore." It was spot on.

I shrugged my broad shoulders, unapologetic of who I was.

"Would you kiss me?" she asked. Her big blue eyes on

mine made me question why I had stupid rules in place at all. Even knowing about my reputation hadn't been enough to scare her off. But most girls still had a belief that they could succeed where no girl had before.

"You've had too much to drink," I reminded her out loud. But it was also for my own benefit to remind myself I couldn't let this get out of hand.

"It's okay...." She shrugged. "I understand."

I frowned, trying to keep my distance so I wouldn't do something I would regret. I dropped my arms to my sides.

"What do you understand?" I found myself asking.

Her eyes lifted to mine and I could see a sadness in them. It wasn't the superficial type that was easily remedied. It reminded me of what I had wrestled with for most of my life. What was haunting her?

"I'm not pretty enough."

I shook my head. "You are...beautiful."

It was the first time I'd ever told a girl that. I'd used the words hot, gorgeous, pretty, but never the word beautiful.

Her eyes looked up hopefully to me. "Really?"

I nodded and found myself taking a step closer to her. I was playing with fire but I couldn't allow her to believe she wasn't good enough for me. The truth was I wasn't good enough for her.

She stood up and I reached for her so she wouldn't fall over. A protectiveness that felt alien to me surfaced. Her hands gripped my shirt as she looked up at me and I fought the urge to cover her lips with mine.

"I want you," she breathed with a sigh. My blood heated at the thought but I shook my head. She was too drunk to understand what she was doing, I kept reminding myself.

I was a lot of things, but I had enough respect for girls to never allow things to happen unless they were able to make the decision without the influence of alcohol.

"We can't," I said, taking hold of her hands. Her skin was soft and I resisted the urge to keep her hands in mine. I guided her back to the bed.

"You can sleep here tonight," I told her as I helped her remove her shoes before tucking her into my bed. I couldn't trust that another guy wouldn't try something with her in the state she was in.

She nodded as she laid her head on the pillow. Her blond hair cascaded around her, making her look even more alluring than before. I was only human and I couldn't take much more. I needed to get away to rebuild my defenses.

"What's your name?" I asked.

"Taylor." It was beautiful, just like her.

The only time girls ended up in my bed was for a night of passion, I'd never allowed a girl to just sleep in my bed. Feeling unsettled, I extracted myself from her before walking with determination to the door.

"I'll be back soon, Taylor," I told her with a backward glance. Outside my room I closed the door and leaned back briefly, trying to rein in my hormones.

I didn't want to go back inside but I was concerned she would throw up in her sleep.

Downstairs, I found Slater having tequila shots with some girls. He drank one and grimaced. His eyes connected with mine. Without any words being spoken he nodded.

I didn't want to tell him about the girl I had upstairs. It would be giving insight into something I wasn't sure I understood myself. He would just assume it was some random girl and that was okay with me.

He headed over to the stereo and turned down the music. A few moaned but Slater pointed to the door. "Party is finished."

I headed back upstairs as Slater began to get rid of people. I hesitated for a moment outside my bedroom door before I opened it and stepped inside.

Beside Taylor's side of the bed I noticed clothes that hadn't been there before. I walked to her side to check on her and she was still awake.

"You okay?" I asked, studying her flushed face.

She shook her head and pulled the covers back to reveal she was undressed and was sleeping only in her underwear.

My eyes swept over her and I was unable to pull my gaze away. She was stunning. The flimsy underwear didn't hide much so her soft curves were there for me to see. I tightened my fists, refusing to allow myself to reach for her.

"I want you," she whispered seductively with hooded eyes.

I reached out and pressed my finger to her lips to stop her from saying anything more. I could only resist so much and I feared she would push me to do something I would regret.

"If you feel the same tomorrow when you're sober then I'll give you what you want," I promised her. I wasn't sure I had the strength to turn her down.

Our eyes held for a moment before she nodded. "You have a deal."

That seemed to appease her. She gave me a dreamy look as she closed her eyes and turned in the bed, burrowing into the pillow. I lifted the covers and pulled them up to her shoulders. For a few moments I stood watching her. I stripped down to my boxers and got into the bed beside her.

I'd never been unsettled by a girl as much, and I was wary of how she made me feel. I liked the control I exercised over my life and who I allowed in.

My mother had called earlier but I had avoided it. It had been enough to put me in a bad mood, bringing back all the memories from a childhood I wanted to forget. But there was no erase button and they seemed to seep back when it was the last thing I wanted to think about.

My eyes drifted back to my bed partner who was sleeping soundly beside me with her hands neatly tucked in under the side of her face. She was the reason why I hadn't invited the other girl to stay the night to keep me busy so I wouldn't have time to think about things that I didn't want to think about.

I lay on my back with my arm across my forehead as unwanted thoughts of my mother entered my mind. She had changed but it still didn't erase her past behavior or how it had impacted on me.

Now that she was sober she was able to give me the love and attention she had been unable to give to me as a child but I didn't have the heart to tell her it was too late. What was done was done and there was no way to take it back. It had given me some consolation that it was something she regretted.

Despite everything she was still my mother and it was the reason I looked after her but for my own sanity and well-being I kept her at a distance. I usually visited her once a month and spoke on the phone with her once a week. Anything more than that I couldn't allow.

The soft murmur beside me pulled my mind back to the beautiful girl sharing my bed.

I let my eyes glide over her fine features while I remembered the softness of her hands in mine. I swallowed when I dropped my gaze to her lips.

Like I had promised her, if she still felt the same way in the morning I would give her a night to remember—as long as she agreed to my rules. Only one night and nothing more.

The next morning I began to surface. Remembering the girl from the night before, my hand searched the space beside me. It was empty and the sheets were cold. She was gone. I opened my eyes and confirmed what I already figured out.

Still struggling to wake up, I rubbed my eyes and yawned. Where was she? She'd been so out of it last night I had expected to wake up with her still sound asleep beside me. Had she gone downstairs to get some food?

I got out of bed and pulled on my jeans. I yawned again as I descended the stairs, listening for any sound that confirmed she was still in the house.

"Morning." The familiar sound of Slater eating a bowl of cereal from the sofa stopped me.

"Hey," I said. I didn't see Taylor but she could still be in the kitchen. My eyes went to the doorway of the kitchen.

"You looking for something?" Slater said, watching me.

I wasn't comfortable admitting to my best friend that a girl had slept over in my bed and nothing had happened.

"Or someone?" he concluded.

"Did she leave?" I asked, knowing he already knew about Taylor.

He nodded as he spooned another mouthful into his mouth.

I hadn't expected that. It was the first time a girl had left before I had woken up. Most girls stayed as long as they could.

"She left first thing this morning. She tried to sneak out."

I nodded, still trying to figure out why she had snuck out like that. I dropped down in the chair across from Slater.

"She didn't want to tell me her name." He was still grinning.

"Really?" I looked at him and he nodded.

"Why are you looking so confused?"

"Usually I have to shove them out the door," I

murmured, still trying to figure out the blue-eyed girl who had left me feeling disjointed.

"She looked quite mortified when I caught her trying to leave," he reminisced with a smile.

There was no sneaking in or out with Slater around. He was usually awake, and when he couldn't sleep he usually spent time on his laptop or watching TV.

His statement wasn't making me feel any better. Was I that bad that she had snuck out so she wouldn't be associated with me? That was a first. Usually girls couldn't wait to boast about bedding me. I didn't like the feeling of inadequacy her actions made me feel.

Was she embarrassed that she'd been so drunk? I began to think back to the night before. She had looked pretty sober when I had left to go to the kitchen during the party. I hadn't been there long and when I had found her again she had been so out of it. I frowned. I had an uncomfortable feeling that maybe someone had given her something.

"You okay?" Slater asked, watching my thought process across my face.

"Yeah," I said. I wasn't ready to analyze Taylor and how she made me feel. I didn't want to look closer for fear of where it could lead.

But what if someone had planned to do something to her? The thoughts that followed only angered me.

I left Slater to go back upstairs. While I showered I debated all the reasons to track her down to check on her and all the reasons to keep as far away from her as physically possible. Even though the reasons to keep my distance outweighed the reasons to locate her, I found myself downstairs asking if he had ever seen her around before.

"Nope," he answered. "But I could probably find out."

"Thanks."

A cup of coffee later and he had given me the dorm

number of where she was staying.

"I'll see you later," I told him as he dug into his second bowl of cereal.

"Later," he said with a mouthful of food.

The dorms were close by so I walked. It would also give me some time to prepare before I saw her again.

This is not a good idea, I reminded myself but I ignored my own warning.

Something beyond what I understood drove me forward. *I'm just making sure she got back to her dorm safe.* It was a blatant lie. The truth was I wanted to see her again and I couldn't explain why.

Slater had told me she was rooming with Jordan so I knew I wouldn't be getting a friendly reception if Jordan answered the door. Surprisingly Slater had never met her before. It was a good thing because his reputation was as bad as mine so she would detest him as much as she did me.

I took the stairs to the second floor. A couple of girls passed me on the way and gave me inviting smiles. I nodded politely but I was only there to see one girl.

I searched for the right room as I walked with my hands shoved into the front pockets of my jeans. There was no mistaking the tightening in my stomach. I was nervous. It wasn't a feeling I liked at all.

A few doors down I found the right room number and knocked. Jordan answered with a glare.

"Whoever you're looking for isn't here," she said with her usual hostility she always showed when dealing with me.

I looked over her shoulder and found Taylor sitting on her bed with an open book in her hands, looking a little surprised to see me. Her blue eyes were wide and her mouth was slightly open.

My visit was unexpected. Most girls would be fawning over me, but she looked like she would rather be anywhere else but here. She blushed at my direct gaze and Jordan noticed. She stepped back and looked between us.

Jordan's reaction told me that Taylor hadn't told her about last night. It confirmed that she was embarrassed and that did nothing for my growing feelings of inadequacy when it came to her. She didn't do anything like other girls, which made me feel like I was out of my depth.

See, she's fine, I told myself. *You can leave now.* But I didn't move.

Taylor stood and dropped the book onto her bed. She walked over to the door and her roommate moved back. She paused in front of me. Our eyes met for a moment before she stepped past me. I followed her down the passageway. She was probably looking for somewhere more private to talk.

A few girls walked by us as I trailed her but my full concentration was on her and the other girls passed in a blur without any acknowledgement from me. Taylor opened the door to the stairway and I followed in behind her. The door closed behind me as we faced each other.

Chapter Three

"How did you find me?" she asked.

"It really wasn't that difficult," I answered. "I asked around."

Slater had a network of people around campus. He could find anyone.

"What are you doing here?" She looked anxious as she dropped her eyes to the floor. She shifted slightly. My presence was making her nervous.

"I wanted to check on you." The answer came out huskier than I had planned.

Checking on her had been part of the reason but the truth was I was curious about the girl who didn't behave like the others. Although it was disconcerting, she was a breath of fresh air. But it made her more dangerous.

"Why?" she asked with a frown as she crossed her arms.

Granted I had used it as an excuse to see her again but to me it was a valid one. Why would she be questioning it?

She'd been so drunk and I had been a complete gentleman by taking care of her the way I had. Some guys would have tried to take advantage.

"It was just one night. Why would you need to check up on me?" she asked with suspicious eyes.

She wasn't making any sense.

"What are you talking about?" I shook my head.

"Last night was fun and...thanks," she answered, sounding unsure.

Then I began to figure out why she seemed to be on a different page than me. I cocked my head to the side, brushing my lip ring with the tip of my tongue as I studied her.

"How much of last night do you remember?" I asked.

Her hesitation confirmed what I already suspected.

"You don't remember," I murmured as I studied her.

She clasped her hands together then shook her head. "No, I don't."

"Trust me—sleeping with me isn't something you'd forget," I assured her with the usual confidence I had with girls.

She looked at me thoughtfully.

"I don't understand," she finally said. "If we didn't sleep together, why did I wake up in bed with you?"

"You were out of it last night, and you could barely stand," I reminded her.

She frowned slightly.

"I'm sorry," she mumbled as her cheeks heated with embarrassment.

There was still one thing nagging me about the night before. Maybe she would be able to shed more light on it.

"Did you take a drink from someone last night?"

She looked a little confused at my question.

"Why would you ask that?" she asked.

"I don't think you were drunk," I answered cryptically. The thought that someone had tried to give her something to incapacitate her to do something underhanded burned me inside my chest and I folded my arms as I dealt with the negative emotion.

"Do you think someone spiked my drink?" she asked with a frown.

I nodded and watched her reaction.

"Why would someone want to do that?" she asked.

The more time I spent with her the more innocent she came across. Surely spiked drinks would be something she would be aware of.

"You can't be that naive," I said, struggling to believe she didn't know that there were bad people out there who would do bad things to people. All you had to look at was the rape statistics for colleges across the country and it was usually some guy no one ever suspected. Not all bad people looked evil.

It annoyed me that she could have been innocent enough to take a drink from a stranger.

"There are bad people out there. People who will do really bad things given the opportunity," I tried to explain to ensure she never made the same mistake again. Next time I might not be around to stop it.

"That was why I took you up to my room. I don't want to think what would have happened to you if I hadn't," I added, dropping my arms to my sides as my hands balled into fists.

"Thank you," she mumbled, digesting the information.

"You're welcome," I mumbled back, not used to being thanked. Feeling uncomfortable, I shoved my hands into the pockets of my jeans. My eyes dropped to the floor briefly.

"Why was I only dressed in my underwear?" she asked, nervously meeting my gaze.

"You were trying to take advantage of me," I answered, unable to stop the smirk I gave her when I remembered how she'd made it clear she'd wanted me.

She blushed. Her response boosted my confidence.

"I'm sorry." She looked mortified.

"Don't be," I said with a shrug of my shoulders. "If you hadn't been out of it, I probably would have taken you up on the offer."

Her eyes widened in surprise.

Standing in front of her now, I felt the same instant attraction I'd felt for her the night before. My eyes drifted over her, openly appreciating her feminine figure. I knew we would be great together, the sex would be amazing, I could just tell.

"Uh...well...thanks," she stuttered, clasping her hands together nervously.

She acted like she didn't have much experience with guys and I liked that. She wasn't overconfident or clingy. Hell, she'd been the first girl to sneak out of my bedroom while I had slept.

"I'd better go," I told her, needing to put some space between us. The way she affected me with one slight look was enough for my self-preservation to kick in, telling me to get as far away from her as possible.

Despite the warnings, though, I wanted to see her again. I stopped by the door and looked back over my shoulder at her.

"If you ever want to take advantage of me when you're in a sober condition, you know where to find me," I offered with the confident smile that girls swooned over.

She looked transfixed, confirming the effect I'd wanted. I left, allowing the door to slam closed behind me.

On the way back out of the dorm a girl handed me her number and I pocketed it. Before, I would have been interested, but sleeping with her didn't hold the same appeal as it would have before.

Big blue eyes in my memory reminded me of why I was feeling so disjointed. Thinking about her only increased the nagging feeling in the back of my mind that I was playing with fire and this was one interlude I wouldn't walk away from unscathed.

When I got back to the house Slater was dozing on the sofa. My brief encounter with Taylor was still thrumming through me. The new feeling agitated me. I went to my room and closed the door, needing to be alone so I could keep a handle on my emotions.

I opened up my laptop and tried to concentrate on the assignment I was busy with but I kept reading the same sentence over and over again without the meaning sinking in.

Frustrated, I closed the laptop and stood up. I decided to go downstairs and I slipped into the garage. I had installed a punching bag a few months ago. Not only did I get a workout from it but it helped me work through emotions and memories that were difficult to deal with. I closed my fist and hit the bag. Again and again. Sweat beaded my forehead as I increased the speed of my punches. Left, right. Jab low, jab high.

My muscles tightened and flexed with each movement. My sole focus was hitting the bag as hard as I could, making me block out my emotions with the physical strain.

I stopped for a moment. Breathless, I held on to the bag and tried to catch my breath. Sweat poured down my face so I lifted my shirt and wiped my brow.

When the door that led to the house opened I discarded my shirt on the floor.

"You want to talk about it?" I felt Slater's gaze from the doorway.

"No."

But the door didn't close, and my best friend remained where he was, watching me.

"Someone spiked her drink," I finally admitted.

He knew who I was talking about.

When I finally looked at him, he was looking thoughtfully at me.

"You sure?" he asked.

"Yeah," I said, nodding as I tried to catch my breath.

"Who do you think did it?" he asked.

"I don't know." I shrugged. I didn't like that someone had come into my house and tried to do that to an innocent girl. My fists tightened.

But no matter how much it angered me, there was no way to know who had done it. I couldn't even prove that it had happened at all. I trusted my gut feeling that there was no way she could have gotten that drunk that quickly.

Thinking of her and what happened last night only reaffirmed what I had already noticed. She was innocent—far more so than the girls I usually associated with.

Even with the warnings going off in my head she still piqued my curiosity. Before, the first sign of innocence and I would have shut it down before it had a chance. Hell, I had given her an open invitation. What was I doing?

My mood hadn't improved later that day when my mom called again. For a few seconds I debated avoiding this call but I let out a sigh before I answered it.

"Sin." Her familiar voice breathed my name. Each time she said my name I was reminded of why she had named me that. I was a constant reminder of a mistake that had been life-changing. It didn't matter that I hadn't really had any part in it, yet I still carried the burden of it.

Most people would be comforted by the sound of their parent's voice, but not me. It set me on edge with an undercurrent of anger. I raked a hand through my hair as I leaned back in my chair, still facing my laptop. I'd been busy with an assignment.

"Mom," I said tightly, trying to soothe the anger that she created in me.

I understood she wasn't the same person but it didn't just erase a past I was trying to forget. But I could still feel that old, familiar fear of being alone with my stomach grumbling for my next meal. I gritted my teeth as I rode the spike of anger in my emotions.

I didn't owe her anything. But something stopped me from cutting her out of my life. Was it the fear that I would feel worse if I let her die without forgiveness?

"How are you?" she asked stiffly.

We didn't have a close mother-and-son relationship. We were still trying to fix years of problems.

"I'm fine," I said tightly, unable to pretend I was happy to hear from her.

She was sober now. But it was only because she had to give it up or die.

"How's college?" she asked.

"It's busy," I said as I stood up. Feeling restless, I began to pace my room.

"I miss you."

Her words cut right through me. Why hadn't she missed me when she had left me on my own to fend for myself? I hated how she could affect me still. The tightening in my chest made me want to disconnect the call and shake off the memories I didn't want to face.

"How are you feeling?" I sidestepped her previous statement, trying to push through the conversation like she hadn't said it.

"Some days are good, some days aren't."

I nodded as I held the phone tighter, biting back the retort that she had brought it on herself. Most days of my childhood had just been bad. I looked out the window, trying to concentrate on the activity outside, wanting to be anywhere but here talking to my mom.

"Do you need anything?" I asked before thinking it through.

Usually I kept our conversations short without any avenue to deviate into a deeper, more meaningful talk that I tried to avoid at all costs.

The silence only increased the foreboding that she was going to take the chance to ask for more than I could give her.

"No, I'm fine," she replied, letting me off the hook.

I suppressed a deep sigh.

"I have to go." The sooner I got this conversation done with the better.

"Okay...I love you."

Closing my eyes briefly, I rode the wave of unwanted emotion her words created in me. For her it was easy to say those words but I hadn't felt loved. I couldn't say words without meaning them and I wondered if I ever would be able to say those same words back to her.

"Bye, Sin."

"Bye."

I disconnected the call and sat down on my bed. For a few moments I stared at my phone, trying to get rid of the feelings I was experiencing. The urge to throw my phone against the wall and watch it shatter was difficult to fight.

I didn't know if we would ever get to a place where I wouldn't still feel anger at her. Alcohol had made her a completely different person. While she had been swinging the bottle and stumbling around in a drunken state, she hadn't cared about anything other than where her next drink was coming from.

The story of a young girl falling for a mysterious rich man only to be left pregnant and alone wasn't new. The strength and character of the girl would shape how she handled it. My mother had spiraled downward and she had never recovered from the rejection. I had been a constant reminder of that.

None of it had been my choice but I had paid the highest price.

The only thing I could thank her for was the fact that she hadn't brought other men into my life. She had been too deeply scarred by my father to allow another in.

Letting out a deep emotional breath, I tried to clear my thoughts. I didn't like to think about the man who was my biological father. He hadn't wanted me and even now it still hurt as much as it had growing up.

Raking my hand through my hair again, I felt my agitation grow.

The young boy who had been forced to toughen up because there had been no adult around to care still lived inside of me. It had been a couple of years since my mother had stopped drinking. Not enough time had passed to even consider forgiveness. But I wasn't sure it was something I would ever be able to do.

My assignment was still open and only half finished but I couldn't concentrate. I got up and went downstairs, needing time before I could tackle the rest of the work.

Slater was playing Xbox. When I slumped into the chair beside the sofa, he stopped his game.

"You wanna play?" he asked.

I shook my head. My mind was still tied up in the phone call.

"I spoke to my mom," I revealed.

Slater put the game controller down on the table. "How's she doing?"

I shrugged. "Same."

He studied me but didn't say anything. He knew me well. There was no need to push me, I would talk when I was ready.

"It's like she's waiting for me to forgive her." My eyes leveled to his. "And I don't know if I can."

If there was anyone in the world who understood, it was Slater.

"You don't have to," he reminded me. It was still my choice.

Would I have regrets if she died and I never got a chance to tell her that despite a crappy childhood and lack of love I forgave her? I didn't want to have to live with more guilt.

There was already plenty of guilt loaded on my shoulders. I had done things I wasn't proud of to survive.

"I didn't forgive mine," he said softly. The haunted look in his eyes reminded me that his had been worse. "And I don't care if I ever see them again."

My situation wasn't the worst. If Slater could deal with his, I could deal with mine.

He reached for the game controller and leaned back into his seat. The conversation was over.

My eyes caught a familiar tattoo on his tattoo sleeve. I looked down at my exact same tattoo. A star with the number seven in the middle.

Although it was surrounded by other tattoos, it stood out for us. It wasn't just some picture or design we had admired and decided to ink into our skin. No, it was more than that. For us it had been a path we had chosen. There hadn't been any other options at the time. Our survival had depended on it.

I didn't allow my thoughts to delve deeper into what the

tattoo represented for both of us. I had to find a way to keep my mind clear of things that only brought negative emotions. The only way to do that would be to concentrate on something that would erase all of those thoughts.

An image of the blue-eyed girl with platinum-blond hair appeared, suppressing anything else I had just been thinking about. The heaviness in my chest and the weight on my shoulders lifted. Not only did she look like an ethereal angel, she was just as innocent. Untouched by the harshness of this world.

I wanted her. There was no doubt about it. But if I touched her, I would taint her. Playing with a girl who didn't understand the rules would only bring trouble and pain. I rubbed my temple.

The right thing would be to walk away from her and make sure our paths didn't cross again. But a pull I couldn't explain made me hesitate.

Chapter Four

A week later I was still trying to shake off the feelings that remained after the phone call with my mom. I had pushed through every day, refusing to allow it to consume me. A lot of people didn't have it easy so there was no excuse, no giving up. With every hurdle I had ever faced I confronted it head on, but this was different. There was no black and white so I had ignored it, hoping time would allow me to push it to the back of my mind.

I had ensured I kept busy. If I wasn't working on an assignment I was hanging out with Slater. The girls had been plentiful. Between girls shoving their number into my hands or openly vying for a place in my bed, I hadn't had a shortage of attention from the opposite sex.

Usually I wouldn't have thought twice. Girls gave me a temporary reprieve from my thoughts and being alone. They gave me much needed peace even if it was only for a few hours. But not this week; for some reason they didn't hold the same appeal that they had before.

I don't know what was wrong with me. The cute blonde who had given me her number with a suggestive wink on Monday hadn't done anything for me. Neither had the brunette who had invited me back to her place for a one-night stand Wednesday night when Slater and I had gone out.

I was still feeling unsettled when Slater suggested we go to a party on campus. Maybe that was what I needed to get me out of my rut. Loud music, lots of people and girls who could help me forget everything for a few blissful hours.

At the sound of the heavy thumping music I led the way into the party with Slater following behind us. I gave a brief nod to a few people I recognized as I made my way to the kitchen to get a drink.

"What do you want?" I asked Slater when I surveyed the options in the iced buckets.

"A beer."

I got two out and handed one to him. I twisted the top off and took a gulp. We went back out to the living room and I allowed my gaze to flit from one girl to another.

"See any you like?" Slater mused beside me.

"There are a couple with potential." I gave the one closest to us an appreciative look.

She in turn swept a seductive gaze over me. I gave her an inviting smile. She was attractive but there was something missing. I couldn't quite put my finger on it.

Get a grip, I told myself. Since meeting Taylor, I was looking at girls differently and I didn't like it one bit. I didn't want change, I wanted my life exactly how it had been before.

Girls and parties with some studying in between so I could prove I was more than just some fucked-up kid with a bad childhood who had inherited loads of money from a father who hadn't given a shit.

Just thinking about that darkened my mood.

"That girl is here," Slater said, nodding in the direction of the front door.

I was about to ask him which one when I caught sight of platinum-blond hair. My eyes focused on the girl who had been in my thoughts regularly since I had last seen her. She was talking to her friend, Jordan, with a drink in her hand.

Keep away, the alarm bells blared in my mind, warning me to keep my distance from her. While she was distracted I let myself take in how the skinny jeans she wore left little to the imagination and the blue top complemented the exact same shade of her eyes.

But I knew she looked better without anything on. Images of her scantily clad in only her underwear when she had slept in my bed had been burned into my mind. I remembered how soft her porcelain skin looked and the slight point of her mouth that made me want to cover her lips with mine.

Stop it! I told myself. The quickening in my veins was a reminder of how attracted I was to her.

Why don't you screw her and get it over with? Could it be that simple? If it was, why was I still standing here debating whether it was a good idea or not?

The struggle inside me was making it impossible to make a clear decision when it came to her. I knew she was innocent but I kept telling myself she couldn't be that innocent. There were few girls who made it to college with their virginity intact.

Despite my attempts to keep my distance, I found myself making my way to her. Jordan was still glued to her side and there was no way I would approach her with her there. So I hung back, keeping my options for the night open with a few girls who had made it clear with bold looks in my direction that I was guaranteed a bed partner for the night.

But none of them kept my attention like Taylor did. As hard as I tried to resist, my eyes felt a magnetic pull to her.

Her big expressive eyes scanned the crowd. Jordan wasn't with her anymore. Before I knew what I was doing I was headed in her direction. I crept up behind her. The gentle sway of her hips to the music made me look at her appreciatively despite all the reasons to keep away from her.

I put my hands on her hips and slid them around her small waist. She smelled like an array of flowers on a spring day. My lips neared her ear.

"I didn't expect to see you here," I whispered huskily.

She leaned her body into mine and I had to fight the urge to spin her around. And do all the things I had been dreaming about, starting with a kiss that would take her breath away.

But my conscience made me release her slowly and turn her to face me. She lifted her eyes to meet mine. There was no doubt about the effect she had on me. It was like taking a step out of a plane without a parachute strapped to my back and free-falling.

The need to still touch her made me keep my hands loosely on her hips. I smiled at her, trying to mask the inner struggle between what I knew was the right thing to do and what I wanted to do. In response to my smile her eyes fluttered slightly, proving she was as affected by me as I was by her.

"I hope you haven't taken any drinks from strangers tonight," I told her, allowing my eyes to drop momentarily to her soft pink lips that I wanted to kiss.

She bit down on her lip, pulling her lip between her teeth. It wasn't helping me trying to do the right thing instead of embracing my attraction to her and throwing caution to the wind. She shook her head. Thank goodness she had learned an important lesson. The sight of Jordan returning caught my eyes and I knew it was time to make myself scarce.

"I'd better go before your friend gets back." I leaned forward, my breath fanning her cheek.

"I'll see you around, Taylor," I whispered before I left her standing in the same spot as I disappeared in among the crowd at the party.

On the outside I kept my composure but on the inside I was shaken. The brief encounter with Taylor still had my heart racing and I could still feel the softness of her skin beneath my hands.

Now there were more reasons to stay away from her. She was far too innocent for me to taint and I knew no matter how brief any encounter with her would be it would leave a lasting impression. We hadn't even slept together yet and she was constantly creeping into my thoughts uninvited. How bad would it be if I tasted her lips and felt her naked skin against mine?

With that, I made up my mind. I was still trying to make a life for myself and there was no room in it for a girl who I could feel more for than I was prepared to.

I got another drink and focused on finding someone else to help me forget about Taylor.

There wasn't a shortage so it didn't take long before I had a girl's undivided attention. I made myself kiss her like I wanted no one else, but I was fooling myself.

In between flirting with the girl looking up at me with a promise of sex for the night, my eyes drifted across the crowd, looking for a glimpse of Taylor. But before I could stop myself I saw a guy trying to chat her up.

I didn't like the way it made me feel. I frowned. My hand balled into a fist and I smothered my first reaction to beat the crap out of him. It was a territorial feeling that felt so foreign and I had no right to feel it. The twisting of my insides as I watched her talk to him was agony. Girls never held my attention long enough to feel that way about them. It only confirmed how dangerous Taylor was to me.

Let her go, my instinct told me but I struggled to pull my attention away from her.

"You okay?" the girl in front of me purred, pulling my attention back to the girl I was planning on spending the night with.

"Yeah," I said, ensuring all evidence of my reaction was gone.

Even with my attention on the girl gliding her hand up my chest I was still mentally trying to shake the image of Taylor with another guy.

No matter how much I tried to argue with myself and all the reasons to stay clear of her, it was difficult to ignore the impulse to watch her.

While talking to the girl, I found myself looking at Taylor and relief flooded me when the guy walked away, leaving her alone. But my relief was only momentary. She was beautiful, I could see guys already circling her. She wouldn't be alone for long.

You're playing with fire, I warned myself. To help myself remember what it felt like when I let someone get close and what inevitably followed, I allowed myself to remember a memory, one of many, when my mother had promised to clean up her act. I had been hopeful, talking myself into it even though she had told me the same thing many times before, but I had been young enough to believe it.

The disappointment I had experienced when I had found her only a few hours later when she had passed out on the floor, an empty bottle of vodka in her hand, was devastating. I could still remember the stench of cigarette smoke that hung in the air and the combined smell of alcohol confirming she had spilled some on the carpet while she had tried to drink herself into a stupor.

The feeling of disappointment was sharpened by the realization that I wasn't enough for her to try to change her ways. Eventually I had learned that people didn't change, and letting anyone close enough would only cause me to end up with heartache and pain.

I had conditioned myself to go from one girl to another, never making a deeper connection, to allow myself to always be in a position where I could walk away without a second thought.

Remember that feeling of pain. If you let her in that's what will happen. I swallowed as I fought to gain my control. I wouldn't allow some girl I barely knew to affect me like this.

She was dangerous and the only way to keep myself safe was to avoid her at all costs. My thoughts confirming what my instinct was telling me should have kept me from searching for her but no matter what reason I used I couldn't stop my subconscious from looking for her or control how I reacted when I saw her.

I could tell we would be amazing in the sack. The way my blood heated at the vision of her in nothing but her underwear was enough to confirm I was more attracted to her than any other girl I had ever encountered before. Was it the innocence in her that made her more attractive, because she was forbidden?

Enough. I shut my thoughts down. I was going around in circles and it was doing my head in.

"Your place or mine?" the girl asked me, brushing the slightest kiss against the side of my mouth.

The usual thrill of what was to come wasn't there but I wasn't going to allow myself to pass up a chance to bed the gorgeous girl in front of me. I didn't even remember her name but all I needed was to lose myself in her for a couple of hours.

That's what mattered.

"Only one night," I told her. She had to understand the rules I played by.

She nodded greedily. "One night," she confirmed, her eyes holding mine.

She was blond but it was darker than Taylor's. I shoved the thought out of my mind. I refused to compare. Her eyes were a light green and striking. There was no denying she was attractive.

I leaned closer. "You won't regret it."

She giggled nervously but I gave her a reassuring smile that told her I would rock her world, for only one night. With the terms laid out and agreed, I made my move.

I took her hand in mine and pulled her to a dark corner by the stairs. I leaned closer and pressed my mouth to hers. Her lips moved beneath mine. She slid her hands up my chest to link around my neck, pulling me closer. Her mouth opened slightly, inviting me inside. My tongue delved deeper, needing more.

Any unwanted thoughts were pushed to the back of my mind as I slid my hand to her knee and lifted it to rest against the side of my hip, giving me better access to her as I pressed my body against hers. She groaned against my lips and smiled. There wasn't a lot I was good at, but this was one of them. I knew my way around a woman's body and how to ensure they left as satisfied as I did. My hand moved to cup her butt as I continued to kiss her.

At that moment my eyes drifted and caught Taylor's gaze. She stood watching me make out with another girl.

The exchange was like the thrum of an electric shock through me. I had never experienced that type of effect without even touching a girl. The chemistry we shared was explosive. Her gaze held mine. She stood transfixed and I couldn't stop myself from smiling against the lips of another at the thought that she seemed unable to keep herself from watching me.

Then Jordan pulled Taylor's attention away from me.

"I need you," the blond girl whispered against my lips.

It was like a bucket of cold water over me and any drive to bed her went straight out the window. I broke the kiss and surveyed the willing participant in front of me. What was wrong with me? I shoved a hand through my hair as I tried to figure out why I felt like something was changing and I had no way of stopping it.

There was no way to explain my way out. There was only one thing to do and that was to leave. I turned on my heel and went straight for the kitchen without another word to the girl I left standing open-mouthed at my sudden change in action.

"You having fun?" Slater asked when I entered the kitchen.

The scowl on my face made his easy-going smile straighten out. He raised an eyebrow at me but I couldn't explain what I didn't entirely understand myself.

"I'm going," I told him tersely, feeling the tension knot the muscles in my shoulders.

He gave me a nod. "I'll get a lift back to the house."

I gave him a brief nod before I left the house out the back door, hoping I wouldn't run into Taylor or the blonde I had left in the middle of making out.

Inside the car I sat in the driver's side with my hands gripping the steering wheel. It felt like I was drowning. I inhaled sharply as my lungs froze. With my eyes tightly gripped closed, I leaned my head against the steering wheel, trying to pull myself together so I could get out of here before I saw someone I didn't want to see.

There is nothing you haven't faced before, I reminded myself, trying to exhale. My eyes opened to see some people heading out of the house, looking worse for wear.

Remember what you overcame. With the pain of my childhood I felt the strength that I had earned tackling insurmountable odds against me. *There is nothing you can't fight. You control your life now. No one else.*

My breathing eased and I felt a restoration of some control. I started up the car and reversed. I put the events of the evening down to chemistry to a girl I was set on avoiding for my own survival.

It is lust, nothing more, I told myself.

Chapter Five

I'd spent most of my morning working up a sweat, needing the physical exertion to close off my mind. I didn't want to analyze the events of the night before and try and figure out what had unsettled me so much.

My muscles ached and sweat poured down my body. I was like a machine that kept going, on and on. Determined.

By mid-day, after a shower and doing some of my assignments, I was feeling better. More in control. I brushed off the night before as a once-off that I would not allow to happen again.

Slater and a couple of friends were playing games but I wasn't in the mood. *You haven't been much in the mood for any of your usual vices*, I couldn't help thinking distastefully. And, besides, I needed to get some work done.

I had learned patience and control over time and I wouldn't allow it to be shaken by anyone even if they had pretty blue eyes and legs that went on forever.

I was leaning back in my chair, staring at the same sentence for the last ten minutes on the screen. I straightened up and rubbed my eyes. My concentration was shot so there was no point trying to push what wasn't working. Resigned, I closed my laptop with the intention of trying again later after I'd had a break.

My body was tired and so was my mind.

"Sin!" I heard Slater yell from downstairs. My bedroom door was open. If it hadn't been, I wouldn't have heard him. I stood and left my room.

At the top of the stairs Slater was by the front door and there stood Taylor standing nervously when my eyes met hers. I hadn't been expecting her. The sight of her was a surprise but I hid my reaction. She was in my territory this time, and after last night I wasn't going to allow her to affect me. I was in full control now.

I descended the stairs with my eyes on her. Slater went back to the living room to his friends again. She was dressed in causal blue jeans and a shirt, less revealing than I was used to seeing her in. How could I forget the mini skirt she had worn the first time I had met her?

"I never expected to see you again," I said when I came to stop in front of her. I wasn't sure what she was doing in my house or why she was looking for me.

She looked nervous as hell and my curiosity was piqued despite my decision to keep her at a distance.

"Hi..." she said, throwing a nervous look at the guys watching our exchange with curiosity.

"We can talk upstairs," I told her, shaking my head at them. They weren't even pretending they weren't eavesdropping. The only way to talk to her without an audience would be to take her up to my room.

I wasn't totally comfortable with bringing her into my personal space again but I didn't seem to have much choice in the matter. She was silent as she followed me up to my room.

Once she was inside, I closed the door and faced her. She looked even more nervous than before. I cocked my head slightly as I watched her. Her cheeks flushed. She looked like an innocent lamb being led to slaughter.

"You don't have to be nervous," I said, stepping closer.

I had a profound effect on the opposite sex and I had left enough girls tongue-tied but there was something about seeing her nervous that pulled at something inside of me.

"I wanted to...ask...you," she stuttered. She had my undivided attention.

"What do you want to ask me?" I prompted, wanting to know why she had sought me out. I stood confidently, waiting for her to get to her reason for seeking me out. She swallowed.

Then she blurted out, "I want to take advantage of you in a sober state."

I hadn't expected that and I couldn't hide my surprise at her request. She wanted me to take advantage of her. The suddenness of her words and what she said made me smirk at her. She had guts being so direct with me, especially knowing how innocent she was. I bet she had never done this before.

"You want to take advantage of me?" I asked, my smirk widening into a smile.

She nodded.

Her eyes held mine before I dropped my gaze to sweep over her from head to toe, remembering how beautiful she had looked beneath her clothes. And here she was asking me to take her to bed.

The temptation was there. But no matter how screwed up I was, I lived by rules I never broke. I was finally facing what I had already been suspecting. I had never bedded a virgin before. It wasn't just the emotional attachment that kept me far away from them. It was more than that. I had lost any innocence I might have had at a young age. Seeing the things that I had, living the childhood I had, ensured I knew how bad the real world really was. Fairytales and happy endings didn't exist.

I didn't want to be the one to take her innocence from her. All I could offer her was one night of steamy sex and then nothing else. Even if she agreed to my rules it would be much more difficult for her to be able to distinguish between the emotional and physical side of sex.

My reputation preceded me but I knew in the cold light of day when I turned my back on her after a night together it would be too much for her to handle.

But you want her. But I wouldn't take her innocence and hurt her in the process. Let her find someone special to share it with. There was obviously a reason why she had kept it for so long. I took a moment to find the right words to brush her off without hurting her feelings. I don't know why I cared, but I did.

"I'm not one to turn down an offer like that," I started to say and she watched me with big hopeful eyes. "But you don't look like you've ever taken advantage of anyone."

She looked a little stunned. I wasn't sure if it was because of the fact that I figured out she was a virgin. Or maybe it was because I was about to turn her down. There was no way to know.

"So what?" she said, trying to sound blasé about it.

If I were some other guy, I probably wouldn't care and I would have had her on the bed already. I had to shut down the image of my mouth closing over hers as I pressed my body against hers. Just thinking about it made my jeans tighten uncomfortably.

"As stunning as you are and as much as I'd like to take you up on your offer..." I began. Her face fell slightly when she realized I was going to say no. "I don't do virgins."

She looked hurt but I knew I was saving her more heartache. I was doing the right thing even if I felt a bit shitty at that moment, watching her reel from my decision.

"Okay," she mumbled and tried make a hasty escape but I caught her arms.

"Find someone special to share it with," I told her, searching her eyes.

"No, it's fine. I'm sure I'll find someone who can help me," she replied and yanked out of my grip. And then she was gone.

I raked my fingers through my hair.

You did the right thing, I assured myself. I knew I had even if it made me feel like an asshole for hurting her.

And she will probably never speak to you again. So in effect I had killed two birds with one stone. She wouldn't approach me again, not after this rejection. And wasn't that exactly what I wanted—her keeping her distance from me? *Yes,* I told myself, even though I wavered for a few moments.

I heard the door slam as she left the house. The sound vibrated through me, making me feel worse. In a few days I would get back to my normal self like I had been before I had met her. Then I could move from one girl to another again, finding temporary solace from my childhood demons.

The next few days did nothing to lighten my dark mood. My mother had been extra clingy, calling me more often than usual. It only put me under more strain because I was unable to give her what she wanted from me.

Couldn't she understand that years of neglect couldn't be wiped away with a couple of years of sobriety and love? She told me she loved me often enough but, with her actions, I didn't feel it. I'd spent most of my life feeling unloved and unwanted. Maybe I wouldn't be so screwed up if at least my father had played some part in my life. But I had been an unwanted mistake.

I was on my way into class when a girl I knew from one of my classes approached me and asked if I had some study notes.

It was a ploy to talk to me but I played along. Besides, I needed a distraction from the ongoing torment of my life and the blond girl who had been plaguing my thoughts constantly. She had made me question my actions.

I leaned against the wall as the girl fluttered her eyes and smiled at me sheepishly, loving the attention I was getting. It was feeding my ego and after my upheaval of emotions over the last two weeks I needed it.

It was one of the reasons I loved sex. It was a purely physical act for gratification. There were no emotions to mar or confuse it. Just skin against skin, one body against another. The rush and for a few moments an ecstasy that superseded any other emotion or physical reaction. I could understand why people wrestled with sex like a drug addiction. You took drugs for the rush, it was the same with sex.

Something pulled my attention from the girl and my eyes meshed with familiar blue ones. My immediate reaction was a stutter in my breathing. She still had a way of affecting me with just a look. No other girl had ever been able to do that. Then my insides twisted when I saw the guy standing beside her.

He looked like the type of guy she deserved. No tattoos, piercings, well dressed with a bright future ahead of him, possibly taking over a family business. The preppy type, who drove the right car and could give her everything I couldn't. Yeah, I had money but I couldn't give her dating or feelings. My future was uncertain.

She blushed, reacting to the boldness of my stare. She

was the first one to look away, focusing her attention back on the preppy guy. It only reinforced what I already knew, he was better suited for her than I was. It should have confirmed any doubts I had wrestled with before, but it only made my chest ache with that same feeling I'd experienced when my mother had reached for the bottle, turning her attention away from me. I tensed my jaw as I worked through the feeling, being careful not to show it.

I should have looked away but I couldn't drag my eyes from her as she walked past. Maybe I was hoping she would look back at me, but she didn't.

"You want to go to a movie sometime?" the guy asked her. I waited for her to answer even though my attention was back on the girl still trying to chat me up.

"Yeah, that sounds nice," she answered lightly.

It wasn't unexpected but the sharp pain that ran through me was. I had no idea what I was feeling but I didn't like it one bit. That was the thing. With her I felt way too much and I needed to find a way to stop it.

He was the right guy for her but knowing she was going to go out with him messed me up in a way I struggled to handle.

Packing up and moving somewhere else held a lot of appeal at that moment. It was the only way to ensure I never set eyes on her again. But I liked the area and I had settled in nicely with Slater. I couldn't just up and leave. And how would I explain that to Slater? I had to figure it out and deal with it. I was no coward and there had to be a way to fix the unsettledness she had created in me.

They disappeared into their classroom and I was left with the girl frowning at me.

"You okay?" she asked, stating the obvious fact that I had been unable to keep my emotions guarded.

"Yeah, but I think we might be late for class."

We made it into class just as the lecturer was about to start. He glared at us above his glasses on the bridge of his nose and we took our seats.

I couldn't remember what he had said the entire class. My mind had been focused on Taylor and the guy she had agreed to go out with.

The following few days I was determined to prove I didn't care what she did. She was an adult and she could do what she liked. It had nothing to do with me. She saw me talking up another girl but I had refused to allow myself to look in her direction. I was sending a clear message that I was unaffected by her.

When Friday finally arrived I was looking forward to putting any complicated thoughts of Taylor behind me and let loose. It was time to get back to the guy I had been before. I would find a beautiful willing girl to help me unwind for a few hours. Maybe that was why I was so worked up about Taylor? I'd never gone this long without sex.

The party was just starting when Slater walked in with some more beer.

"I invited that girl," he said as he put the six-pack on the counter.

"Which girl?" I asked.

"The one who came around the other day—Taylor."

I frowned. I was looking forward to a Taylor-free evening and now I was annoyed that I would have to keep up my guard again.

"Why did you do that?" I asked, unable to hide my irritation.

Slater studied me as he straightened up. "Is there a reason I shouldn't have?"

I shook my head. I wasn't getting pulled into a conversation I was far from ready to have.

"No."

While the party started to get busier I drank a beer, telling myself there was a chance she wouldn't even make it and I was getting all wound up for nothing.

Relax and have fun, I told myself. I wasn't going to let her ruin my night.

I was eating those words a few hours later. I couldn't take my eyes off her no matter how hard I tried. She was dressed in a skirt and a fitted top. She looked hot but that wasn't the reason my attention was glued to her.

She was drunk. The unsteadiness of her feet and the glowing smile on her face was a dead giveaway that she'd had a few drinks already.

Slater was dancing beside her and I wasn't happy about it at all. Once I had a girl I didn't care who had my seconds but this time was different. I saw the way other guys looked her up and down with a hunger I shared.

Damn it! My control was slipping and I didn't know how much longer I could hold on. My anger simmered beneath the surface. My night was getting worse with every minute that passed.

Why couldn't she go off and find someone nice to lose her virginity to? But she was gazing up at my best friend. Slater treated girls the same way I did. I had already decided I wasn't good enough for her and there was no way in hell he was. In some ways he was more messed up than me.

The moment he leaned closer to say something, I broke. Before I even realized what I was doing I was headed toward them. I caught her wrist and she looked at me with surprise. I focused all my anger in a glare at my best friend.

Slater lifted his hands in mock surrender, understanding that I wasn't finished with this girl.

I pulled her off the dance floor, ignoring the curious looks we were attracting. I led her up to my bedroom.

Inside my room, I let go of her as she entered and closed

the door behind me, blocking out the world, leaving us alone. I faced her in time to see her wobble slightly as she sat down on the edge of my bed. Any anger that had only moments been directed at Slater was now solely focused on the tipsy girl staring up at me with confusion.

Chapter Six

"What the hell are you doing?" I asked her, needing to cross my arms to stop me from reaching for her and shaking some sense into her.

"Whatever I want," she shot back recklessly.

She didn't know the world like I did. I had lived through the darkness and had come out the other end scathed with the reality that bad things happened to good people all the time.

For goodness sake, she had been naive about someone spiking her drink and here she was getting drunk. Did she not care that there could be someone out there with an intent to hurt her? I felt like an adult looking at her disapprovingly like a mischievous child who didn't know any better.

She crossed her arms and glared at me.

"I told you to go and find someone special to share it with," I reminded her, not hiding the anger I felt. "Not to go to a house party, get drunk and see who you end up with."

"Who do you think you are?" she asked, matching my

anger.

I was no one to her.

"You know what? You don't get to lecture me," she said, standing up on unsteady legs. "I already have one protective brother and I don't need another one. Your friend invited me to a party and I came to let loose and have a little fun. What I do and who I do it with is none of your business." She was right. I had no right to tell her what to do and it didn't sit well with me at all.

I should have let her go when she made a move to walk past me but I stopped her.

"I'm not trying to lecture you. It's just there are bad people out there, and you just seem so naive," I explained. Feeling more agitated, I raked my fingers through my hair.

"I was talking to your friend," she said.

"Slater and I are not good guys," I stated.

If she had an idea how bad we had been she would keep her distance, but I couldn't bring myself to tell her the dirty details of the childhood we were still trying to outrun.

Our eyes held.

I had done everything I could to fight what I felt for her but I couldn't do it anymore. She was determined to lose her virginity to someone and I had no control over who she would pick, so that left me with only one choice.

There was only a moment of hesitation as I flickered my tongue against my lip ring but an image of some guy taking advantage of her and treating her far worse than I would made me step up.

"I asked you to have sex with me and you told me no. That doesn't mean you get to tell me what to do," she reminded me.

I wasn't the best choice but the fear that someone else would do more damage made me decide to do something I had never contemplated before.

Her gaze dropped to my mouth before she tried to walk past me again, but I wasn't letting her go. My hand wrapped around her wrist and she turned to face me.

"I changed my mind."

She looked at me not quite understanding what I was talking about.

"I want to take advantage of you," I whispered, allowing myself for the first time to freely embrace the attraction I felt for her.

"In a sober state," I finished. My eyes dropped to her lips. I had lost count of how many times I had imagined how it would feel to kiss her. Would her mouth feel as soft as it looked? It was time to find out. I stepped closer.

She looked undecided despite the way she looked at me, like she was ready for me to kiss her.

"Who says the offer is still on the table?" she shot back.

My rejection had hurt and I knew this was her way of protecting herself. What she wanted was written in the way she looked at me. She wanted me as much as I wanted her.

But there was only one way to prove to her that there was no more time for games. No more denying what had sparked between us and continued to burn. Even if we didn't like the truth we couldn't ignore the chemistry we had.

I backed her up against the wall, caging her in with my arms on either side of her. The moment I had been waiting for had arrived and I leaned closer. Our eyes held and then I looked down to her mouth. She was breathless as she waited for me to kiss her.

She closed her eyes when I touched her lips with mine. Her lips moved against mine. I had kissed more girls than I could remember but I had never shared a kiss like this. My tongue swept along the seam of her mouth and she opened her lips.

She tasted so sweet and I had the urge to groan. My lip

ring pressed against her lip as I increased the pressure, needing more. Where I was sure in every action as I continued to kiss her, I could feel her inexperience as she responded to me.

It felt so good I couldn't remember why I had been fighting it for so long.

I gathered her in my arms, needing to be closer to her as I caressed her tongue with mine. The tidal wave of want swept through me. I held her like an anchor that kept me from being knocked off my feet. Her arms linked around my neck as I pressed her up against the wall, loving the feel of her against me.

Any reason I had come up with to keep my distance went straight out the window and I nearly gave in to the urge to lift her up and carry her to my bed to do what I had wanted to do from the start.

But the slight taste of alcohol reminded me she wasn't sober. I wanted to ignore it but I couldn't allow myself to take her in the current state she was in. For once I rued the morals I had put into place and refused to budge on.

I pulled myself away from her before I did something I would regret.

She looked dazed and I smirked at the effect I'd had on her. Her lips were slightly red and I had the urge to brush my fingers along them but I was already playing with fire. She was lethal. One taste of her and I was willing to throw away every rule I had ever put into place to keep myself safe.

But like she had already shown me, if I wasn't going to do it she would find someone else who would. I was experienced so I knew I would make her first time good. It wouldn't just be a few minutes of some guy pumping into her before leaving her unsatisfied with a bad view of sex. At least when I left she would know how good it could be.

I was still trying to calm my breathing. Her chest rose

and fell just as sharply. The physical chemistry between us was explosive. There was no disputing she still wanted me and I was going to have her.

"Tomorrow night," I told her. I reached out and caressed her cheek with the slight touch of my knuckles.

"You've been drinking tonight, and I want you to be sober," I said. She looked at me with the same innocence I had spotted the first time I had met her. My only consolation in the guilt that I was doing something I had been trying to fight from the beginning was that I was protecting her in some way. Maybe it was only trying to give myself a way of having her and allowing myself to sidestep the guilt I was feeling.

"Go back downstairs and enjoy the rest of the party. Meet me here tomorrow night."

She nodded in agreement. I studied her for a few seconds before I surprised myself by pressing my lips momentarily to her in a brief kiss.

I watched her leave my room with a growing sense of fear that I was getting myself into something I wouldn't be able to walk away from.

For the rest of the party I kept a low profile. It was easier than dealing with curious looks from anyone who had seen me with Taylor. Besides, I also didn't want to have to brush off any advances from other girls. There was only one girl on my mind and she was the only one I wanted. And if I was entirely honest with myself, it was the reason no other girl had held any appeal lately.

You can work her out of your system, I told myself. I rolled my shoulders, feeling the tension in them. I could keep lying to myself but I already had a feeling that this thing with Taylor wouldn't be the same as the others before her.

Despite the fear, I couldn't walk away. I was going to go through with it and hope afterward I could carry on like I had before.

Much later when everyone had left I went downstairs. Slater was busy cleaning up. He dumped the plastic cups in the trash bag. When he noticed me, he stopped and straightened up.

"You need a hand?" I asked. He nodded.

We had never had a disagreement before and my odd behavior over Taylor was foreign. I picked up a few empty cups and discarded them into the bag he held out to me.

"So are you going to tell me what happened earlier?" he asked softly.

There was no ignoring that something had changed even if I couldn't quite figure out what that meant.

"There's something different about her." I rubbed the back of my neck, feeling agitated by having to put into words what was going on inside.

He watched me tentatively.

"I don't know what it is or why," I added, feeling the need to explain as much as I could to him.

Our friendship was more important to me than anything else and I owed him an explanation.

"All I know is that I won't share her." I held his unwavering gaze. He gave me a slight inclination of his head.

"I won't touch her." They were simple words but I knew he would stand by them.

In comfortable silence we cleaned up the rest of the house.

I was nervous. That unsettled feeling growing in the pit of my stomach was making it worse. I stood up and paced my room.

Get a grip, I told myself. I hadn't felt this way about a

girl before. Usually I met a girl and after a night together I walked away. So waiting for a girl to arrive was something I wasn't used to but it still didn't explain why I was nervous.

I was good at sex. I'd had plenty of practice. What the hell was I nervous about? I knew by the chemistry alone that tonight would be amazing. I had already realized she was different but I was still going to go through with it despite any misgivings I had.

I had told Slater she would be coming tonight and he had ensured the house would be empty. If he had acted the way I had over a girl, I would have thought he was crazy and I don't know if I would have been as supportive as he was being.

The sound of a knock at the door pulled me out of the array of emotions I was sifting through.

She was here.

My heart started up at the thought of her on the other side of the door waiting for me.

I rolled my shoulders back slightly, mustering the courage to tackle this with my usual detached confidence. I opened the door and the sight of her in a blue top and jeans quickened the beating of my heart and I smiled to cover the anxiousness I felt.

"You came," I said.

"Hi," she greeted, looking so nervous I wanted to reassure her that she could stop this at any time. I didn't want her to do more than she was ready for.

It was one thing talking about it and making the decision but it was different actually going through with it. And losing their virginity was usually a big deal for girls.

Then what the hell are you doing getting messed up in this? But I ignored my conscience. I had told her I would and I stood by my decision. Even if my survival instinct told me to run as fast as I could before it was too late.

I let her into the house and closed the door. She scanned the empty living room.

"Where are your roommates?" she asked.

"They're out." And I was so glad we didn't have an audience right now.

She looked more nervous than before.

"Do you want a soda?" I offered, keeping my gaze focused on her. I didn't know how to ease her nervousness. I was used to girls who knew what they were doing.

She shook her head. I watched her, trying to figure out if she was having second thoughts.

"Are you sure you want to do this?" I asked softly, giving her the opportunity to stop before we started.

She nodded. She was determined to go through with this and that meant there was no backing out for me either. *Remember it's either you or some other guy who would only use her for his own gratification.*

"Okay." I reached for her hand and led her upstairs to my bedroom. The feel of her smaller hand in mine made me feel protective of her.

She surveyed my neat and tidy room. Her eyes fixed on the bed and I saw a slight frown in her features.

"The sheets are clean," I told her, knowing she was probably wondering about all the girls who had been with me before.

"Good," she said swiftly. She clutched her hands tightly together.

"Relax," I told her as I walked to her. She looked up at me.

She is so beautiful, I thought to myself as I studied her for a moment.

"Breathe," I instructed, giving her a smile to put her at ease. She let out the breath she had been holding.

It was time.

I reached for her hand and tugged her closer. My hand went to her waist as her body touched mine. After fighting it for so long it felt strange being able to hold her and do all the things I had wanted to. She looked up at me with a trust I wasn't sure I deserved. But I wanted her so much I would give her anything she wanted at that moment.

"I know this is your first time, and you're nervous. But you shouldn't be." My words did nothing to ease the anxiousness I could see in her eyes.

"I'm going to try and make sure it feels as good as possible," I reassured her.

It was my responsibility as the more experienced partner to ensure I did everything I could to make sure she had the best first time she could. I was not used to the responsibility of another on my shoulders.

My eyes flickered to her mouth. It looked so inviting, any strength I had to fight the urge to kiss her and make her mine was gone. I closed the distance between our lips and kissed her. Seconds later I felt her hands on my chest and I began to explore her mouth.

I stroked her tongue with mine and she bunched my shirt in her hands. She tasted so sweet, like strawberries with a hint of apple. Every touch, every breath, only intensified the beating of my heart and my senses.

I wanted to bury myself into her as quickly as possible but I stopped myself. *Take it slowly.*

We had way too many clothes on and it was time to remedy that. I pulled away to unbutton her shirt. When I pushed the fabric off her shoulders she shrugged out of it.

My eyes slid over her half-naked form, allowing myself to take in every beautiful curve on display for my enjoyment. I was so turned on and it was intensified by the mirrored heat in her eyes. I wanted to free her breasts from the confines of her bra. I wanted to tease them with my mouth and the scrape of my teeth.

Whatever happened tonight between us was what we both wanted. There was no hiding it or fighting it.

It would happen, and afterward wasn't something I wanted to think about right now.

Chapter Seven

I pulled my shirt over my head. Her eyes drifted over my tight torso and I saw her appreciation. I knew I looked good both in and out of clothes. It was a side effect of working out my emotions with the punching bag.

Tentatively she lifted her hand and touched my chest. My skin tingled beneath her touch. I tightened my muscles in growing anticipation and I flicked my tongue against my lip ring. She trailed her hands down my abs and I allowed her to explore me like I intended to explore her.

Her eyes found mine and I put my hands on her hips, bringing her closer. The feel of her body against mine, skin to skin, was electrifying. Even the slight brush of her breath against me only intensified the need to get her screaming my name while I gave her her first sexual experience.

I glided my hands though her hair, bringing her lips to mine, and I covered her mouth with mine. Our kiss heated and was more urgent than before. Gently I sucked her tongue.

With my mouth still working against hers, I rested my hand on her hips and steered her backward to the bed. I laid her down onto the mattress. The sight of her there, with her hair spread out and her eyes darker than before, made me realize she had never looked more beautiful.

It made me question why I had been fighting this from the beginning.

I wanted her naked. My hands went to her jeans and unbuttoned them. She lifted her hips to help me remove her clothing and I dropped it to the floor. I discarded my jeans. I watched how her eyes went to my boxers and the evidence of how much I wanted her was there for her to see. It reminded me that this was unknown territory for her.

Needing her to feel as out of control as I was, I joined her on the bed and hovered slightly above her. I kissed her urgently before sliding my tongue along her neck between soft kisses. Did her skin burn under my touch like mine did for her? She shivered when I kissed the bottom of her neck. Then she groaned.

I liked that I had her quivering beneath me, enjoying what I was doing to her.

"Do you like that?" I murmured, repeating the action to see if I got the same response. She closed her eyes as she rode the wave of anticipation.

My attention focused on her bra. I slid my tongue down the valley between her breasts as I slipped my hand under her to unclasp her bra. She stiffened. Had I moved too quickly for her?

"It's okay," I murmured gently, easing the straps from her shoulders and discarding it.

Damn. I swallowed when I surveyed her half-naked form.

"You don't have to be shy; you're perfect." The nervous look she shot me made me want to assure her that she had no need to feel nervous.

My mouth took in her nipple and I sucked gently.

"I...." she stuttered before I took her other nipple into my mouth and repeated the action. She closed her eyes and gasped.

She was hot for me by the time I reached her panties. Her hands fisted the sheets as my hands skimmed down her thighs and opened them.

"Any time you're not comfortable with something, all you have to do is tell me to stop and I will," I felt the need to tell her. She had to know that she was in control of what was happening.

"Okay," she replied when I kissed just above her panty line.

I kissed each thigh before I made the move to remove her last remaining item of clothing. I eased them off slowly, not wanting to rush her.

She tensed when she realized she was naked beneath me. No barriers, vulnerable to me.

"Relax," I told her.

She gasped when I flicked my tongue against her. She tried to wriggle free, uncomfortable with my attention, but I kept her from moving away. My finger slid into her, testing to see if she was ready for me. She stilled and I worked her with my tongue. I felt her quiver and tense before she came, trying to stifle a gasp.

I had held on long enough and was ready to burst at any moment. There was no way I was even sure I would last to give her another orgasm. She looked at me with a dazed and satisfied look that made me feel proud that I had been able to do that for her.

I moved above her, fitting my body against hers, lining us up. Slowly I touched her lips with mine, pressing myself against her, needing her to feel how much I wanted to be inside of her. She ground against me.

"Are you sure?" I asked her. If she stopped me now, even a cold shower wasn't going to help with the hard-on I had.

"Yes," she breathed.

I left her long enough to get a condom and discard my boxers to roll on the protection. Her eyes widened when she saw me for the first time. I moved onto the bed again and covered her body with mine as I dropped a kiss to her lips to ease her nervousness. I settled between her legs.

"I'm going to go slow so I don't hurt you too much," I assured her softly. Her eyes widened slightly when she felt the tip of me at her opening.

Unable to talk, she nodded, looking up at me nervously. Trying to distract her, I kissed her again as I began to enter her as gently as I could, hoping to keep any pain she would feel at a minimum.

"Are you sure?" I asked, feeling the strain of keeping my control, which was hanging on by a thread. Instead of answering, she pushed onto me as she kissed me.

God, she felt so good. Her warmth enveloped me. Her breath hitched when I pushed through the barrier of her innocence.

"Are you okay?" I stilled. I wasn't sure how much pain I had caused.

"It's okay," she said.

With the last of my restraint I eased out and reentered her as slowly as I could. She seemed to adjust to me and I increased the tempo slightly.

When she wrapped her legs around me, I lost the last of my control. I grabbed her hands to hold them above her and began to thrust into her faster, needing to bury myself to the hilt.

The headboard began to bang against the wall but I couldn't slow down even if I wanted to. I was so close but I was determined to make her come again before I did.

She was so damn tight. Her body quivered and tensed. She was close. She bit her lip as she reached her peak. I pushed into her, needing my own release, and trembled as I spilled into her. My breathing was rapid as I rode the rush I craved.

Afterward I was still trying to catch my breath but she lay unmoving, our bodies still intertwined. I kissed her before I rested my forehead against hers.

I knew we would be good together, the chemistry between us foretold that. But that had been the best sex of my life—and with a virgin. I still couldn't wrap my mind around it.

"For your first time, you were pretty awesome," I told her.

She gave me a smile that pulled at something in my chest. It was the first time she didn't have the nervousness or anxiousness for the unknown. She looked satisfied and relaxed. And I had to admit I liked seeing her like this, especially in my bed.

"You weren't too bad yourself," she shot back, making me laugh. I shifted off her, needing to get rid of the condom. I walked to my bathroom and discarded it.

When I joined her back in my bed I lay beside her. I pulled the covers over her. Physically I was satisfied and tired. It had been an amazing night but after such an intense experience, I was exhausted. And there was nothing better than falling asleep with her beside me.

She'd done it again. I was annoyed. Twice I had woken up to find the spot beside me empty. She had left while I had slept.

I don't know why it made me feel the way it did. If it had been any other girl, I would have been relieved. I got up and raked a hand through my messy bed-hair, trying to make sense of why I cared. It was a question I kept asking myself and so far I had failed to answer.

It didn't help my mood when I found Slater smiling at my obvious annoyance when I went to get some coffee.

"Don't."

"I didn't say a word," he told me, holding his hands up. I ignored him.

He didn't have to. I knew what he was probably thinking. I felt like my whole axis had been shifted and I was still trying to figure out where I was. Lost. That's exactly how I felt. In a world I had never been in before.

I got a mug and set it down so forcefully it banged against the counter. I was losing control and I didn't like it one bit. It reminded me of a time when I'd had no control over my life and that had been the scariest time of my life.

After making some coffee I took a gulp, burning my mouth slightly but at least it distracted me from whatever was going on inside my chest.

Quietly, Slater watched me from the doorway. I bet he was trying to work out what was wrong with me.

"What time did she leave?" I finally asked. I didn't want to ask but something compelled me, reinforcing my lack of control in the current situation.

Our night was over. Her virginity was gone and I'd had the best sex of my life. I didn't do more. She hadn't stayed and made the morning after uncomfortable.

So what exactly is the problem? I asked myself.

"Four a.m."

I shot him a raised eyebrow, alarmed that she had left in the dark. Didn't she know it wasn't safe for a girl to walk around when it was dark?

"I walked her back to her dorm," Slater revealed, much to my relief.

I held his gaze, trying to read his motive behind it. He was my best friend, I trusted him more than anyone, but I didn't like the idea of any guy around Taylor.

"I didn't think it was safe for her to walk alone." He gave me a dismissive shrug like it wasn't a big deal.

I could read him well enough to see his intentions for what they were and not what my crazy mind was trying to come up with. Feeling like an asshole for even thinking he would do something underhanded made me murmur, "Thanks."

"Do you know what you're doing?" he asked, taking me by surprise. His expression was concerned.

My behavior was out of character and so were the emotions building up inside me. If he had been acting like I had been the past few weeks I would be asking him the same question. But hearing the words out loud only put more weight behind what I was struggling to admit to myself.

"No, I don't," I admitted truthfully with a heavy voice. I dropped my eyes to study the contents of my mug, feeling defeated that everything I had tried hadn't worked up to this point.

I had no idea how to fix any of it. And sleeping with her had just made it worse. I could still feel her velvety soft skin under my hands, hear her gasp in ecstasy and remember the bliss of losing myself in her.

Even after working out for a few hours I still couldn't clear my mind of her. It didn't help that my sanctuary had been tainted with memories of her. Where I had first met her. The first time we'd kissed, and more.

Later, feeling like I was going to go crazy if I didn't get out, I suggested to Slater we go out and do something.

"Yeah, sure," he said. He was always up for going out.

We both needed the distraction.

"How about we go to Joes?" I suggested.

It was our local hangout.

"Let's go," Slater said, standing up and getting his jacket.

It was like old times when we got there and started playing pool. He would set up the balls and I would break. We were both really good at it. After six games we were tied.

A couple of girls approached us, wanting to play against us. One was a redhead and the other had long auburn hair. It wouldn't be fair but I was pretty sure the way they were looking us up and down they didn't care about the game.

Slater raised an eyebrow at me and shrugged. If he wanted I would play along so he could score but I wasn't sure I had it in me. The only girl I wanted was still cycling through my mind, reminding me that no matter how much I didn't want to admit it I wasn't ready to let her go.

"I'm Casey," the one with the auburn hair introduced herself to me, putting her hand out to shake mine.

I shook hands. "Sin."

"Really?" she asked, looking at me suspiciously, not convinced it was my name.

I nodded with a smile. It was the usual response when I told people my name. No one could quite believe a mother would give her child that name. It reminded me of the events that had led to my existence and how I reminded my mother of that with every breath I took.

"Wow."

Slater partnered with Casey's friend Victoria, which left me with Casey. She was pretty funny and she attempted to flirt with me but I wasn't interested in her, despite my denial of having a girlfriend. We played a few games. Slater and Victoria were too busy flirting to pay much attention to the games, so it was pretty easy to beat them.

Slater suggested we go outside because the inside of the

bar was getting stuffy and hot. Victoria went to the restroom and Casey remained outside with me while Slater went to get drinks.

She said something funny and I smiled. It was probably the first time I had interacted with a girl with no play to get her into bed.

Then I looked past her to see Taylor and Jordan walking toward us.

There seemed to be no way to get away from her. I had come out with Slater with one goal of keeping myself busy so I didn't have time to think about her and here she was walking toward me. Her usual open and friendly features were closed off.

Even dressed casually she was still so striking. The girl beside me didn't hold a candle to her. And suddenly it felt so wrong to be standing with another girl while Taylor and her friend approached.

It wasn't what it looked like but there was no way to explain that without revealing I cared what she thought.

I remembered our great night together. My gaze swept over her and I could still smell her in the bed beside me. The closer she got the more I studied her stoic features. She smiled at me but I never saw it in her eyes.

"Hi," I greeted. Casey turned to see who I was talking to. I saw the way Taylor looked her up and down.

"Hi," Taylor said and Jordan nodded her head.

The vibes coming off Jordan were enough to tell me all I needed to know even if I didn't fully understand why.

"Where are you guys headed?" I asked.

"To the movies," Jordan answered stiffly.

The frostiness from Jordan made it clear there was no reason to prolong the awkward conversation. In her mind I was living up to my reputation.

"Well, it was nice seeing you again, Taylor," I murmured

to her.

She gave me a nod and looked away. She linked her arm through Jordan's and I watched them walk away.

I wrestled with the need to assure her that I wasn't trying to hook up with Casey but that would be giving away more than I was prepared to acknowledge.

Chapter Eight

Mommy?

There was no answer. I opened the door to her bedroom. Fear of what I would find made me hesitate before I mustered the strength to keep going. Maybe she was hurt? She needed me, I convinced myself.

I peered into the room slowly as I spotted her on the floor.

"Mom!" I yelled, running to her. I touched her back with my small hand but she didn't move.

"Open your eyes," I told her but there was no response. I shoved her, hoping to wake her but there was no movement. Feeling my rising fear, I bent down and looked closer at her face pale. Her eyes were open.

"Mommy?" I whispered softly, not understanding why she wouldn't say something.

Then I realized she was dead.

Tears blurred my eyes as I lay down beside her and put my small arm around her, hugging her close.

"I love you," I pleaded like it was enough to bring her back, but it didn't.

I shot up in bed. Still feeling the rawness of my grief, I looked around and realized I was in my room.

My heart was still slamming in my chest at a rate that made it difficult to breathe. With one hand to my bare chest I threw my covers off, hating that the nightmares could spin up all the old feelings from my childhood of a boy who had been so scared.

It wasn't a memory. My mother was still alive and kicking.

It had been fear—my biggest fear when I had been growing up. Each time I had found my mother passed out in a drunken stupor, I had been so scared she would drink herself to death. It had stripped me over time, leaving an emptiness inside and eventually I couldn't care anymore.

In the dream I had been alone but in reality I'd had Slater by my side every step of the way. He'd been there when I'd had no one and I had stepped up to be there when he needed me.

He was my family.

I felt frustrated that I had no control over these dreams, and they seemed to be happening more often. I rubbed my chest as I paced my room. I knew exactly who had stirred this up. Whatever was going on with Taylor was affecting every aspect of my life even though I had kept my distance, even missing a couple of days of classes to ensure I didn't see her.

I had the urge to hit something so I strode downstairs without acknowledging anyone I passed, my sole focus to punch something until the pain stopped me.

Slamming the door of the garage behind me, I walked over to the punching bag with a determination to work the suffocating emotions out of me before I lost all control. Again and again I slammed my tightened fist into the bag. Pain jolted in me with every contact of my hand against the firm object.

Eventually I couldn't do it anymore. My muscles ached from the punishing movements. My fists were numb and when I looked down at them, with my chest rising and falling sharply, I realized they were bleeding.

But no matter how much I tried to chase the demons of my childhood away, I couldn't wipe the memory of the dream or how heartbroken and sad I had felt.

I walked backward and dropped down onto the step before the doorway into the house. I bent my head into my hands and focused my attention on the concrete floor below me.

No, I couldn't do this. But I had no idea how to stop it.

Taylor. An angelic image appeared of her looking at me with those big blue eyes and those lustrous lips of hers. But it was more than that. It was the way she looked at me and the way it made me feel.

I didn't want to feel anything. I wanted to be numb so I didn't care and so the invisible barrier that seemed to stop me from moving on to another girl would vanish and I could carry on with my life on my own terms.

The door behind me opened.

"You okay?" Slater asked.

I nodded, not wanting my voice to give my inner turmoil away. Before he had stood with me and shouldered my problems with me but this he couldn't help with. I had to get through this on my own.

The door closed softly.

Slowly the feeling returned to my hands as I flexed them, feeling the pain that I had inflicted.

I found myself standing in Joe's again. Slater had insisted I could do with a night out. Hoping that getting out would help, I gave in and allowed him to drag me with him.

Usually I was pretty good at pool but I couldn't shoot anything properly and Slater was kicking my ass. It only reminded me of what was bugging me.

"You suck," Slater noted when he beat me for the sixth time.

"I'm just not feeling it tonight."

My friend studied me from across the table before he walked over to me, still holding the cue.

"Something's been bugging you for a while. Maybe talking will help." I shook my head.

I knew he meant well but verbally admitting what was happening wasn't something I was prepared to do yet. I didn't know if I would ever be ready.

Flexing my still aching hands, I studied the slight bruising from my exertion with the punching bag earlier.

Being out in public, away from the house, had done nothing to settle what was going on in my head. I didn't want to be here. I wasn't sure there was anywhere I did want to be.

An image of Taylor appeared in my mind and I scowled. I couldn't get away from her. She was the person who had caused this and even keeping away from her hadn't lessened her impact.

"I don't think I'm up for any more games," I finally admitted as I straightened up from leaning against the wall. I reached for my jacket.

Having an audience wasn't helping me with my darkening mood and I wasn't very good company anyway.

We decided to go outside to finish our last drink before we left.

Slater smiled when he looked at something behind me and I turned to see Taylor with the preppy guy I had seen her with on campus. The one I had decided was the type of guy she deserved. Not someone who couldn't keep their shit together.

An unwanted possessiveness struck me. I smiled, trying to soothe over the sudden urge to tear her away from him.

"Hi," she greeted. She introduced the preppy guy as Caleb.

While I eyed him, Slater shook hands with him and said, "Nice to meet you."

I didn't want to play nice but I didn't want to create a scene that would lead to questions I didn't want to answer. Or, more truthfully, didn't know how to answer. There was no way I was going to shake hands with the guy so I gave him a brief nod instead.

"Where are you guys headed?" Slater asked, detracting attention from me as I studied the couple closer.

I remembered how she had looked at me after our night together. Did she look at him the same way? That thought turned my stomach. Had they slept together? *It doesn't matter. You don't care*, I told myself. She can do what she wants with whomever she wants.

But no matter how many times I told myself that, I didn't believe one word. I cared way too much.

"To the movies," she replied nervously.

The atmosphere was awkward but I didn't care. Keeping a lid on red-hot emotions that were bubbling inside of me was more important. I wanted to wipe that confident look of Mr. Preppy's face. I dug my nails into my palms as I resisted the urge to rearrange his perfect face with my fists. I had no right to feel the way I did. I had no right to her. If I wanted that I would have to give her more, and I couldn't. The memories of my nightmare stopped me.

She glanced down at her watch. "We'd better go, otherwise we're going to miss the show."

My eyes focused on her hand intertwined with his. The ache in my chest worsened. I wanted them to go.

"We're having another party on Saturday. Why don't you come? Bring Caleb and your hot friend, Jordan," Slater said as they started to walk away.

I shot my friend a glare before focusing back on Taylor.

"I will," she replied as she gave Slater a short wave.

Our eyes met briefly before she left, leaving me with a rawness inside. After they disappeared out of my line of sight I turned to Slater.

"What?" he asked when he saw the annoyed look I gave him.

"Why did you invite them?" Only a few moments of seeing her together with Mr. Preppy had been hard to handle, I didn't want to spend a whole evening watching them together.

"I wanted to see her friend again," he admitted with a slight shrug of one shoulder.

"Jordan?" I asked. She didn't like me much because of my reputation. I couldn't see her being okay with Slater's reputation.

He nodded.

"I don't think she's our usual type." I felt compelled to warn him. In fact I was pretty sure she viewed him as a lowlife player like me.

He shut down the rest of the conversation with a shrug. He clearly didn't want to talk about it and I wasn't going to push it.

Seeing Taylor had turned my mood and I wasn't interested in being around people. Slater seemed quieter than usual so we went back to the house earlier than we had planned.

Alone in my room, my phone started to ring. I stood watching the flashing name of my mother as the insistent ringing put me on edge. The nightmares made it impossible to work through my feelings of abandonment from my past. Now I was even further away from finding a way to forgive her than I had been before.

I put my hand to my chest and rubbed the rawness that seemed to be spreading inside. Much to my relief my phone eventually stopped ringing. I sat down on my bed, trying to sort through the chaotic memories from my childhood and the thoughts of Taylor.

There had to be an explanation as to why I was still so wired over Taylor. What was it about her that kept her in the forefront of my mind, leaving no room for any other thoughts?

My eyes settled on the carpet by my feet as I contemplated possible reasons why I couldn't forget Taylor like the rest of the girls I had slept with. What set her apart from the rest? She was the most beautiful but looks were only skin deep. There had to be more than that.

I rubbed my chin as my mind explored the possibility that somehow her being a virgin had affected me more than I had wanted to admit. Being her first lover had given me a responsibility I had avoided with others, so what had made me step in and accept it? Fear of someone hurting her. But why did I care?

These were all questions I had asked myself before but I had been unable to come up with answers. I didn't even know much about her. Although I could remember every inch of her from our night together.

I suddenly had a thought. Was it my attraction to her? It still only took one look for me to feel my blood thicken at the thought of having her again. My attraction for a girl only lasted for the one night, and after that I wasn't interested. Clearly that wasn't the same with Tay.

No. Taylor, I corrected myself. I wasn't going to shorten

her name like a nickname. It implied she was more to me than a girl who I'd bedded and was going to ultimately discard.

I went back to my previous thought about how I could still feel so attracted to her. I felt like I was on to something. One night hadn't been enough. Maybe I needed more. I rubbed my chin as I began to contemplate my new explanation of why I was struggling to move on from her.

Those thoughts stayed with me for the next few days. I saw Taylor briefly and I kept my interaction with her short and sweet, still not being completely convinced that sleeping with her would work her out of my system and would set me free to go back to my life before we'd met.

The upcoming party stayed in the back of my mind. I still hadn't decided how to deal with the pretty blue-eyed beauty who had dominated my mind despite every attempt I had made to forget about her.

I had contemplated giving the party a miss but then I decided I wasn't a coward, and I didn't run from things that were difficult to deal with. I faced them head-on and with the determination that helped me survive a bad childhood.

This would be no different.

The moment she stepped inside my house my eyes focused on her, taking in the mini skirt she was wearing. My heated gaze slid down her bare legs, remembering how good it had felt to feel them wrapped around me. I swallowed. Her eyes drifted over the crowd and I wondered if she was looking for me. Then I noticed the guy who was with her and I frowned. Caleb.

The crease in my forehead stayed as I watched her, along with her date and Jordan, making their way to the kitchen.

I glanced momentarily at the girl who I had been trying to chat up before Taylor had arrived. Her mouth was moving as her eyes glittered up to mine.

I had stopped listening. It wasn't her conversation I was interested in. She was a beautiful redhead but I didn't feel the usual pull I did to the opposite sex. I think her name was Sarah or Stacy. I couldn't remember. I wanted to test the possibility that pushing myself to sleep with her would end whatever lingered with Taylor.

I glanced back at the kitchen door to see Taylor and Caleb. My eyes narrowed as I took in every interaction between the two.

Then her eyes found mine. Feeling like a charge of electricity bounced between us threw me, leaving my heart beating a little faster than usual. I still wanted her as much as I had wanted her the first time I'd met her. Having her hadn't eased the attraction I felt for her.

My eyes slid down her, remembering exactly what she looked like underneath. Her pale skin and the softness as my hands glided down her body. I gritted my teeth, trying to keep a lid on what I was experiencing. When our eyes met again there was no doubt she felt the same way even if she was with another guy.

Our connection was broken when Jordan and Slater joined them. I briefly watched Slater with Jordan. I'd seen him with more girls than I could count and I could tell there was something different in the way he looked at her.

Taylor whispered something into Jordan's ear and then she left, headed in the direction of the bathroom. Before I could even make the choice, I followed a safe distance behind her. The bathroom downstairs was busy so she went upstairs, with me only a few steps behind her, not even sure what I was going to do.

There was only a brief moment when she walked into the

bathroom and turned to close the door. I pushed the door slightly, stopping her from closing it. Her eyes met mine as I stepped into the room and closed the door.

We stood staring at each other. She looked surprised, with her mouth slightly open. She didn't say a word.

But this wasn't the time to talk. It was time for action. I wanted her and I wanted her now. It wasn't something I could explain.

Then I closed the distance between us, feeling our attraction pull me closer to her. Like we were magnets gravitating to each other with no control over it. The slight brush of her tongue on her lips broke me into action.

My mouth was against hers. My hands held her body against me. There had been no time to think the action through or to contemplate the repercussions. There was only my mouth moving against hers.

There was no resistance from her and when she started to kiss me back, it confirmed that she wanted this as much as I did.

Chapter Nine

My tongue darted into her mouth, loving the familiar taste of her. My hands gripped her butt and she wrapped her arms around my neck. This was what I wanted: to bury myself so deep into her that nothing else mattered.

My lip ring pressed into her lip and she shivered. I loved that I could make her react like this. Her body responded to mine like it remembered our night together. I didn't even allow myself to even consider the thought that she might have already slept with Caleb. Just the thought was enough for me to see red.

No. If it had taken her this long to lose her virginity, would she have moved on so quickly?

I lifted her off her feet and her legs wrapped around my hips, pressing her body against mine. She fit perfectly against me, like she'd been made for me. My hands dug into her, keeping her tightly against me before I set her down on the bathroom vanity. My mind was already racing ahead on how

I would take her and make her groan my name.

My hands cradled her face as I kissed her hungrily, letting her know with my actions how much I wanted her. And then she pulled her lips from mine, breaking the spell I had been under. I rested my forehead against hers while I tried to even my breathing.

"I can't," she whispered, shaking her head. It felt like someone had punched me in the chest. I reeled from the feeling of rejection I hadn't been prepared for.

As I studied her, I pulled away. I should have known I wouldn't be enough compared to the preppy guy she had waiting downstairs for her. I wanted to argue that if she was here kissing me like she had just moments before, she couldn't really be serious about Caleb. Surely it was as simple as that.

I put my hands on the vanity on either side of her as I waited for her to explain, not sure I could cope with it. Inside I felt raw, vulnerable and fearful that she had the power to hurt me.

It was another reason I had always kept girls to one-night stands because it meant there were no emotions, no expectations and it didn't leave me vulnerable. Exactly the way I was feeling now, staring into her eyes.

"Why?" I asked, flickering a gaze to her lips. I wanted to kiss her again and finish what we had started.

"Caleb," she answered. It was like a cold bucket of water over me extinguishing the heat I had felt for her.

The anger ignited inside of me. Anger at her and myself for allowing myself to get into a situation where I was open to it. If I had kept to my usual plan we wouldn't be here right now. No, I would have been screwing the redhead, already craving the rush and peace it would momentarily give me.

I clenched my jaw as I worked myself though my anger.

"You can't deny what's between us," I told her, crossing

my arms.

If she was really into Caleb, she wouldn't have responded to me the way she had. Then it occurred to me. He was rich and handsome. He was the type of guy who could give her the type of future she deserved.

To her I was just some bad boy covered in tattoos with some piercings who only looked for a good time briefly with multiple girls. I wasn't exactly relationship-material. I was the one-night-stand king.

"I'm not." I wanted to believe her but I didn't.

She hopped off the counter and I stepped backward, keeping her at a distance.

"It's just—"

"What is it?" I asked, feeling the hurt squeeze my lungs and burn my throat. "Yeah, don't worry, I get it."

Her rejection was a reminder of what I had been wrestling with for most of my life. Feeling inadequate. I hadn't been good enough for my mother to love me, I hadn't been good enough for my father to want me and now I wasn't good enough for her.

Needing to get as far away from her as I could, I reached to open the door and she stopped me. Turning my attention back to her, I sneered at her.

"Don't worry, I get it. You prefer the preppy, rich guys," I told her angrily, pulling my wrist free.

She didn't deny it. Instead she looked speechless as I walked out.

There was only one action on my mind when I descended the stairs and searched the room for the girl who had been flirting with me earlier. I wanted to find another girl to help ease the burning hurt I was feeling and to show Taylor she was just another girl in a long line of them. It would also lessen the ache I was feeling in the middle of my chest.

Just as I made it down the stairs, a girl who had tried to flirt with me earlier stepped into my path. The seductive look she gave me left me with no doubt that she was up for anything I wanted.

There was no need for words as I reached for her and she lifted herself up onto her tiptoes and kissed me. There was no spark, I could have been kissing my sister for all the response I was feeling, but I was determined to give Taylor the message that she was dispensable like all the other girls before her.

As I kissed the girl, out of the corner of my eye I saw Taylor descend the stairs. The moment she spotted me, I felt the heat of her gaze. She hesitated as she watched us for a few more seconds before she rejoined her group.

From the surprised look in her eyes, she had received my message loud and clear. I couldn't stop watching her from the corner of my gaze while she took a drink from Jordan and sipped it quietly.

Caleb. I glared at him as I remembered her saying his name. He was the reason she had stopped.

The girl I was kissing pulled away and I turned my attention back to her, giving her the confident smile I knew would make her putty in my hands. *This is what I need*, I told myself.

"What's your name?" I whispered to her, looking at her like she was the most important person in the room.

It wasn't like I was going to remember anyway.

"Paige," she answered.

"You have a pretty name." It was a line I had used before.

New is dangerous, old is good, I reminded myself. I only had to remember what had just happened in the bathroom with Taylor to be reminded of that.

Briefly, out of the side of my gaze, I saw Taylor rub her temple. I hardened myself inside, refusing to be pulled in by the hurt look in her eyes.

Paige looked up at me dreamily and I kissed her again. She didn't taste as sweet as Taylor did. I shut down my thoughts, refusing to compare everything I had felt with Taylor with every other girl.

I had to close the door on Taylor and lock it so there was no reopening it again. Paige wrapped her arms around my waist, making me feel like a noose was tightening around my neck but I didn't push her away. I needed her to shield me from Taylor.

Taylor made her way out of the party with Caleb. She looked back at me one last time. I didn't look away or pretend I didn't see her. I met her gaze with my unyielding one as Paige laid her head against my chest. My eyes took in Caleb beside her briefly before I set my attention back to her.

I wanted her to hurt like I was and I was convinced I saw it in her eyes when she saw Paige getting cozy with me. She left the party, following Caleb out of my house.

I didn't need her. Any other girl could fill the gap she left, I told myself. I was trying to convince myself it was the truth. I felt annoyed that my whole evening had been ruined by the incident with Taylor. I spent another half hour with Paige before making up an excuse and making an exit up to my room.

I wasn't in the mood for company. If I didn't have a house full of people, I would have gone straight to the garage to work out some of my frustration and anger with some boxing. Instead I was pacing my room, trying to work through emotions I wasn't used to.

Raking a hand through my hair, I let out a deep breath, trying to expel the negative emotions building up inside. She had left with Caleb and that fact twisted my stomach.

It was one of those times I wished I could get drunk, then I would be able to numb the pain I was feeling. But spending years cleaning up after my mom, I couldn't bring myself to have more than a few drinks. Besides, I liked to be in control and I needed a clear head for that.

This girl is screwing with your mind, I told myself. I couldn't think straight because all I could think of was Caleb kissing her, or worse. No. I couldn't even think about that.

My physical reaction only affirmed the reasons I had kept rules in place. To protect myself from girls and them from falling for me.

A knock on my door stopped me wrestling with my thoughts. Had Paige come looking for me? Feeling annoyed, I walked to the door and opened it.

Momentarily I was taken by surprise. Taylor stood outside my bedroom, looking nervous. But then I remembered her rejection earlier. That was enough to harden myself toward her.

"Ah, you're back," I remarked.

"I need to talk to you," she said softly.

I frowned slightly, not sure I wanted to talk to her. As I thought about it, I stood unyielding in the doorway to my room. It was only curiosity that made me consider allowing her in. I studied her as I tried to decide if I wanted to hear what she had to say. My tongue flickered against my lip ring.

What had made her come back? I had watched her leave with Caleb, but not even an hour later here she was outside my bedroom door.

It only took me a few seconds to step back and motion her inside. I watched as she entered my room and closed the door. I leaned against it as I allowed my gaze to sweep over her.

She had her arms crossed as she stared back.

"So talk," I told her firmly.

She licked her bottom lip and I couldn't stop myself from following the motion, sending a thrill through me.

"You never gave me a chance to explain why I stopped

you," she began to say.

On the outside, I was the calm self-assured playboy, but on the inside I wasn't. The only tell-tale sign was my nervous habit of touching the tip of my tongue against my lip ring. It was a habit when I was unsure.

I watched how her eyes were drawn to the action before she made a point of looking me straight in the eye. I waited for her to continue.

"Caleb and I went out a couple of times. I didn't want to start something with you before I could make it clear to Caleb that I just wanted to be friends and nothing more."

She finally shed light on the reason she had stopped me in the bathroom.

"With me it's not 'something,' it is just sex," I felt compelled to tell her. By stating the words out loud, I wasn't allowing her to misread my actions even if this thing with her was unchartered territory for me. I never went back and here I was ready to pick up where we had left off.

"I know."

She shifted slightly as the silence continued. The time for talking was over. I closed the distance between us with intent and purposeful steps toward her. She was nervous despite her attempt to hold my bold gaze.

"This thing with you... I want more than one night," I told her softly, stopping in front of her.

I wasn't going to touch her until we agreed on my terms. I still had to hold some control over what was happening between us for me to even consider going forward. If she disagreed I would show her the door and keep my distance. It was all or nothing with me.

"Okay." She nodded.

"This has to be exclusive, though. I don't want you to touch another girl while this is going on between us," she added with a slight frown.

For a few moments I considered her request. It was reasonable. Besides, I wasn't going to tell her that I hadn't been attracted to another since I had met her.

"Fine. Exclusive fucking," I agreed. "Any more rules you want to put in place?"

"No," she said.

"No feelings, just sex, and when it ends we walk away," I reminded her on the terms we had agreed to as I took another step closer. She had to look up at me to hold my gaze.

"Yes."

Finally. I reached for her slowly, not wanting to rush things. My hands threaded through her hair, preparing to kiss her. My breath brushed against her lips as I leaned closer before touching my mouth to hers. She slid her arms around my neck as we kissed tentatively. When she opened her lips and my tongue brushed against hers, I felt a rush of heat at the taste of her sweet mouth.

The urge to take her quickly and bury myself as deep as I could took hold but I stopped myself. She wasn't a virgin anymore but I couldn't be rough with her. My hands lifted her off her feet. Her legs wrapped around me, securing herself against me.

With our mouths fused together, I caressed her tongue with mine. My fingers dug into her soft skin. I wanted her exactly the way we'd been earlier, so with my focus still on her, my one hand left her long enough to open the door and I carried her down the hallway to the bathroom.

Once inside, I closed the door behind us. The only time I released her was to set her down on the counter and to lock the door so no one would interrupt us. My heart was beating with excitement as I opened her legs and stepped between them. I was in complete control and she looked at me nervously.

"I want to pick up where we left off," I murmured before

I kissed her. My hands rode up her legs, pushing up her skirt. I gripped the sides of her panties and slid them down her legs. Once off, I discarded them on the floor.

I lifted her top and she took it off. It was the next item to be dumped on the floor. Her eyes glittered and I covered her mouth with mine, harder than before, my actions more urgent. The need to have her was too difficult to fight. It was like swimming against a tsunami—impossible. My own arousal strained against the confines of my jeans.

She needed to be ready or it would hurt. I trailed my mouth from her lips down the side of her neck and she groaned. The sound warmed the inside of my chest. I pulled her bra down and flicked my tongue against her nipple. She gasped and I smiled at her, enjoying how I could make her react. Her hands gripped my shoulders tightly as I straightened.

"Are you ready?" I whispered against her lips. My hand went between her legs, seeking her heat. My eyes held hers as I slid a finger into her. She gasped. She was more than ready.

"Yes," she gasped when I added another finger. She moved her hips in rhythm to my fingers pumping into her.

"Tell me what you want," I said, increasing the tempo and watching her briefly close her eyes.

"I... want," she tried to say.

"You want me here," I said firmly, pressing my fingers harder into her.

"Yes," she panted. Her heavy-lidded eyes fixed on mine.

I'd waited long enough. I removed my fingers from her to undo my jeans and drop them to the floor. My boxers followed closely behind. I got a foil packet and ripped it open with my teeth before rolling it down my length.

I allowed my eyes one quick sweep of the trembling girl I was about to take to new heights. She gripped the counter as I leaned forward and kissed her hard. I opened her legs wider and as I stepped between them she pressed her legs against my sides.

My heart was beating so fast when I lined up our bodies. I watched her react as I nudged her before I began to enter her slowly. Then I gripped her butt and pulled her closer, sliding into her to the hilt. God, she felt so good.

"I can't take it slow," I warned her softly, briefly pulling out to slam back into her.

"I need to fuck you," I rasped, holding her in place with my hand holding tightly onto her hips. I thrust back into her harder.

At this rate I wasn't going to last long. She felt better than I had remembered. But I wanted her to come before I lost my load. I pounded into her, trying to angle our friction against her clit.

"Harder," she instructed as I felt her tense, knowing she was going to climax soon. I kept the angle, feeling the building up as I continued to fuck her.

My tongue brushed against my bottom lip as I watched her anticipating her climax. Then she came, gripping me tighter. I pushed into her a few more times before I trembled with my own release.

Chapter Ten

After we finished, I got rid of the condom and zipped up my jeans. I watched Taylor find her panties and slide them on again. Just watching her made me hot for her again. It was mad that such an innocent action had me hungry for her. It wasn't like she was actively trying to seduce me, even I could see that.

"It's hard to believe you haven't done this much," I said, watching her, but she just gave me a dismissive shrug. The way her eyes caught mine before she looked away told me she was still nervous. It was incredible that we had just been as close as two people could be and she still didn't feel completely comfortable.

I wasn't even going to analyze how I felt around her. The warning lights were going off in my head. *Let her go. Let her walk out and keep your distance from her.* But I ignored it. After tasting her, I needed more—a lot more.

I was done analyzing or thinking. I was going to go with

my instinct. I wanted her and I would have her.

"I'd better go," she said, making an attempt to leave when she reached for the door handle.

"It's too late," I told her, stopping her with a hand to her wrist. My touch was firm but light. "Besides, I'm not finished with you yet."

Her eyes met mine and every intention I had for her lay open for her to see in my eyes. She swept her tongue across her bottom lip. I reached out a hand and she put hers in mine. My fingers closed around hers and I took her back to my room.

I let go of her hand to get my phone from my desk.

"What's your number?" I asked, briefly looking up at her.

She rattled it off and I programmed it into my phone. I ignored the fact that I had never asked a girl for her number before. *This is just about sex,* I told myself. *Great sex.*

"Give me your phone," I told her and she gave it to me.

I put my number into hers under my name—Sin.

"So how does this work?" she asked when I handed her phone back.

It was difficult not to look at her like I wanted to take her right back to bed and do all the naughty things I had planned for her. My blood thickened with the thought.

"Whenever we need relief, we call each other," I explained and she blushed, a reminder she wasn't like the experienced girls I was used to. But there was something primal about being her first. I moved closer and raised my hand to feather a touch to her cheek as I smirked at her.

"And no hooking up with other people," I said, restating the rules we had agreed on. "No feelings, just mind-blowing sex. And when we're done, we both walk away."

I did feel some satisfaction that Mr. Preppy and other guys who I had seen check her out would not be able to have her, at least for the short time we worked each other out of our systems.

It would be the first time I would be having exclusive sex with someone and it didn't fill me with the fear I had expected. Anything restrictive on what I did and with whom was something that was important to me and I thought the loss of it wouldn't be something I could deal with. But here I was, making plans with Taylor without feeling like there was a noose being tightened around my neck.

Now that the talking was over it was time to get physical. I kissed her, capturing her lips and with the gentle sweep of my tongue she opened her mouth. Our tongues brushed against each other and I needed more. Her hands went to my chest and my heart beat increased under the splay of her one hand.

I walked her back and lowered her down on my bed. All thoughts and warnings emptied out of my head the moment I began to discard her clothes.

I hadn't had enough of her, not by a long shot. My clothes followed hers onto the floor. She looked at me shyly as I stood confident in my nakedness. Her eyes ran over me as she lay naked on top of my bed.

"Tell me what you want?" I asked her as I lay down beside her. My hand drifted down the curve of her breast to her hip.

"I..." She began to stutter.

"This is just you and me. There is no need to be nervous."

She didn't have much experience and I wanted to give her a chance to explore her sexuality, let her figure out what she liked and what she didn't.

Her eyes dropped lower.

"Do you want to touch me?" I asked huskily, feeling myself rearing for her touch.

Her tongue swept quickly across her lips and she nodded.

I lay down on my back and put my hands under my head, giving her complete control to do what she wanted.

"Touch me," I encouraged. Her eyes met mine nervously.

She knelt beside me and tentatively wrapped her hand around me. I closed my eyes briefly as I enjoyed the light touch of her fingers.

"Is this okay?" she asked softly, her movements slow as she moved her hand up and down.

"Yes."

As she began to become more confident in her actions, she increased the tempo. I gripped my hands under my head as the motion began to make me want to take control of the situation and bury myself in her in one swift motion.

Then her tongue swept against me and I held my breath, trying to keep my control. I opened my eyes to watch her take me into her mouth. Gritting my teeth, I tried to hold on as she worked me slowly with an explorative tongue.

My muscles strained while I watched her. It was the most erotic thing I had ever experienced. Her hand gripped me more tightly and I squeezed my eyes closed when I could feel the familiar tightening just before I was about to lose my load.

"I won't last if you keep that up," I told her, my breathing hard from the exertion of trying to control myself. I was only hanging on by a thread.

"Really?" she asked me with those innocent blue eyes.

I couldn't take it anymore; I had taken control. My mouth found hers and I kissed her hard as I got a condom from my side table. My teeth scraped against her bottom lip. I pulled away only long enough to put on the protection.

The throbbing of need pulsed through me while I pushed her down onto her hands and knees. My hands caressed her butt as I found her heat first with my fingers to ensure she was ready to take me. I held her hips, trying not to hold her hard enough to leave bruises as I slid into her. She groaned and I gave her a moment to adjust before I began to rock into her. Slowly at first and then I sped up.

Her hands held on to the sheets and she panted as I slammed into her. Over and over again. My muscles strained. Her body tensed and then she cried out as she came.

I only lasted a few seconds more when I shuddered through my orgasm. I allowed myself a few moments to ride the rush of peacefulness that followed. My cheek was against her back as I tried to even my breathing. Then I got off the bed and left her, to get rid of the condom.

When I reentered the room, she was lying on her side and her eyes were closed. The steady rise and fall of her chest told me she had fallen asleep. I smiled to myself when I thought about how thoroughly I had worn her out. My eyes drifted over every inch of her as I walked to the bed. *She is beautiful,* I thought to myself when I got in beside her and pulled the covers over the two of us.

I woke her up with kisses before I made her shatter one last time.

And for the third time, she slept beside me in the bed. That night, instead of tossing and turning, wrestling with the dark memories from my past like I did most evenings, this time I slept peacefully.

In the middle of the night I awoke to find myself lying on my stomach, half on top of Taylor. For a moment in the darkness only lit by the moonlight, I let myself take in her peaceful sleeping features. But I stopped myself from trailing my fingers across her face. Instead I tightened my hold around her waist, allowing myself to hold her closer.

I ignored the thoughts that questioned my actions. I was done justifying things to myself. I knew what this was with Taylor and after we were finished it would be over. As simple as that.

A few hours later when I rolled onto my back and opened my eyes, I wasn't surprised to see the space beside me empty. But this time I didn't feel that familiar unsettled feeling at her missing presence. It was probably the fact that we now had an arrangement in place.

I rubbed my chest while I thought about my night with Taylor. A smile touched my lips as I thought about how satisfied she had been when she'd finally fallen asleep. This was unknown territory for me but I was looking forward to spending a few more nights teaching Taylor about sex and how good it could be.

But it wouldn't last forever. I would get bored, it was only a matter of time. And when that happened I would cut her loose like every other girl before her.

The only thing out of place when I went downstairs later and found Slater eating his favorite cereal was the smile on his face.

"You look like you had a good night," I said to him as I got some orange juice from the fridge and poured some into a glass.

He ate his last spoonful before he put his bowl and spoon into the sink.

"I did."

"With who?" It had to be a girl.

He turned to lean against the counter, his hands on either side.

"Jordan."

"Taylor's roommate?" I asked, not quite believing that the girl who pretty much hated me for the way I lived my life would be getting friendly with my best friend who lived his life the same way I did. We both had reputations.

I took a drink of the orange juice as he confirmed with a nod.

"I thought she hated us?" I murmured, trying to read what he wasn't saying.

"Apparently not." He gave me a dismissive shrug.

"So what happened between the two of you?" I asked. Usually we didn't discuss details, but this girl was different.

"We talked," he murmured softly like he had done something he shouldn't have.

My eyes narrowed as I watched him. He was worse with commitment than I was and he had spent the whole night just talking to a girl? The red sirens in my mind were going off in my head for him.

"Be careful." I set down my half-empty glass of juice on the counter. I felt compelled to warn him.

"The same way you have to be careful with Taylor." He was only stating what I already knew but I wasn't about to lay it out for him to analyze.

I had already spent so much time going over it again and again in my head, and I was sure I was making the right choice. Besides, I couldn't walk away yet. I hadn't had enough of her. Just the thought of her last night, naked in my bed, filled my chest with a warm, prideful feeling.

"I know what I'm doing," I assured him as I crossed my arms. Despite my words he did not look convinced.

"It's just sex. That's it." I raked a hand through my hair.

"I hope for your sake it is," he said and I frowned.

It was.

His warning lingered in my mind as I tried to work on an assignment later, but after thirty minutes I gave up, deciding to retry the next day.

I checked my watch. It was late afternoon. I was due for

a visit to my mother and with the uncertainty I felt with Taylor, I decided to pack for a short visit with my mom.

Just before I left, I called her to tell her I would be there a little later. The excitement in her voice scratched the surface of my skin like a knife. It felt like a physical pain. Once I ended the call, I asked myself if I was doing the right thing by going to see her.

You need to remember what happens when you let people in. If you care, they have the power to hurt you. Even my father, who I had never meant, had hurt me with his rejection.

"Where are you going?" Slater asked when he watched me descend the last couple of steps with a bag packed.

"My mom's."

"You want company?" he asked, studying me as he put the game controller down.

I shook my head. I knew it was his way of protecting me but I knew how seeing my mother reminded him of a childhood he didn't want to remember either.

"I'll be back tomorrow."

I usually only spent one night, ensuring I limited my exposure to my mother. Seeing her would reopen the wounds that would remind me of what was at stake.

"Call if you need anything," my best friend said as he went back to the game he was playing.

I left the house and dumped my bag in the back of my Jeep. The sight of my car reminded me of a time when I had just inherited more money than I had known what to do with. Initially overwhelmed, I had spent it on a red Ferrari. Back then I had more money than sense. After wrapping it around a pole and surviving it with only some bruises, I swore I would never do that again.

So now I only bought what I needed, not enough to let anyone suspect I was well-off. The car was nice but it didn't scream 'rich.'

I put the radio on when I started the car up and backed out of the driveway. I cranked up the music, hoping it would keep my mind off the growing feeling of dread in my stomach.

There had been so many times I had seen what normal families looked like and wished I'd had the same. But all the wishing in the world hadn't changed anything. The only thing that didn't send me into a spiral of panic was the fact that I was in charge of my life now. The fear of being put into foster care was gone, as well as the daily fear of possibly finding my mother's lifeless body.

When I finally arrived in front of the house where my mother now lived with a nurse who could take care of her, I sat for a few minutes, building up the courage to get out of the car.

It was difficult to deal with the fact that every time I was around my mother, I was transported back to the young boy who was fearful of what was going to happen.

I let out a deep emotional breath before I got out of the car and got my overnight bag from the seat. Even though I had my own set of keys, I knocked on the door. I had bought and furnished the house for her but it didn't feel like a home for me.

"Hi, Mr. Carter," Sally, my mother's live-in nurse greeted me when she opened the door and ushered me inside. She was an experienced nurse in her late thirties who had come highly recommended.

"Sally," I greeted her with a nod. My eyes swept the living room to find my mother sitting with a blanket over her legs. Her eyes lit up when she saw me. She looked so happy to see me and I felt a pang of guilt that I didn't feel the same.

I dropped my bag by the entrance and made my way to my mom to give her a kiss on the cheek. Her hands gripped my face as she pressed a kiss to the side of my face.

"It's so good to see you," my mom said, releasing my face to tightly grab my hand. It was like she was scared to let me go.

"You look well," I said. I looked a lot like my mom. She had the same dark hair as me but her eyes were a dark brown. I hadn't met my father but I assumed my blue eyes were inherited from him.

She looked much older than her age. Her skin was pale and drawn, adding at least ten years to her features.

"I feel good," she added and her smile increased. "Especially now that you're here."

I wanted to feel the same but I didn't. And I wondered if I ever would.

Chapter Eleven

It was there, sitting beside my mother, looking into her glittering eyes filled with excitement, that I had a thought. If I failed to embrace what I could have with her now, I was throwing away the second chance we had been given.

There had to be a reason she had survived to clean up her act. It couldn't all be for nothing.

It made me look at her differently while she told me about her week. Her smile was infectious and I found myself smiling too. I also noticed a light in her eyes that I had never seen there before. For the first time, I looked at her as she was, not the drunken mother who hadn't been able to cope with the responsibility of a young child who had been a constant reminder of one mistake that had changed her whole life.

I would always have the difficult memories from my past, but I couldn't allow them to shadow my future.

That night Sally retired to her room after I assured her I

would put my mom to bed later. I stayed up for a while, talking to my mom. It was way past her bedtime when I helped her to her room and pulled the covers up to her shoulders.

"I love you," she murmured. There was so much emotion in her eyes that I found it hard to pull my eyes away from her and sever the connection between us.

I wanted to say the same back but I couldn't. Even if I had realized I could give her more than I had before, I wasn't ready to say those words to her. I still needed more time.

I gave her a kiss on her cheek before switching off her light.

Letting out a deep breath, I sat down in the living room. My phone started to ring and I answered it before it could wake anyone else.

"Boss," the voice said and I instantly recognized who it was. Besides, there was only one person who called me that.

"Jeff," I greeted, leaning back into the chair.

"You at your mom's?" he asked.

"Yeah."

The call abruptly disconnected and then there was a faint knock at the door. I got up and answered it. Jeff stood outside. His head was shaved and the array of tattoos that covered his body only added to the aura of danger that surrounded him.

He was a good friend of mine and Slater's who we'd met when we had joined a gang. Unlike a lot of the other members, I had seen some good in him. Like Slater and me, he had only joined the gang for survival. And I trusted him.

It was only after I had inherited the money from my father that I had the freedom to pay our way out of the gang. And there was no way I was going to turn my back on Jeff and leave him to a dangerous life. He was my friend and had pulled me out of more than a few dangerous situations.

"It's good to see you," I said, bumping fists with him.

"I saw your car." He nodded in the direction of my Jeep.

"Yeah, it was a last-minute decision." I shrugged.

Employing Jeff had been the next logical step for me. It was a way for him to earn a living and keep him on the right side of the law. I had someone to watch over my mother. Not many people knew what I was worth but there were a few unsavory people who did and that was one too many for me. Jeff was my security.

From the start of our arrangement he'd gone from calling me by my name to 'Boss.' I had told him it made me feel like a Mafia boss but he had refused to call me something different. He regularly checked in on my mom and kept an eye on things for me.

We talked softly, standing outside on the porch. He lit up a cigarette. It was a habit I was glad I had never picked up.

There hadn't been much going on but I could not let my guard down. I didn't know if there would ever be a time when I wouldn't be looking over my shoulder. It came with the territory of having been in a group of law-breaking individuals who had no conscience when it came to getting what they wanted.

Drugs and guns had only been the tip of the iceberg.

"You wanna beer?" I asked. He shook his head.

"I need to go." I nodded, knowing he had responsibilities. He had a sister he looked after. She was younger than him and I knew she was still in high school. I didn't know why his parents were missing in his life. It was something he had never opened up about. Looking back at my childhood, I don't know how I would have coped if I'd had the responsibility of a younger sibling. Getting through it on my own had been difficult enough. It made me respect Jeff more.

He left, disappearing into the night, and I went back

indoors.

When I finally made it into bed I was tired. I had come here thinking I would hate every minute of being in my mother's company but it hadn't been that bad. I rubbed my chin as I looked back on my conversation with her.

I didn't feel that usual resentfulness or simmering anger. Somehow I had managed to view the relationship with my mother a little differently and it had made it easier to be around her. We were still a long way off a normal mother-and-son relationship, though.

I tossed and turned for a while before I fell asleep.

Even Slater was surprised at my good mood when I got back from my overnight visit with my mother. Usually when I got back I was moody and irritable.

With a frown, he had asked, "Did it go well?" He could tell something was different but he couldn't tell what.

"Yeah." I didn't go into the details of why I seemed to hate my mother less. I understood why but I couldn't explain it to someone else.

My good mood continued for the next couple of days until the moment I was leaning against the wall, waiting to see if I could catch a glimpse of Taylor. Then I spotted her walking toward me. Just the sight of her was enough for me to stop, but it was the guy she was talking to that turned my mood. Mr. Preppy.

She laughed at something he said and I felt the jealously jolt through me. And then her hand rested on his arm for a moment. My eyes fixed to the action as I felt the jealousy roll through me, leaving me feeling raw inside.

Then Taylor looked up and caught my gaze. She gave me a tentative smile but all I could concentrate on was the guy standing beside her. A possessive feeling I wasn't used to flared inside of me, making me want to mark her as mine.

And while we were in an arrangement, she *was* mine. I wasn't going to share her.

She didn't seem to know whether to approach me or not. Caleb noticed she was looking in my direction and leaned closer to her to say something to her while I continued to glare at him.

Our eyes met again when I pushed off the wall and strode over to them.

"Hi," I said to Taylor, giving her a smile to try and cover the anger I felt. I didn't want her to see how affected I was.

"Hi," she replied huskily.

Caleb touched her arm again and I had to fight the urge to remove it. Anger like hot lava burned through me and I exerted all my control not to let it loose.

"I need to talk to you," I said firmly.

"Sure," she said before she turned to face Caleb.

"I'll see you tomorrow," she said to him. I frowned. I didn't want her around him.

The smile he gave made me tense my jaw as I held on to the last of my control. But when he glared at me, I glared right back, making it clear I didn't like him one bit.

"I'll see you tomorrow," he said to her before walking off.

I tongued my lip ring as I fought for control over my raging emotions. Taylor turned to face me and I had the urge to brand her as mine. To assure myself that she only belonged to me, and there was only one way I knew of for how to do that.

I grabbed her hand and looked for some privacy. Then I remembered a janitor's closet nearby. I strode with determination, pulling her along. Without exchanging a word, we turned the corner and I saw the door to the closet.

Once I opened the door, I pulled her inside the dimly lit room and closed the door behind us. My heart was beating faster with anticipation mingled in with my tense mood.

When she faced me, she opened her mouth but I didn't give her a chance to say anything. My mouth covered hers with only one intention in mind.

My hands went to her hips as I continued to kiss her. She raked her fingers through my hair, pulling me closer. She groaned when I increased the pressure of my mouth against hers as my tongue entered her mouth and slid against hers. I needed her more than I ever had before. The intensity of it took me by surprise but there was no stopping it. All I could do was feel, with no rational thought. There was no decision-making, no choices, there was only action as I lifted her by the waist and her legs wrapped around mine.

I needed her now. There was no time for foreplay or undressing. I had to get inside of her as quickly as possible. It was all that mattered. I would only have the reassurance that she was mine when I was buried as deep as I could be in her heat.

My mouth moved down her jaw before my tongue touched the spot just below her ear that made her gasp. I knew exactly how to play her to make her hot for me. She ground her body more insistently against mine. I wasn't going to last long if she kept that up.

I pushed her up against the wall and held her there with my body as I slipped my fingers below her skirt and between her legs. I could feel her wetness through the thin fabric of her panties as I ran my finger lightly over the material. She was ready for me. I could smell it. With her hot breath against my face, I moved her panties aside and slid one finger into her. Then I added another. Her hands dug into my shoulders as she trembled while I pumped my fingers into her. She moved against my hand, panting with each movement, straining for the release only I could give her.

A warmth filled my chest at the thought that no other guy had ever been this intimate with her.

I kissed her again, addicted to the sweet taste of her lips. It was a mixture of peppermint and vanilla.

"Please," she begged in a whisper.

I stopped to remove my fingers from her before I eased her down to stand. She held me tightly like I was going to leave her but I wasn't going anywhere. I reached for the foil packet in the back of my jeans and tore it open with my teeth. I unbuttoned my jeans and dropped them to the floor. Then I freed my erection from my boxers to roll on the protection.

The sound of my heavy breathing intermingled with Taylor's when I kissed her again. My hands lifted her with only one goal in mind. When her legs wrapped around me again, I lined myself up with her before she sank down on me. The warmth of her tightened around me as she gasped. Sheathed inside her, my lips found hers and I groaned as I began to fuck her. My thrusts were hard and quick.

She is mine, I thought as I drew back and reentered her. Her hands were on my shoulders and I was watching her expression as I took her up against the wall.

The slight tensing of her body against mine told me she was close and then she shattered, biting her lip to stop herself from crying out as she climaxed. Now that she was done, I concentrated only on my own release. My movements were more aggressive as I thrust into her again and again.

I felt the tightening just before I came, shuddering as it swept through me. I leaned against her for a moment, my breathing hard.

The anger that had driven me had dissipated, leaving me to analyze my actions.

I eased her down to the floor. She was wobbly, still

struggling to stand. I leaned my head against hers for a moment with my hands on either side of her as it began to dawn on me what I had done.

My lips touched her gently like I could erase how roughly I had just taken her. I felt remorse.

And then the need to get away took hold. I pulled away from her. Her eyes met mine for a moment and I felt the weight of the guilt on my shoulders. Her lips were red from the force of my mouth against hers.

I had never lost control like that with a girl before and it scared me. I got rid of the condom in a nearby trashcan before getting dressed. The need to escape was urgent when I felt my lungs restricting. I couldn't even look at her again so I kept my eyes on my hands as I fastened my jeans.

Feeling the rising bile in the back of my throat, I couldn't even bring myself to look at her one last time. And I didn't know what to say so I just opened the door and walked out.

I rubbed my hand over my face as I strode away.

Only when I reached my car did I stop long enough to get in. For a while I just sat in the driver's seat, trying to sort through the mess of thoughts and memories in my head.

Seeing her with Caleb had pushed me to prove she was mine. And I had. I had taken her roughly, ensuring my ego that I was the only one she had ever been physical with. The loss of control I had felt had scared me. I didn't like the feeling of not being able to rein myself in and I didn't know how to deal with it.

Memories of her gasping as I slid into her replayed in my mind and I closed my eyes, briefly hating the wave of self-loathing I felt. I gripped the steering wheel tightly.

She was dangerous and with every interaction her hold over me was growing.

It's just lust, a physical reaction to her, I told myself. But I wasn't totally convinced.

Before, I hadn't cared who they screwed before or after I was done with them.

The feeling of possessiveness over her had been an alien feeling. In my mind I tried to work out why I felt that way.

We had a physical arrangement to sleep together. Was I only acting this way because I had felt Caleb was encroaching on my territory? It wasn't about feelings or emotions. No, she was mine to have when I wanted her. A purely physical thing, I convinced myself.

Each time with her only reinforced our attraction. Even though I had taken her roughly it had been mind-blowing. But still, I could have hurt her. Had I been too rough? I replayed through the scene, finding no evidence that I had.

Now that I had somehow rationalized my emotions, I could breathe easier. The tightness in my chest loosened. My hold on the steering wheel slackened and I leaned back, letting out a deep breath.

This was new and now I was unsure of how to tackle it. The jealousy and my response had been alien to me. She had that way of making me do things I hadn't done before. It unsettled me.

Chapter Twelve

I don't know what made me drive to Taylor's dorm after I pulled myself together enough to see my actions for what they were—an act of possession, needing reassurance that despite what I had seen she was still only mine.

I found myself parking a few streets away. A feeling of nervous apprehension stirred in the pit of my stomach at what she might say to me.

I didn't do *this*. I didn't apologize for my actions. But here I was, headed to her room, ready to tell her I hadn't meant to be so rough or to leave her so abruptly without a word being said. I could still feel the impression of her lips on mine from kissing her so hard. It only reminded me of my loss of control.

There was a chance that words wouldn't be able to fix this. I wasn't even sure if she was there, but I felt a need to set things right even though I had no idea what I was going to say.

It was only when I neared her building that I looked up. The sight stopped me in my tracks.

The anger I had experienced before resurfaced as I watched Taylor talking to a guy I didn't recognize. He looked too old to be a student. Perhaps he was a new lecturer. The casual clothes he wore screamed money. Whoever he was, money wasn't in short supply.

My eyes narrowed as I studied their interaction. He hugged her and their closeness made me frown as I continued to watch them.

I wasn't the jealous type but this was the second time in less than an hour I had felt the burning emotion that fogged logical reasoning. I had trust issues and it didn't come easy. It was difficult to trust that there wasn't more going on with them than a friendly interaction between two people.

Then he released her.

Was he competition? Taylor was beautiful so it wasn't a surprise that she had so much interest from the opposite sex, but I didn't compete. Before, there had been no need to.

They knew each other. I could tell by their easy and familiar exchange that Taylor knew him well. Who was he?

Like some sort of stalker, I stood there, unable to walk away, watching them closely. I analyzed every look between them. She smiled at him and I frowned. They began to walk and I contemplated whether I was going to follow them.

What's wrong with you? I asked myself, refusing to act like some jealous guy. If I turned and left now she would have no idea I had come back to talk to her. But no matter how much I urged myself to distance myself, my feet were like concrete, unable to move.

It's your own fault, my conscience reminded me. *You broke your rules and this is the consequence.* Deep down I knew there was some truth to the warning going off in my mind. They walked a few feet before coming to a stop.

You're overreacting. We had agreed to be exclusive while we were trying to work each other out of our systems. She had been a virgin, for crying out loud. I couldn't believe she was two-timing me. But I had to admit I didn't like seeing other guys around, especially in Caleb's case, since I could see by his body language that he wanted her.

My fear was that maybe I wouldn't be enough. I had never kept a girl around so there had never been a need to keep them. What if I couldn't hold her attention until I was ready to cut her from my life?

They were having a serious conversation. Then she took his hand in hers.

It tugged loose something inside my chest. The pain was like a raw, open wound that winded me. I unclenched my one fist to touch my chest briefly, assuring myself the pain was inside.

For a moment I was transported back in time to when I was a little boy who still had hope that his mother would love him enough to pull her life together. That hope hadn't survived for very long. The cold, hard reality of my life had been hard to ignore after empty promises from my mother. They had just been empty words.

I swallowed, trying to bring myself back to the present. Reliving the hopeless betrayal from my past was enough to make me want to turn and leave.

She tugged him forward by his hand. I continued to watch as I tried to shake off what I was feeling, like I didn't care. And if it had been any other girl, I wouldn't have. Then as if in slow motion her eyes found mine. I also caught the attention of the blond stranger, who studied me with interest.

Any previous thoughts and guilt were replaced by a feeling of betrayal so intense it still burned in my chest. My eyes only left hers to look down to where her hand was still intertwined with the stranger's. Here I had been prepared to tell her I was sorry for how I had treated her but all I wanted to do now was get as far away from her as possible.

I shook my head, still feeling Taylor's watchful gaze. It was too much. I had to get away. Finally I turned around and walked away.

Twice in one day I had spotted her with other guys. I wasn't the jealous type but even I recognized the strong emotions I had felt.

She is just a girl. One of many, I told myself to downplay my response. She was replaceable. But even I recognized I was lying to myself. She wasn't just some girl. She was a girl I was attracted to enough to want her more than once.

I still hadn't managed to work through the emotions that I'd had to deal with in the last couple of hours.

"Rough day?" Slater asked when he saw me walk through the front door.

He could read me better than anyone. I briefly nodded, disappearing up to my room, needing to be alone. I felt like a caged animal as I paced the length of my room.

I rolled my shoulders, trying to get rid of the tension. I got my phone and some earphones, scrolling through any playlist to find something loud enough to drown out my thinking. I kicked my shoes off before lying down in my bed and selecting a song from my favorite heavy-metal band. I hit play and looked up at the ceiling.

The intro to the song was slow but then the drumming and singing from the lead singer drowned out any rational thought. It was the only way to calm the chaos inside. I drummed my hand against my leg in beat with the drums.

I listened to music for well over an hour before the song got cut off by the insistent ringing of my phone. It was Taylor. My thumb hovered over to answer it but I couldn't bring myself to speak to her. I wasn't ready and I wasn't even sure if I could.

When it stopped ringing I pulled the earphones from my ears and threw them in the drawer beside my bed. Was she calling to explain who the guy was? Even if it was innocent I was still too worked up to listen.

Needing to work off some of my anger, I changed into some sweats, not bothering with a shirt, and then headed downstairs to work out. It was one of the few things that helped me work through my emotions.

Avoiding emotional attachments wasn't healthy but I couldn't bring myself to risk getting hurt. I didn't love Taylor. But in the short time I had known her, I had gotten far more attached than I wanted to admit.

"You want some company?" Slater asked as I descended the stairs.

"Sure." I didn't really want company but Slater wasn't just anybody. He had a way of knowing when to talk to me and when not to.

He followed me into the garage. I faced the boxing bag and gave Slater a chance to hold it with both hands before I tightened my hands into fists. I began to pound the bag, imagining the smug face of Caleb. I wanted to wipe that self-assured smile from his face.

Slater remained quiet, knowing I didn't want to talk. So instead he held the bag so I could hit it with everything I had. Sweat poured down my strained muscles. I hit it again and again until the pain in my muscles made it impossible to keep going.

I leaned my head against the bag with both my hands resting on it as I tried to inhale. It was difficult. My lungs burned from the physical exertion.

"That bad?" Slater said, breaking the tense silence.

"Yeah," I breathed, lifting my head long enough to look him in the eyes.

I inhaled and held the breath before allowing the air to

rush from my lungs.

"It's Taylor, isn't it?"

I refused to answer but he could read me. He already knew it was about the pretty little blonde who had me all tied up in knots. I didn't need to confirm it to him.

"Maybe you need to end things with her." He let go of the bag and studied me.

I shook my head. I didn't smoke or overindulge with alcohol. But I was addicted to Taylor and giving her up before I was ready wasn't an option.

"I can't. Not just yet."

They were only a few words but it confirmed that in the end I would let her go and move on. It was just a matter of when.

Later, after I had a shower, I sat at my desk and toyed with my phone in my hand. I still wasn't ready to return her call. Maybe tomorrow after I got some sleep I might feel I was in a better space to be able to talk to her.

I didn't want to admit to anyone—even myself—that I had been jealous seeing her with other guys.

It was Friday night and it was party night. The house was already filling up. Slater stood beside me with a beer bottle in his hand.

"I invited Jordan." I shot him a questioning side look.

He didn't face me, but he nodded.

"I told her to bring Taylor."

I wasn't mad. The truth was I wasn't sure how I felt. I still hadn't called her back. I didn't know how to approach the situation and it just seemed best to let it work itself out. She would show up later with her friend and we would talk. Or not. There were other things I wanted to do with her.

But after seeing her with Caleb and the stranger, did I still trust her? It was difficult to think of Taylor as a liar so there was a part of me that trusted her. But the part of me that had been damaged by my mother's constant lies didn't.

I didn't even quite understand it myself so it was more difficult to explain to someone. And besides, I didn't talk about my past or what I had been through. Girls didn't want to hear about my sorry past. All they were interested in was here and now. They wanted Sin Carter, the bad boy who would give them a night they would never forget.

And so far I had lived up to my reputation. There was no need to make it more complicated.

It would be the same with Taylor. I was determined to give it a few more weeks, and when I tired of her, I would tell her that our arrangement was over. It would be the end.

Any doubt that I still only wanted Taylor was confirmed when a stunning brunette cornered me with an offer and a seductive smile. She held no interest and I disentangled myself from the situation to make a swift exit.

I was biding my time until Taylor arrived.

"Taylor's not coming," Slater said when he came to stand beside me. "I need to go and pick up Jordan."

I digested the information with an uneasy feeling in my stomach.

She was at it again. Doing the unexpected. Why couldn't she just do things the way other girls did? Was it the fact that she wasn't like other girls that held my attention? Like a shiny new toy.

"Sure." I gave him a brief nod.

"I won't be long," he assured me before he left me standing, wondering what my next move was going to be.

She wasn't going to come to me so that left me with only one course of action and that was to go to her.

I waited until Slater came back with Jordan before I put

my half-empty beer down on the first available surface and headed for the door.

"Where are you going?" Slater asked as I approached where he was standing with Jordan. She gave me a disapproving look, which left me with no doubt that she knew there was trouble between Taylor and me.

"Out," was my reply. I didn't want to go into details of where because then there might be a reason to explain why and I didn't want to talk about it.

The drive to her dorm was quick and before I knew it I was standing outside the door to her room. I didn't allow my unsettledness to delay me. I knocked gently and waited, shoving my hands into the front pockets of my jeans.

She opened the door a few moments later. Why had she not asked who it was? I could have been an axe-wielding murderer. She was dressed in an old pair of sweats and an oversized shirt that looked a couple of sizes too big for her. It even had a few well-worn holes. My anger was momentarily suspended by the sight of her.

She looked surprised to see me.

"I could have been a rapist or a murderer and you just opened the door without asking who it is," I told her with a frown.

It reminded me of her naivety.

"If it's my time to go it's my time to go," she replied flippantly.

"That is a strange outlook to have." I assessed her features to tell if she was mad at me.

She shrugged.

"Aren't you going to invite me in?" I asked, looking briefly past her but she was alone. It wasn't like I was expecting her to be with someone else.

"Are you going to rape or murder me?" she asked with a mischievous sparkle in her eye that made it difficult to stay angry with her.

"Not tonight," I shot back. She let me in and closed the door behind me. The room was small and I took in the nervous way her hands soothed over her shirt.

"Why are you here?" She was getting straight to the point. She tucked her hair behind her ear. I studied her, trying to figure what to say. Her teeth bit into her bottom lip. I had to yank my concentration back from thoughts of kissing her.

"I was expecting you to come to the party with Jordan. I wanted to talk to you."

"So when I didn't show, you came here?"

"Yes." I nodded.

Her reception was frosty. She wasn't going to make this easy. But I liked a challenge and I wasn't going to back down.

Yeah, I wasn't perfect. I had more issues than most. There were so many reasons for me to let things go and walk away but I couldn't. Like I had said to Slater, I wasn't ready yet.

"So talk," she said, crossing her arms, confirming she was not happy with what had happened. Was she angry that I had left her without a word in the janitor's closet? Or was she angry that I had walked away when she had been with the blond stranger? Or was she angry I hadn't called her back?

I pushed my tongue against my lip ring as I studied her, trying to decide what to say. This wasn't a familiar situation, needless to say I didn't do a lot of apologizing, but here I was ready to take responsibility for my actions.

"I wanted to apologize for the other day," I began. There, I had said it. My words took her by surprise. Her eyes widened as they held mine.

Chapter Thirteen

"I didn't mean to be so rough the other day in the janitor's closet," I said, watching her, trying to gauge what she was thinking but she was difficult to read. The nervous knot in my stomach tightened.

"I liked it," she said, taking me by surprise.

Who knew the innocent virgin I had first met would like hard up against the wall in a janitor's closet. I smiled. Maybe there was a naughty vixen inside her that was waiting to be set free. I would enjoy every moment of freeing her inhibitions.

"I'll remember that." My gaze went to her lips momentarily.

In the air, our chemistry sizzled between us, charged by the way she was looking at me like she couldn't wait for me to do it again. She swallowed. She was just as turned on as I was.

"Why did you just leave without saying a word?" she asked softly.

I studied her while I tried to find the right words to

explain my actions.

"I'm very territorial. I don't like to see the girl I'm fucking being hit on by another guy." I didn't trust Caleb at all. He did nothing to hide the interest in his eyes every time he looked at her.

She looked at me thoughtfully. I would have paid good money to know what was going on in her pretty little head.

"Caleb wasn't hitting on me. He is just a friend." She was still so naive.

"Are you sure he knows that?" I said, looking skeptical. I was a guy. I knew how guys operated and there was no doubt in my mind Caleb wanted her.

"Yes." She gave a slight nod.

Now that we had discussed the first incident of seeing her with another guy, it was time to approach the subject of the blond stranger she seemed to know too well for my liking. "Who was the other guy you were with?"

"He's my brother."

Well, I hadn't expected that. A brother. It hadn't even crossed my mind when I had watched them. But looking back now with that information I began to see the similarities. It also explained the affection and the ease at which they had interacted.

"When we put rules in place for this arrangement, we both agreed that we would be exclusive," she reminded me.

"I know, it's just like I said before...I'm territorial," I said, shrugging my shoulders. I didn't want to explain why I had trust issues. It would entail talking about my childhood and that wasn't something I opened up about. I didn't want her sympathy.

"When I agreed to being exclusive, I meant it." The tone of her voice left me with no doubt she was being sincere.

Not wanting to continue talking about it, I gave a brief nod.

"Have you eaten yet?"

She shook her head.

"Do you want to go and get something to eat?" This was a first and even took me by surprise. Clearly she hadn't been expecting it either, from the expression on her face.

"It's just food, not a date," ensuring she knew the difference. Our arrangement had an expiry date and she had to remember that. I didn't want her reading more into my actions.

"Sure. I just need to get some other clothes on."

I let my gaze sweep her from head to toe.

"You look fine," I argued. She would look beautiful in anything she wore. Even in her comfy clothes that had seen better days my hormones were raging.

"I need five minutes," she said, unconvinced.

"Meet me downstairs when you're ready." If I stayed we wouldn't be going anywhere. Besides, it gave me time to think over our conversation.

I was leaning against my car when she appeared, dressed in a pair of jeans and a shirt with sandals. There was only the slight smear of lip gloss on her lips. It made me want to kiss her but I refrained.

When she neared, I pushed off the car and opened the passenger side for her. She got in and I closed the door.

"I know a little place close by that makes killer burgers," I suggested when I got in the car.

"Sounds good." The fidgeting of her hands told me she was nervous.

There wasn't much talking while I drove to a nearby burger joint I had first discovered with Slater. On the outside it didn't look like much but their burgers were good. I gave Taylor a side glance to see her take it in.

"It might not look like much, but they make the best burgers," I told her after I parked the car and helped her out.

We went inside and ordered our food, and I paid the bill. I carried our drinks and straws out to any empty table outside. There was only one other couple eating on the patio.

"So why did you decide to go to college?" I asked just as we sat down. I gave her a soda before I opened mine.

"It just seemed to be the next logical step. What made you decide to go to college?"

"I wanted to prove I could do it," I answered.

College wasn't something kids in my neighborhood aspired to. We were lucky if we reached adulthood without a drug addiction or getting shot in a gang war.

"Who are you proving it to?" she asked tentatively, like she knew she was treading on a sensitive subject.

I considered her question for a few moments before I answered, "Myself."

I had wanted to prove that I was more than a guy with a bad childhood who had made some bad choices for survival.

"Why?" She frowned slightly as she asked the question.

"It's a long story." I wasn't going to divulge further into it.

It was time to steer the conversation away from me. "I want to know more about you."

"What do you want to know?" She shrugged.

I was used to feeling uncomfortable about people prying into my past but she looked a little apprehensive now that the spotlight was on her. Was she hiding something? Her slight discomfort at my question piqued my curiosity.

"Tell me about your family," I told her. It seemed to be the best starting point for the conversation.

I studied her closely, trying to read her body language, which was telling me she wasn't comfortable with the question I had asked. Was she hiding a family secret?

Had something happened in her childhood? I was confronted with the thought that maybe she had experienced something as bad, or worse, than I had.

"My parents are dead." Her revelation blew me away.

I couldn't imagine having no parents although if I looked back I was pretty much an orphan anyway. My father hadn't wanted any part in my life and my mother had spent all her time staring at the bottom of a bottle. No one had cared. Something twisted in my chest at the thought that Taylor had experienced that.

"That sucks," I said.

"Yeah, it does. My brother Connor looked after me." At least she hadn't been alone.

"How did your parents die?" I asked, needing to know more, despite knowing she didn't really want to talk about it. Could I blame her? No. I didn't want to talk about my crappy childhood so I understood why she didn't want to either.

"They died in a car accident," she shared.

"My father died." I don't know why I told her but the words were out. Was it to ease the glimmer of pain I had seen in her eyes? Would knowing that I had also experienced pain in my childhood make her feel less alone in her grief? To most people 'father' meant something more, deeper, but to me it was just a word to describe a stranger.

Unable to keep her gaze, I looked down at the straw I was still fidgeting with.

"I'm sorry," she said. I don't know why people said that.

"It's okay—he was an asshole." I lifted my eyes to meet hers. I could feel the muscles in my shoulders tense. Talking about him only reminded me of that feeling of abandonment I had experienced.

"So how long have you and Slater been friends?" she asked, trying to steer the conversation to a safer subject.

I smiled.

"We used to live next door to each other and we've been

friends from the time we could walk." Technically he had been about six when he had moved in next door to me.

"Do you have any siblings?" she asked.

"No, I'm an only child." I shook my head. Honestly I was glad I hadn't had a brother or sister to suffer along with me. It would have made it harder. Besides, Slater was as good as any blood sibling I could have had.

Our burgers arrived and we started to eat.

"Mmm," she sighed when she took her first bite.

At least she wasn't one of those girls who complained about their weight while pushing rabbit food around their plate.

"I told you," I said with my second smile in a matter of minutes. Not only did she have a way of tying me up in knots, she also had a way of making me feel more relaxed and peaceful when I was with her.

The rest of the conversation died away as we finished our food. Afterward I walked her back to my car and I drove her back to the dorm.

At the entrance of her dorm she turned nervously to me. I didn't want the night to end yet. I wanted more of her but I wanted her to be the one to make the move. After the quickie in the janitor's closet she needed to be the one to make clear what she wanted.

"Thank you, that was nice." She looked up at me with those pretty blue eyes that made my blood thicken.

"You're welcome." My gaze was intense.

"Do you want...to come in?" she asked, nervously brushing her hair aside. She didn't have to ask me twice. I allowed myself to embrace our attraction and I closed the distance between us. Her eyes lifted to mine as I cupped the back of her head. I kissed her gently and then our tongues caressed each other.

But one kiss was never enough with her. I needed more.

But I had to be clear about what was going to happen if I came upstairs. I broke the kiss. It was her naivety that made me want to spell it out for her.

"If I come in, we won't be talking," I whispered against her lips huskily. In my mind we were already naked in her bed.

"I know."

"I need to get something from my car." I needed protection.

"I'll meet you upstairs." She sounded breathless. I nodded as she walked to the building. I jogged to my car and opened the front door. In the glove compartment I found my stash of condoms and pocketed a few.

I hurried to the entrance of the dorm and went straight to the stairwell. I remembered someone complaining about the elevator still not working. There was a muffled sound that seemed strange as I ascended the first few steps.

Then the sound of a girl crying out sped me into taking the steps two at a time. Something was very wrong. My heart thudded in my chest.

When I made it to the landing, I saw Taylor sitting down on the floor, rubbing her side.

"Taylor?" I said, unsure of what had happened.

Pure terror filled her eyes as they began to water. I rushed to her with concern. Tears streamed down her face as she sobbed. She tried to stand up but winced in pain.

I had just left her a few minutes ago. What had happened? Had she fallen? But that didn't explain the terror in her eyes?

"What happened?" My hands went to her as I scanned her face. She was shaking like a leaf. She seemed to be in shock and was unable to tell me exactly what had happened.

She began to cry again and trembled with every sob.

"Shh." I put my arms around her and held her, trying to

calm her down. I kept her close until she managed to calm down and her crying eased.

Taking in her tear-streaked face felt like a knife in my chest twisted. I brushed her tears away. She trembled when I put an arm around her shoulders and led her the rest of the way up to her room.

Inside her room I steered her to her bed and she sat down, keeping her gaze down on the floor. I bent down in front of her and lifted her chin with a finger to align her gaze with mine.

"What happened, Tay?" I asked softly. I ignored the pang of warning that my mind set off with the use of a nickname for her. It was too personal.

She pressed her lips together as she seemed to struggle to keep her composure. Her eyes watered again and she brushed the tears away with the back of her hand.

"You have to tell me what happened," I encouraged gently, keeping her gaze connected with mine. I couldn't help her if I didn't know what happened.

A sense of foreboding uncurled in my stomach when I stared into her eyes and I knew I wasn't going to like what she was about to tell me.

"Someone...a-attacked me," she stuttered huskily.

Attacked? My mind reprocessed what had happened to try and piece together what she was telling me with what I had seen. In just minutes from leaving me in the front to when I had entered the stairway, she had been attacked. Was the person responsible still in the building? My jaw tensed when I felt a protective anger rush through me. Who would do something like that?

"Did you see who it was?" I asked, trying to sound calmer than I felt. She shook her head.

"He came up behind me and I couldn't..." Overcome, she put her hand up to cover her mouth to smother the sob that rose up in her.

"I need to call the cops," I told her like an adult would speak to a small child. I reached for my phone in my back pocket. She gave me a defeated nod, knowing it was the right thing to do.

I usually avoided cops but this situation called for the men in blue. I had the urge to call Jeff but squashed the thought. This might not just be about Taylor, and to protect the rest of the female students it needed to be reported so the college could take steps to up security.

Maybe Taylor was just in the wrong place at the wrong time. I didn't want to think what would have happened to her if I hadn't arrived when I had and scared him off. I swallowed my fear.

I stood up and dialed the cops. I paced, raking my hand through my hair while I reported the attack with as much information as I had. They told me they would be sending someone over right away.

She clasped her hands in her lap and I had the urge to cover them with mine to remind her I was here. But I wasn't the dependable kind. I was the opposite. After I finished the call, Taylor lifted her vulnerable eyes to mine and any thought of disentangling myself from the situation went up in smoke.

Besides, there was no guarantee the guy wasn't still in the building. What if he tried to attack her again?

I walked over to her and sat down beside her. I wasn't going anywhere. She leaned into me as I put a protective arm around her and she rested her head against my shoulder.

"They're on their way," I murmured to her.

She didn't say a word while I held her and I tightened my arm around her, drawing her closer. Thoughts of what could have happened if I had taken longer than I had went through my mind. What if he had dragged her onto another floor? I would have had no idea.

I still couldn't shake the feeling that this hadn't been some random attack. The more I thought about it the more it just didn't sound like some potential rapist taking an opportunity that had presented itself. It had only been a window of a few minutes.

Something nagged in the back of my mind.

Chapter Fourteen

I stood to the side as one of the officers named Johnson questioned Taylor.

Instinct borne from being in a gang urged me to get away as quickly as possible but I couldn't leave Taylor on her own. It didn't help that cops reminded me of some choices I regretted, but there was nothing I could do to wipe it from my past or memory.

I kept my concentration on Taylor beside me. She still looked pale and frightened but at least she had stopped crying. Seeing her this vulnerable tugged at something in the middle of my chest, bringing out the protectiveness I felt for her. But I told myself it was normal to have empathy for her. It was a natural human emotion.

"What's your name?" the officer asked.

"Taylor Price."

"Taylor Price," he murmured as he jotted it down in his small notebook. "Your name sounds familiar. Have you had any run-ins with the law?"

For some reason she looked nervous but there was no reason for her to feel that way. She was a victim. Only people who were hiding something needed to be nervous. My eyes narrowed on her.

She swallowed.

"What happened?" Officer Johnson asked just before he shot me a questioning look.

Not only did I have that look about me that seemed to shout to law and order that I was up to no good, I had in fact lived up to that expectation. But for once I wasn't in the wrong and I refused to allow the cop to intimidate me. I kept my features schooled as he studied me briefly.

The scared look in Taylor's eyes made me move closer to her to put a supportive arm around her shoulder.

"Did he say anything during the attack?" The officer's question brought her attention back to him.

"He said that I was his whore," she said after a slight hesitation.

Whore. Anger sparked to life. I couldn't associate that word with the beautiful and innocent girl who I knew. I wanted to erase the word from her memory. Who on earth would say something like that to Taylor? The same type who would try and hurt her.

"Did you get a look at him?" the officer asked.

"No." She trembled as she wrapped her arms around her body like she was trying to hold herself together. It stoked the anger brewing inside of me.

"Was there anything you noticed that would help us identify the attacker?"

She shook her head and looked defeated. Despite her not answering the question, the officer scribbled down something on his notepad.

"Have there been any other incidents that you think

might be related to this?"

Then I remembered how I was convinced Taylor's drink had been spiked the first night I had met her. How could I have forgotten? Was there a chance it was related to this attack? An uneasy feeling settled over me and I stiffened.

"Yes," she said, rubbing her forehead. "There have been a few weird incidents."

A few?

"Take your time and start from the beginning," the officer suggested.

She told him about the night she'd passed out at my house party but she couldn't remember drinking that much. But when she revealed another incident that involved finding her underwear on her bed with the word 'Whore' written in red marker on them, it took me by surprise. I looked down at her, wondering why she hadn't said anything? What else had she kept from me?

Why would she confide in you? You're not her boyfriend. But I still didn't like that I had no idea what had been going on. I tightened my arm around her.

"Why didn't you report your drink being spiked?" the officer questioned.

"I couldn't prove it," she replied.

"Did you keep the underwear?"

She shook her head.

"Do you have somewhere to stay in the meantime?" Officer Johnson asked.

She rubbed her forehead as she mulled over his question. I frowned.

"Ma'am?" the officer prompted.

"Yes, she does." My words were out before I realized I had spoken. She looked up at me but my attention was on the cop. "She'll be staying with me."

I didn't miss the way the officer looked at me before he

nodded. It was something I was used to. A few years ago he would have been right, but I was different now.

The cops left and I waited while Taylor packed some things.

"I can stay in a hotel," she said, unable to look at me.

I shouldn't have been surprised. I had made it abundantly clear that we only had an arrangement of sex that had an expiration date. She was abiding by the rules of our agreement and I felt like such an asshole.

"You've got some crazy nut after you and you want to go and stay in a hotel where he might find you?" I argued, not wanting to tell her that I wanted to keep her close because I didn't trust anyone to watch her like I would. It reminded me of the protectiveness I had felt the first night we had met.

Her eyes held mine for a moment with real fear.

"We both know what would've happened if I hadn't come back and frightened him off," I added, needing to ensure she was going home with me.

She went a shade paler. Her eyes watered and she swallowed. I felt like a bigger asshole for scaring her but she needed to understand the severity of the situation she was in. When a tear escaped down her cheek, I felt like someone had sucker-punched me in the stomach.

"I'm sorry." I gathered her into my arms and she pressed her cheek against my chest.

"I didn't mean to make you cry," I whispered softly. I pulled away to look down at her tear-soaked face. Knowing I had made her cry made me feel like crap. I wiped the tears from her cheek before I held her again for a few minutes.

"I'm sorry." She broke away from my embrace and I dropped my hands to my sides.

I was quiet as I watched her.

"What about your roommates?"

"It will be fine." I shrugged. She didn't know that I

owned the house and I wasn't about to share that piece of information.

She looked like she was still trying to decide if it was a good idea to come back to my house but she didn't realize I had already made up my mind and she didn't really have a choice.

"Okay." She relented.

She packed a bag quickly and we left the room. I couldn't wait to get her out of the building, away from the memories of the incident that had still left her shaken.

When we reached the stairwell, she hesitated. I held my hand out to her and she took a deep breath like she was building up the courage before she put her hand in mine. All the way down the stairs I held her bag in one hand and her hand in my other.

The drive back to my house was quiet. I kept looking at her, worried that she may have another meltdown, but she kept herself together.

I had forgotten about the party that was taking place at my house. It was still going when we pulled up in front of my house. I got out of the car and got her bag. She got out of the passenger side and I walked her into the house.

"Hey, man, where have you been?" Slater asked when I entered first and then when Taylor followed behind he said, "I didn't think you were coming tonight."

Taylor attempted a smile but Slater could pick up on the undercurrent. "What's up?"

"Taylor is staying with us for a couple of nights," I told him. He shot me a surprised look.

"Sure, no problem. Do you want me to close up the party?" he asked. He could tell I wasn't in the party mood. I gave him a nod.

"Tay," Jordan squealed and hugged Taylor. She was unusually happy, which meant she'd probably had too much to drink. Clearly they had been enjoying the party.

"Were you planning on taking Jordan back to the dorm room?" I asked Slater when he slung an arm around her.

"No." He gave me a questioning look.

"Good," I said, not wanting to go into all the details in front of Taylor. It was time to get her upstairs and settled.

Even as I ascended the stairs, I was already coming up with reasons why she was safer in my room than the guest bedroom a few doors down from me. But when we got to the top, I led her to my room. I opened the door for her and switched on the light before closing the door behind her.

She looked so nervous as she surveyed my room and it pulled at the protectiveness I felt for her. I ran a hand through my hair, trying to figure out why she made me feel the way I did. I tested my lip ring with the tip of my tongue as I watched her.

She looked so vulnerable. I walked to her.

"How are you doing?" I cradled her face gently, searching her eyes.

"I'm okay." But I could tell she wasn't and she had every reason to feel the way she did.

"Do you need to shower?" I asked, dropping my hands to her hips.

"Yes." Her eyes dropped to my lips.

"Get what you need together and I'll put a clean towel in the bathroom for you." I let her go when I felt the familiar attraction to her despite the circumstances. She needed a shoulder to lean on not a roll between the sheets.

"Okay." She picked up her bag and began to get some things out.

I left to get a clean towel and I left it in the bathroom before I went downstairs. The music was off and Slater was still ushering some people out the door. Jordan was sitting on the sofa, watching. Her slightly glazed look confirmed my

135

earlier suspicion that she was drunk.

I waited until the last person had left before pulling Slater into the kitchen.

"What's going on?" he asked with a crease in his forehead.

"Taylor was attacked tonight." I rubbed my chin as I fought with the snap of emotion it released in me.

"What happened?"

"Some guy tried to attack her in the stairwell at the dorm but I scared him off."

He swore. "Did you see him?"

I shook my head. "He heard me enter the stairwell and let her go."

"Did you call the cops?"

I nodded. There hadn't been any other option.

"He apparently pushed her up against the wall and told her she was his whore." Just thinking about it made the anger rush through me. I curled my fists like I wanted nothing more than a few rounds with the guy. I would teach him a lesson he would never forget. "I thought it was a random incident that the college would need to be aware of so they would be able to protect the girls on campus."

Slater frowned. "Thought?"

"Yeah. But it wasn't a random attack." I leaned against the kitchen counter. My friend waited for me to continue. "Someone tried to spike her drink."

He nodded. "Yeah, I remember."

"Someone also broke into her room and took her underwear and wrote the word 'whore' on it."

The worry I felt was mirrored in his eyes.

Feeling that the situation wasn't within my control only set me more on edge, increasing the tension knitting into my shoulders. I rolled my shoulders, needing to ease the buildup. I felt like the small boy who hadn't been able to control the situation with a drunk mother who had struggled to cope.

"You think it's something you should get Jeff to look into?" He rubbed the back of his neck.

"Yeah," I replied distractedly. "It's either a stalker or it has something to do with her past."

She was beautiful so it could easily be some guy who had taken more than a shine to her. But my gut was telling me it was more than that. I believed it had something to do with her past.

But the only way to find out was to ask her. I remembered our conversation earlier over burgers when I had asked about her parents. Her reply had been curt and short. Was she hiding something?

Our physical arrangement was blurring into something more and I wasn't sure I could even stop it anymore. With the threat of someone trying to harm her, I was forced into finding out more so I would be able to do my best to protect her.

"What do you think?"

I pressed my lips together for a moment. "I think it has something to do with her past. Has Jordan mentioned anything about her?"

Slater shook his head. "No."

"It might not be best to tell Jordan about what happened until tomorrow."

"I wasn't planning on saying anything to her tonight." There was a light in his eyes when he spoke about her and I wondered if that happened to me when I spoke about Taylor.

"You getting serious with her?" I studied him.

"I like being around her." And that was all he was prepared to admit. He shrugged.

I wanted him to be happy but there was also a part of me that didn't want him to get hurt. He had been through so much already and I wasn't sure he could cope with more.

Like me, we'd had our fill of the dark side of life, so any more and there was a chance we would spiral out of control.

"You need help clearing up?" I asked when I surveyed the kitchen, which looked a mess with empty cans and cups.

"No. I'll get Eric to help me."

Slater began to clean up and I exited the kitchen. Jordan had passed out on the couch. I studied her for a moment, hoping she wouldn't hurt my friend. But there wasn't much I could do other than give him advice. It was his life to lead.

I hadn't planned on being gone for that long but when I re-entered my room, Taylor was curled up asleep with her phone in her hand. I took her phone slowly from her and put it on the bedside table. I picked her up gently so as not to wake her and opened the covers to settle her in the bed. She moaned softly against my neck and I tightened the hold on her, only allowing myself to savor it for a few moments before I laid her on the bed. Still sleeping peacefully, she tucked her hands under the pillow while I pulled the covers over her.

Then I stood back. At least with me I could protect her but I couldn't be with her every moment of every day. The worry I had felt earlier returned and my mind began to work through possible solutions but I was still hoping Taylor would be able to throw some more light on the subject.

Feeling tired, I kicked off my shoes and stripped down to my boxers before I switched off the lights and I got in beside her in the bed.

For a while I lay there unable to go to sleep but eventually the soft breathing beside me lulled me to sleep.

Half asleep, I reached out and put my hand on her hip. The movement beside me jolted me out of my semi-sleeping state. My eyes adjusted to the darkness to see Taylor sitting up beside me. She was breathing hard like she had just woken up from a nightmare.

"Hey, it's just me," I soothed, sitting up. I hadn't meant

to scare her when I had reached for her. It had only been to assure myself that she was safe beside me.

She breathed in sharply like she was going into a full-blown panic. She put her hand to her head. Needing to ease her fear, I pulled her close to my chest and held her. She wasn't alone and I wasn't going to let anything happen to her.

After a few minutes, I could feel her heart beat slow down and her breathing return to normal.

"I'm sorry," she mumbled from the safe cocoon of my arms.

"It's okay." Absentmindedly I stroked her hair. She looked up at me as I released her.

She looked every inch of the innocent and naive girl I had met the first time. I tucked a stray piece of hair behind her ear. I watched as her tongue swept across her bottom lip.

It was difficult to suppress my body's response to her but now wasn't the time for that. Then, before her movement registered, she kissed me, taking me by surprise.

Chapter Fifteen

Even though I wanted nothing more than what was happening between us, I held back, unsure she was in the state of mind for what she was pushing for.

She increased the pressure of her mouth on mine but I refused to give in to her. She was in a vulnerable state and I wouldn't allow myself to take advantage of her. Finally she pulled back and made me feel like an asshole for not giving her what she wanted.

"What's wrong?" I asked when she moved away from me. I wasn't asking because she was distancing herself physically but I wanted to know why she was pushing for a physical connection so soon after being attacked.

"Don't you want me?" She sounded hurt by my resistance. She had no idea how close I was to giving in to her. I could feel the heat in my veins when I looked at her. The impression of her lips still on mine made it impossible to think straight.

I was trying to be a good guy and it was proving to be more difficult than I had anticipated. I tried to think of the best way to convey my concerns so she wouldn't take offense.

"I'm not sure if this is what you need right now," I said softly. She clasped her hands together as I held her gaze. "You were attacked tonight. You've been through so much, it has been an emotional roller coaster."

"When he attacked me, he pushed his body...against mine," she began to explain. "I need you...to wipe that memory from my mind."

I understood why she thought it would be a good idea but I wasn't convinced it wouldn't only be a temporary reprieve that would cause more trouble later. I wasn't a shrink but she had been through a traumatic event and needed time to work her way through it.

"I don't think that's going to help you deal." I tried one last time to talk her out of it.

"Please." The pleading in her voice was enough for me to throw caution to the wind. I was strong but I wasn't made of stone.

"Come here," I instructed softly in the darkness, already making up my mind that I would be as gentle as possible so as not to scare or hurt her.

My hand touched her arm as she moved closer. I covered her lips with mine as I cradled her face gently in my hands. Her tongue swept against my bottom lip, touching my lip ring. Still fighting to control myself, I inhaled sharply as my tongue touched hers.

I loved the sweet taste of her. It ignited my burning need for her. Her hands settled over mine still cradling her face as I explored her mouth with mine. Light sweeps and gentle caresses kept her wanting more. I could tell by the tremor that vibrated through her that she wasn't in complete control. I kept watching for her to reach her limit and stop me but she didn't.

Then I broke away from her and pushed her gently down to lie on the bed. She bit her lip nervously as I pressed her body into the mattress with the weight of mine. She stiffened and I stilled.

"It's okay, it's me," I murmured to her as I held my weight off her with hands on either side of her. With her eyes on me, she opened her legs and I lay between them. Wanting to keep her in the moment with me and not in the memories of her attack, I kissed her again.

This time my kisses were more intense, wanting her to know exactly who was in the bed with her. I wasn't the stranger who had tried to hurt her.

My lips moved from hers to trail kisses along her jaw. Her breathing was hard and I shifted off her to dispense with her clothing. I pulled her pajama shorts off along with her panties as she lifted her hips for me.

Then I stood up to get rid of my clothes and to get the protection from my side table and I put it on. I returned to the bed and got in beside her to help her discard her top. And then I pressed my lips to her when I covered her body with mine. Skin to skin.

Thoughts of some guy trying to hurt her flashed in my mind but I pushed them away, refusing to think about what could have happened. She was safe here with me and that was how she would stay.

I wanted to make sure she was prepared for my entry so I ensured I worked her up well with kisses down her body. With a slight moan and her hands fisting my hair, I knew she was ready. I moved back to line up my body with hers. She wrapped her legs around me. I pressed against her heat. The moment our lips met again I thrust into her in one full stroke. Her breathing hitched and I gave her a moment to adjust to me before I began to move. Her hands went to my shoulders and she held on.

She was already panting and the slight tensing in her body told me she was close. I strained against her, taking her to the heights that would wipe clean any remains of the stranger's imprint on her.

She groaned when she came and I followed soon after. Trying to catch my breath, I leaned my forehead against hers. Her arms wrapped around me and our breath intermingled as we savored our release.

I kissed her cheek before I moved from her. I went and disposed of the condom before I returned to the bed. She looked so beautiful in my bed, her lips still red from my kisses. She looked so content and it was because of me.

The lines of our arrangement were fading. With her, I lacked my usual control and focus.

I got in beside her. I lay on my back and put a hand underneath my head. She lay quietly beside me, also looking up at the ceiling. I wondered what she was thinking.

"Is Sin your real name?" she asked out of the blue.

It wasn't the first time I had been asked that question but usually I changed the subject so I didn't have to reveal the truth behind my name. For the first time, I wasn't preparing to deviate the conversation to safer subjects.

"Yes." Most people assumed it was short for something.

"It's unusual. What made your mom choose that?" she asked, digging a little deeper.

The rawness in my chest made me want to avoid the subject.

"My mom had an affair with a married guy. She was young and from the wrong side of the tracks when she met a rich, married guy who swept her off her feet. They started having an affair. He kept telling her he was going to leave his wife, but he never did...then she got pregnant with me." I paused. "The day she told him she was pregnant with me was the last time she saw him. She named me Sin so she would always remember how I came into this world."

My throat burned at the hurt that I still couldn't erase. Even now it was hard to look at her and not see the mother who had given me nothing but pain. *But she has changed*, I reminded myself but it was still difficult to see her in a different light.

"That's horrible." She moved onto her side to look at me. In the darkness I could still make out her features. My revelation had affected her. Taylor was not only naive and innocent, she was sensitive too, taking on my pain as her own. I could see the turmoil in her features as she struggled to make sense of it.

"It's okay. I like the name. The girls love it." I tried to lighten the heavy conversation but something I didn't understand compelled me to open up. "It's also a reminder to me that people are human and they make mistakes. My mom made a mistake believing my father's lies." It was the reason I controlled my life to the degree I did so I wouldn't have repercussions to deal with.

I couldn't ignore the fact that I was constantly rewriting my rules for her even though I knew there was a chance I was making a big mistake.

"Did you ever meet your father?" she asked tentatively.

He wasn't someone I liked talking about. It didn't seem right to give him attention in my life when he hadn't given me any in his.

"No," I answered, feeling the weight of the fact that even if I wanted to I couldn't. "He wasn't really a father in the true sense of the word. He was just a sperm donor."

Feeling more agitated, I put both my hands behind my head.

"Did he ever try to contact you?"

"No, and then he died a couple of years ago."

She quieted down as she digested the information. I remembered her telling me that her parents had died. Had I reminded her about their deaths?

"I'm sorry." I reached for her hand and held it. "I didn't mean to remind you about your parents."

"It's okay," she said softly but I could hear the emotion in her voice.

I couldn't imagine having parents who loved me, or losing them.

"How old were you when they died?" I found myself asking.

"I was nine."

She was so young. At nine I was trying to keep things together while my mother continued to spiral out of control.

"Do you still see your mom?"

"Yeah, I check up on her every week. She doesn't live far from here." I moved onto my side and she lay on her side facing me. "She never quite recovered from the rejection from my father. From then on, she tried to find solace in the form of alcohol."

It was one of the few times I had ever opened up about my mother.

"Who took care of you?" she asked.

"I did." It wasn't the answer she was expecting. Even with the death of her parents, she had someone who had loved and cared for her.

"I'm sorry," she said, obviously not knowing quite what to say. The sadness in her voice loosened a warmth in my chest.

"Don't feel sorry for me. I had Slater and he had me," I told her, not wanting her sympathy.

We had been in similar situations and there hadn't been much choice. It wasn't like an adult in our lives was going to care for us so it had fallen on us. And we had done the best we could. There were times when I remembered going to sleep with the hunger pangs twisting my stomach. I tried to physically shake the feeling.

"Does Slater have any siblings?" Her question took me by surprise.

People assumed Slater was an only child but I knew different. When I had first met him, he had been withdrawn and quiet. It had taken a few weeks to break through his protective walls and it had taken much longer for him to open up to me. It was the first time I had realized that despite my crummy upbringing and alcoholic mother there were children out there who were much worse off. It had made me look at life differently.

"He had a sister," I told her softly.

"What happened?" she asked in a whisper.

I had never been tempted to reveal anything about Slater's past on the few occasions I had been asked.

"It isn't my story to tell."

She quieted into a thoughtful silence.

"Did you tell Jordan about all the strange stuff that had been happening?" I asked. It had been bugging me from the time she had revealed the extent to which someone had been stalking her.

She moved onto her back, letting out a heavy sigh like she knew she was in for a lecture. "No."

"Even after the incident with your underwear?" I found myself getting angry that she hadn't confided into her closest friend about what was going on.

She didn't answer.

"Why didn't you tell anyone?" I asked. Any normal girl would have at least told someone. Most would have gone straight to the police. It puzzled me that she hadn't.

"Because at the time I didn't think it was a big deal." Her answer didn't sit well with me. She wasn't telling me the whole truth. But I couldn't come up with a reasonable explanation as to why she would lie. The more I got to know her the more I realized things didn't add up.

"Did you think ignoring it would make it go away?" I asked. The thought that she hadn't taken the threat to her well-being as seriously as she should have only angered me more. She had been irresponsible.

"Hey, I've had a rough day and I don't need you lecturing me on top of everything else," she snapped, sitting up beside me, clutching the sheet to cover her nakedness while she touched her hand to her temple.

My anger dissipated slightly at the sight of her trying to cope with the events of the day.

"I'm sorry. It's just that there is a naivety about you that I've never seen in a person before." But my gut was telling me there was something off about the whole thing. "So naive that I keep worrying that something really bad is going to happen to you.

I paused. "Like not taking drinks from strangers. It's like you haven't experienced anything that most teenagers have and I can't figure out why."

There was a story behind it and I felt compelled by the danger that surrounded her to dig deeper. If I didn't then there was a chance she would continue to do things to endanger herself.

She shifted slightly, fixing her eyes in front of her. It felt like she was distancing herself not only from me but from my questions. She wasn't going to open up to me. The realization hit me hard, opening up an old wound inside me. I swallowed, trying to keep a handle on my emotions.

"You're not going to tell me, are you?" I asked the question already knowing the answer. She wasn't going to reveal to me what had happened in her past to explain her naivety or her lack of experience.

The ache in my chest worsened.

"You're not going to tell me anything, are you?" I asked tightly. "I bared a part of my soul to you, but that doesn't make any difference."

I had promised myself I wouldn't allow anyone to have the power to make me feel the way I was feeling. My anger was directed at myself for allowing this to happen.

I continued to stare at her for a few more seconds, hoping she would change her mind but she didn't. She pulled her knees up to her chest and her eyes met mine. It was all I needed to confirm that she wasn't going to tell me anything.

Feeling angered, I got off the bed and found my jeans on the floor. I pulled them on and faced her.

"I should've known better," I said before I stormed out of the room, leaving her alone in the darkness.

I went downstairs, needing to deal with the building anger that I couldn't seem to control, and I needed space from Taylor. Putting distance between us was the only way to protect myself and allow myself to set up the boundaries that would keep her from getting to me again.

Rubbing my hands over my face, I sat down on the sofa. For once Slater wasn't up and I was relieved he wouldn't see me this worked up over Taylor, since it would be difficult to explain.

Remembering how I had revealed more to her than I had to any other girl only intensified the anger and hurt I was feeling.

You only have yourself to blame, I told myself. If I had stuck to my rules of no virgins and only one-night stands I wouldn't be in this situation. I ran a hand through my hair. Why had I opened up to her? She wasn't the first girl who had questioned me about my past. What had made her different? I wasn't stupid enough to tie sex with feelings. No, it was something else.

Maybe it was because I felt like she had experienced the same type of childhood that I had. One that had repercussions through to adulthood. The death of her parents at a young age would have been devastating but my gut was telling me it was more than just that.

Chapter Sixteen

I stayed up for most of the night, too wound up to find solace in sleep. Eventually I dropped off to sleep but my dreams ensured any rest I got had been restless.

When I awoke on the sofa I yawned and glanced around the room but I was alone. My body felt cramped from sleeping on the sofa instead of my comfortable bed. I stretched the tiredness out of my arms. The sound of voices was coming from the kitchen. It sounded like Taylor and it took me a few more moments to place the voice of Eric.

I sat up and swung my legs over the side. I hadn't heard her come downstairs. How long had she been awake?

I scanned the room. My eyes settled on her packed bag by the door. She had been up long enough to get dressed and pack her things. It only added to the feeling of betrayal that she hadn't trusted me enough to open up about her childhood.

The events from the previous night stirred my anger. I'd

given her insights into my childhood and when I had asked her about herself, she had clammed up.

I stood and followed the voices to the kitchen. The sound of Eric's voice aggravated me. There was just something about him that just didn't sit well with me. I couldn't quite put my finger on it. It was like he was always trying too hard to fit in or be funny. He would probably be easier to be around if he were just himself. I didn't know how people pretended to be somebody they weren't. I couldn't be someone I wasn't, what you saw was what you got with me.

I slowed my footsteps to hear what they were talking about. Eric had never paid any interest in any of the other girls that I had slept with so it piqued my interest that he was talking to Taylor. Maybe it was because I hadn't kept a girl around long enough for him to try.

"You guys have a fight?" he asked her. I frowned. He was stepping over the line by poking his nose into my business.

Why did he care if we'd had an argument or not? I debated whether to step inside the room or to wait a little longer to hear more.

The fridge opened and closed.

"Something like that." Taylor's voice was reserved as she answered his question. She didn't seem to be happy to reveal too much.

"I wouldn't stress about it too much. Girls never last long with him," Eric told her.

It was the truth but his words made me angry. Who the hell was he to interfere in something that had nothing to do with him?

I edged closer, resisting the urge to interrupt before he could say anything more.

Taylor remained quiet.

"Although I've never seen him sleep on the couch before," he added.

I'd heard enough. I stepped into the doorway of the kitchen. Taylor noticed me first. She looked unsure as her eyes met mine. I scratched my chest as I strolled into the room.

Eric took his glass of juice and gave Taylor a slight nod before he left. He didn't even have the balls to look at me as I threw him an annoyed look. We would definitely be having a talk about this later.

Nervously, Taylor set her glass of water down on the nearby counter.

After last night, there was a void between us. I was still feeling betrayed and she was looking at me like she wasn't sure how to deal with me.

"You sleep okay?" I asked, coming to a stop a few feet in front of her.

She nodded. My eyes went to the dark purple bruises on her arms. I reached out and took her one arm in my hands, brushing my fingers over the darkened areas that marred her porcelain skin. I didn't like how I felt at the thought that her attacker had hurt her.

But what scared me more was how I was feeling. I needed to distance myself so I stepped back, releasing her arm like it had burned me.

I couldn't bullshit my way out of this. If I had any way of protecting myself it was time to release her and end our arrangement. When I had entered into the agreement with her, I had never imagined it would be difficult to walk away but now I was discovering how attached I had become.

I knew what I needed to do but I couldn't open my mouth and say the words. So instead I held her gaze in a silence that wasn't comfortable for either of us. I wondered what she was thinking. Was she thinking the same? From the start of our arrangement it had never occurred to me that she might end our arrangement before me.

The doorbell rang, interrupting us.

Feeling like things between us were still undecided, I gave her one last look before I left to answer the front door. I wasn't expecting anyone.

I opened the door and found the blond stranger I had seen Taylor with before, standing with a disapproving look as his gaze swept over me. It was a look I was used to. The slightly surprised look hidden in his frown told me she hadn't told him about me. It shouldn't have hurt or angered me. We weren't anything other than a sexual arrangement.

"I think he's here for you," I said in the laziest tone I could muster. I opened the door farther and Taylor looked like she had been caught doing something she shouldn't have. Me.

I glanced back in time to see the thunderous look her brother directed at her. Even if our arrangement wasn't done I knew it wouldn't survive his disapproval.

"Get your stuff," he ordered her without stepping into the house. I glared at him, not liking the way he was talking to her. He sounded like a father instead of a brother.

He crossed his arms and waited for Taylor to follow his instruction. She sighed and walked over to her bag by the door. My eyes followed her. Briefly she looked at me but I looked away. I didn't want her to see the turbulent emotions inside of me.

Out of the corner of my eye I saw her tremble slightly before she took a deep breath.

"Don't let Jordan go back to the dorm. Tell her I will call her a little later," she said and I nodded, still holding the door open.

"Thanks for everything." She hesitated in the doorway. I don't know what she was waiting for but she wasn't going to get it.

"See you around." This time I looked her in the eyes,

ensuring she knew the full impact of my words. We were over. I didn't allow her look of hurt to shake me or change my mind. It was over.

Our temporary acquaintances with benefits was finished.

As soon as she exited my house I shut the door. I closed my eyes briefly, finally allowing my true emotions to come to the surface. Now that I didn't have anyone watching, I could let myself feel.

Damn it. It hurt and I chastised myself for allowing myself to walk the path that had brought me here. It was my own fault, there was no one else to blame. Taylor was human and flawed. It was her inability to trust me that had hurt. This experience only reinforced why I had put my rules in place to protect myself.

Allowing myself to get closer to her would only spell more pain in the end for me. I let go of the handle and stepped back, trying to figure out the exact moment I had lost control.

I wasn't sure it had been the first night I had looked after her. It was probably the night I had taken her virginity. From that point onward I had continued to break my rules. But it didn't matter. All that mattered was ensuring it never happened again.

A couple of hours later Slater found me in the garage beating the punching bag as if it weren't an object but Taylor's brother. His disapproving look stuck with me. I hated being made to feel inferior and in one look he had been able to do that to me.

"Where's Taylor?" he asked, scanning the room.

"She left." My answer was short. I stopped and looked at him, dropping my hands to my sides.

"You let her go back to the dorm?" he asked, incredulous.

I shook my head. "No."

I was a lot of things but I would never knowingly allow her to do anything to put herself in danger.

"Then where did she go?" he asked with a frown.

He and Taylor had grown closer over the past few weeks. I could tell he had a soft spot for her.

"Her brother came and picked her up." I wiped the sweat from my forehead with the bottom of my shirt.

He continued to frown as he studied me.

"What's going on?" he asked, knowing something was bugging me and it had nothing to do with the attack on Taylor.

I let out a heavy sigh before I dropped my shirt. "She won't be coming around here anymore."

I couldn't exactly say we were over because that would imply we'd been more than we were.

Slater watched me thoughtfully. "She will be back."

It wasn't what I wanted to hear. For my own sake it had to be over.

"I don't want her back." I made my stand on the subject of Taylor clear.

He gave me a slight inclination of his head as if conceding my decision. He didn't push any further.

The door widened and Jordan appeared beside him looking a little worse for wear. She was dressed in the outfit she'd worn yesterday.

"Where's Taylor?"

"Her brother came to pick her up," Slater told her.

She gave Slater a confused look. "She didn't tell me her brother was in town."

Then I remembered we hadn't told her about the full details of the night before.

"Taylor was attacked yesterday." Her big eyes swung to me.

"When?" she asked, trying to piece it into last night's events. She'd had more than a bit to drink so it might not be easy.

"Before I brought her back here."

She shook her head slightly, like she was having difficulty trusting what I was telling her.

"What happened?" Her attention was on me.

"I took her out and when we got back to the dorm she went in first. I followed a few minutes later and scared the guy off."

"Someone attacked her in the dorm?" Her eyes were wide with shock.

"Yes. In the stairwell."

She looked visibly shaken. Slater put an arm around her and pulled her closer to him. It was weird to see him like this with a girl. Getting intimate with a girl was very different from being affectionate or protective like he was acting. He was unable to hold my questioning gaze, which spoke volumes.

"Who was it?" she asked, her eyes still wide.

"We don't know. Taylor didn't get a look at him." I watched the array of emotions play across her features as the new information sank in and what it meant.

If I'd had a good look at him he would have been apprehended already. But the chances of catching him were slim to nonexistent when Taylor hadn't seen him, and there was no physical evidence to lead the police to the culprit.

It could be anyone. And chances were he would try again.

"Someone has been stalking her," I revealed, walking to them. "The cops are going to look into it but without any evidence it's going to be much harder to figure out who it is."

I already knew that she didn't know anything about the underwear.

"I don't understand," she said, looking at me with confusion.

"I think someone spiked her drink the other night." She nodded, indicating that she already knew about that. "Someone broke into your dorm room and left Taylor's underwear laid out on her bed with the word 'whore' written on it."

"Taylor never told me about that," she murmured. "But I remember her asking me about a pair of her underwear that had gone missing."

So it proved that someone had broken in twice: once to steal the underwear and a second time to lay it out on her bed.

It was one thing breaking in once, but the guy had been confident enough to do it twice. That worried me.

Slater's gaze met mine. He was thinking the same thing. This wasn't good.

She trembled and Slater's arm pulled her closer to him. She buried her face against his chest as she tried to handle the news that someone had tried to hurt her friend and had broken into their personal space twice.

"I need to call her," she finally said, pulling away from Slater and disappearing back into the house.

"How safe do you think Taylor is with her brother?" Slater asked me.

I might not have liked the guy but I knew he would do everything to keep her safe.

"I don't think he's going to let her out of his sight."

"Good."

So for the moment she was safe but she would not remain safe if the identity of her attacker wasn't discovered.

Slater and I entered the house in time to hear Jordan say,

"Both of us?" as she cradled her phone against her ear while she paced the living room.

It was difficult to figure out what was being said on the other side of the conversation.

"Okay," she agreed.

She rubbed her forehead slightly while she listened.

"He is only doing it because he cares," she said.

They were probably talking about Taylor's brother. He had money and I knew he would be doing everything he could to ensure she was kept safe.

"Okay. See you soon," Jordan said before she ended the call.

"Taylor's brother is sending a car to pick me up."

"Where are you going?" Slater asked her with a frown.

Just because Jordan wasn't the main target didn't mean she couldn't be caught up in the crossfire. Slater was right to be concerned about her.

"His driver is going to take me back to the dorm to pick up some clothes and then he'll take me to the apartment he is renting for us."

Slater's expression to a stranger would be difficult to read but I could tell he wasn't completely happy with that arrangement. I wondered if it was because he didn't trust them with her safety or if it was something else.

It didn't surprise me that the brother who had glared at me on my doorstep only a few hours before had already put a plan into action to keep his sister safe. Like I had already told Slater, I knew he would do everything possible to keep her from being attacked again. I could at least give him that.

Hearing about her only made me feel worse. *Give yourself a few days and you'll be back to normal,* I told myself. *She can get on with her life and you can go back to yours.*

Despite how things had pushed us to being strangers again I still couldn't stop the feeling that I wasn't finished with her. We hadn't had enough time to work each other out of our systems. I could still feel the attraction just with a memory of her looking at me with her large fluttering eyelashes like she wanted nothing more than for me to rip off her clothes and take her swiftly. I swallowed, trying to ignore the flare of want that burned through me, leaving me with doubt that we were really finished.

I only had to remember the way her brother had eyed me up and down to feel like a dirty secret that she'd been hiding. I was the guy you had amazing sex with, I wasn't the one you took home to introduce to your parents, or the guy you planned the rest of your life with.

No matter what I tried to tell myself or how I tried to explain it away, it didn't ease the hurt that I felt that she hadn't been able to confide in me and she hadn't been up front with her brother about me.

She hadn't broken any of the rules in place. In fact I was the one changing things. I was expecting more than we had originally agreed and it was a very sobering thought.

Chapter Seventeen

Initially I'd been angry and disappointed when I'd shared snippets of my past with her and she hadn't trusted me enough to share any of hers with me. I don't even know why I'd opened up to her. Maybe it was because I rarely felt calm, but I did when I was with her.

My life had always been a rush of activity and noise. Maybe it was because in those moments of quiet I had time to think of all the things I'd done wrong in my life and, trust me, I could spend a lot of time on that.

Taylor.

When I thought back to the first time I'd met her, I couldn't help the affectionate smile that tugged at my lips. She'd been a breath of fresh air the moment I'd laid my eyes on her. She was beautiful—there was no denying that. But a lot of girls were beautiful. Taylor's beauty went deeper than just the surface of her skin. She was like an enigma that I couldn't figure out. It was obvious from the start that she wasn't like other girls her age. There was an innocence about her that had nothing to do with the fact that she'd been a virgin. It was more than that.

Her brother seemed to be the overprotective type, but why was he that way? Had it been the result of her parents' car accident that her brother had become overprotective over her? Plenty of people lost their parents, so it didn't explain the extreme naivety in Taylor. It was like I was sitting with more questions than answers.

"Sin!" I heard Slater call from downstairs. If my bedroom door hadn't been open then, I probably wouldn't have heard him.

I stood up and rubbed my hands over my face. I was tired. Since I'd told Taylor 'I'd see her around' I'd been agitated and nervous. I had no idea what was wrong with me. I made my way down the hall and then down the stairs. I hesitated for a split second when I saw the person standing beside Slater waiting for me. For a moment I'd hoped it might be Taylor, but it was her brother studying me with a reserved expression.

I knew how this talk was going to go before we even got started. He was going to tell me to stay away from his sister. When he'd come to collect his sister the day before, I hadn't missed the looks. He didn't think I was good enough for her and he was probably right. I'd spent my life not being good enough. For my sperm donor, I hadn't been good enough to be a son he could love, and even my own mother struggled to love the reminder of her bad judgment. It didn't matter what I did now or what I had, nothing would change that.

The only person I was good enough for was Slater. I was good enough to be his friend. Maybe it was because he'd grown up in a similar situation to me that had bonded us in friendship and had pulled us through a lot of dark times.

As I reached the bottom step, Slater gave me a

questioning look that Connor didn't see because his eyes were fixed on me. I shook my head at him and he reluctantly left us alone.

"What do you want?" I asked him in a clipped tone as I held his gaze. It didn't matter that I already knew the answer. We stared at each other, neither of us wanting to look away first.

"I wanted to talk to you about Taylor, my sister," he began. And there it was. I crossed my arms over my chest and waited for him.

"Whatever is going on between the two of you needs to end," he stated firmly and I laughed in his face. He looked a little taken aback. He hadn't expected my reaction.

"And why would I listen to you?" I scoffed. I hated being told what to do by people I knew so I didn't take it very well from someone I was meeting for the second time. It didn't matter that I'd pretty much ended things with her. I'd meant it when I'd told her 'I'd see her around'.

With that one sentence, I'd closed the door on our arrangement and made it clear from then on I would only consider her an acquaintance that I would see when we passed in the hallways.

He studied me for a moment.

"I know what type of guy you are," he said. "You'll have your fun and then at some point you'll get bored and then you'll walk away."

I remained silent. He pretty much summed me up. The only difference was that, with Taylor, it had been more than one night and I'd formed a connection with her. I didn't want to admit it, but when she'd been attacked in the stairwell, it had scared me. It was then that I'd realized then that I cared about her. It wasn't like I wanted to date her or anything like that. I just didn't want anything bad to happen to her—it was hard to explain.

"Look, man, I don't know how any of this is any of your business," I retorted, feeling my anger at his outright meddling in his sister's life. She was an adult and she could make her own decisions about her life. There was no need to be difficult, but I couldn't help myself. I wasn't going to let him think that he could control me.

"She isn't like other girls," he tried to explain. I knew that already, but the way he said it piqued my curiosity. There was a somber sadness in his voice that was matched in his eyes.

She'd been so adamant that she didn't want to share her past with me, but I knew that the knowledge of what happened to her would help me understand her better. I didn't know what made me want to understand her. I'd never wanted to know anything about the girls I fucked. There were a few times I wondered whether the fact I'd been her first had made me feel more protective over her.

The fact that she was so naive worried me. It left her more susceptible to something bad happening to her. It shouldn't be my problem, but somehow it was.

"Why isn't she like other girls?" I asked, hoping that he would tell me what I wanted to know.

"Something really bad happened to her...I don't want to go into details, but she had a very protected childhood."

That was all he revealed. I could tell he wasn't going to tell me any more.

"You are going to hurt her and she might not be able to recover from it," he added. That was really weird to say. Girls had their hearts broken all the time and they got over it, though some took longer than others.

I held his gaze for several moments.

"What happens between your sister and me is our business. Stay out of it," I warned. I could be intimidating when I wanted to be, but I didn't feel the need to be. He gave me one last look before he turned and left, slamming the door behind him.

"You okay?" I heard Slater ask as I turned to walk up the stairs.

"Yeah."

My curiosity got the better of me in that moment and I climbed the stairs on a mission to uncover what Taylor was hiding. I wasn't trying to go against her wishes, but I felt that knowing everything would help me understand her and help keep her safe. She'd been drugged and if it hadn't been for me, God knows what would have happened. As soon as I got to my laptop, I started searching the web. I searched her name and it didn't take me long to find the news articles.

My blood ran cold and I felt the horror come alive inside of me as I read the details of her parents' death. After nearly half an hour, I knew enough and closed my laptop. She'd lied about her parents dying in a car accident. It also explained why the cop had recognized her name. I rubbed my hands over my face as I contemplated what to do next. There was a pain in my chest at the thought of what she'd been through and I knew I had to see her.

She'd probably be mad when I told her what I knew, but there was no way I would be able to look at her without thinking about it. It would come out eventually.

My eyes scanned the crowds as I walked to my first class of the day. I was on edge. I had spent so much time going over and over what I had discovered about Taylor's past. My stomach twisted and I stopped for a moment. It made me physically sick when I thought about what had happened to her.

My guilt only worsened it. I drew in a breath and

released it. *Get your shit together*, I told myself. I couldn't let on to what I had done until I had a chance to own up in private. I had made my decision and I would have to face the consequences of the choice I had made.

I couldn't see her anywhere and I was going to be late if I didn't get to my class. I was hoping to at least arrange a meeting with her. The sooner I got it over with the better. I knew there was a chance she might not be able to forgive me. In her shoes I didn't know if I would forgive me.

I raked a hand loosely through my hair. I'd really messed things up. My curiosity had gotten the better of me. It hadn't crossed my mind until her brother had shown up on my doorstep and warned me off. But I couldn't blame him. It had been a factor, but I had been the one to snoop into her past.

I don't know what I had been expecting but it had been worse than any scenario that had ever crossed my mind.

Knowing what happened gave me insight and some understanding into why she was the way she was and it explained why she had fought so hard to keep it a secret. Just thinking of how I had betrayed her trust made me feel even more like the asshole I was.

Every hour that passed only made me feel worse. I just wanted to get it over with so I could face the consequences head on. The fear that she might not be able to forgive me stayed with me the entire time.

She had been unexpected and so was my attachment to her.

There was no more trying to talk myself out of what was going on. We had connected not just in a physical way and I was struggling with that connection that made it impossible not to think about her.

With everything going on in my head I barely made it through my classes. By the end of the day I felt drained, not just physically but emotionally as well.

Like I had for most of the day I looked for her as I left my last class. But there didn't seem to be any sign of her. Had she taken time off? It was a possibility.

Then I saw her. I stopped. The sight of her hit me right in the middle of my chest, making it harder to breathe. This time she looked more vulnerable than before. I was sure it was her secret that made her seem so much more fragile. It only made me feel all the more protective of her.

Her eyes met mine. Could she see I was hiding something? Was she able to read it in my eyes?

The moment was broken when I noticed a guy standing just behind her with his gaze fixed on me. The sight of him got my back straight up. He was tall with light brown hair with touches of blond. His eyes met mine. He was dressed in jeans with a black shirt.

I frowned. Who the hell was he?

There was only one way to find out. I walked to her, determined to come clean and face the repercussions. The slight pain in the middle of my chest reminded me that there was more at stake than I was prepared to lose. I refused to allow the thought to take hold. I had to believe she would be able to see the true intentions behind my actions.

My steps faltered slightly when I looked to the stranger still standing behind Taylor, who was making it clear he was with her. I didn't like that one bit. I pressed my lips into a thin line as I forced myself to face her head on.

I was no coward. I had made the choice and now it was time to lay it all out in front of her to see what happened. But not here and not out in the open. There was no way I was going to broach the subject in public.

When I reached her, I looked at the guy still standing just behind her to one side before moving my attention to her.

"Who is he?" I asked, not beating around the bush.

"Matthew, Sin, Sin, Matthew," she introduced.

I didn't want a name. I wanted to know who he was to her. The tight hold I was exercising over my anger was loosening. I let my gaze sweep over the guy, sizing him up. Then I remembered what was more important and I looked back at her.

"I want to talk to you," I told her. My tone was as tense as I felt.

I wasn't in control of the situation and I didn't like the uncertainty of not knowing how this was going to unfold. There was a chance this was going to blow up in my face and there would be no way to save it.

Our last meeting and the way it had ended didn't count in my favor either. This was bad. I had pushed her to open up and she had refused. How was she going to feel when she found out I had looked her up on the internet?

"I'm not sure I want to talk to you," she told me. I didn't blame her. My eyes searched hers and I took her smaller hand into mine. It felt good to touch her, reinforcing the physical connection we had. I saw her eyes soften slightly and I tried to block out the third wheel watching our interaction.

"Please," I murmured softly and I watched her anger unravel.

"Fine," she gave in and looked at me expectantly like she was ready to listen. But this subject was way too sensitive to discuss in a public place.

"Where are you staying?" I asked, not liking that Matthew was still watching us with interest.

"In an apartment nearby."

I wasn't in the clear yet but I was hoping I was one step closer.

"Could I come by tonight to talk?" I didn't want to spend another night contemplating what her reaction was going to be and how I would handle it.

She made me wait while she considered my request. The anxious uncertainty that settled in my stomach reminded me that I wasn't in control of this situation. She was in complete control.

I held her gaze while she looked at me thoughtfully.

"Fine," she answered and I felt relieved.

Not liking how on edge I was feeling, I shoved my hands into the front pockets of my jeans. She gave me the address.

"I'll be there at seven," I told her. She nodded. I couldn't stop myself from shooting one last glare at Matthew, who had witnessed the whole exchange. His expression was unreadable.

I raked a hand through my hair as I walked away. At least I wouldn't have to wait much longer to see how this played out. I pushed my tongue against my lip ring, trying to work through my agitation.

There were only two choices. She would understand that her brother's warning had pushed me to look her up on the internet. Or she wouldn't and I would lose her.

My throat tightened as I swallowed. If I were a betting man, I would bet against myself.

Chapter Eighteen

There was so much riding on this one moment that I had to take a deep breath before I knocked on the door. At least the wait was over and I would soon find out if she would be able to forgive me.

I could tell myself that I should have heeded all the warnings I had given myself but none of it seemed to matter now. How I felt wasn't something I could change, even if I wasn't ready to label it yet.

Taylor opened the door.

"Hey," I said, trying to smile to hide my nervousness.

She didn't smile back as she stepped back and let me into the apartment. It was not a good sign.

"Hi," she greeted stiffly.

She walked toward the living room and I followed her, letting myself take in her new living quarters. It looked expensive.

A knee-jerk anger hit me when I saw Matthew sitting on

the sofa watching TV. He looked way too comfortable in the apartment. What the hell was he doing here?

"He's living with you?" I asked Taylor. The anger intermingled with my nervousness, sending me spiraling in an already fragile situation.

If you don't calm down you're going to mess this up, I told myself, trying to rein back my emotions.

"Yes," she answered calmly. What the hell?

It felt like everything I thought I had known and felt secure in went straight out the window. I had never felt so unsure of something before. The odds were building up against me.

"Who is he?" I asked, still unable to hide my anger. I studied her closely, trying to read her features. She took a deep breath.

"No need to talk like I'm not here," Matthew said sarcastically. I glared at him but it didn't rile him up like I wanted it to. I wanted nothing better than to slam my fist into his face. Subconsciously I tightened my fist to ride out the urge.

"You came here to talk...so talk," Taylor told me, bringing me back to the reason I was here. She crossed her arms as she gave me her attention.

I gave Matthew one last side-glare before I looked back at Taylor. *Remember why you are here.* This was too important to allow a stranger to derail me.

"I want to talk to you alone."

There was no way I was going to tell her what I had done while a third party was watching. I shoved my hands into my pockets to stop myself from doing something stupid when I felt Matthew watching me. He was baiting me and I wasn't going to let him win. Taylor was more important.

"Fine," she said in a clipped tone before walking into a nearby room.

A sense of foreboding swirled in the pit of my stomach as I followed her into the bedroom and closed the door behind us. Finally we were alone.

She stood with her arms crossed, waiting for me, my gaze holding hers.

Now that the moment had come to tell her the truth, I felt a surge of panic that she wouldn't be able to see my reasons for doing it. But it was time to face the music.

"Your brother came to see me," I said, watching her closely and as I suspected she looked surprised.

"What did he say?" She eyed me nervously.

"He told me to stay away from you." I moved closer but she stepped away, keeping her distance from me.

"He told me you'd been through enough. He said that I'd just end up hurting you and you wouldn't be able to deal with that." Watching the emotions play over her fine delicate features, I wanted to reach out and take her hand into mine to soothe her. Anger darkened her eyes. I was pretty sure her brother would be getting an earful.

"He wouldn't tell me anything about your past," I admitted. The guarded look she gave me made my stomach sink.

It was going to get much worse than that.

She closed her eyes, briefly touching her temple like she was struggling to take in everything I was telling her. And I felt like an asshole for what I was going to tell her next.

For the first time since I had arrived, I allowed myself to remember all I'd discovered about her and her traumatic childhood. I couldn't stop or hide my feelings about what she had gone through and how much I wanted to be able to wipe the darkness from her light.

I moved closer but I didn't touch her. She opened her eyes and looked deep into mine. And there was no more hiding what I knew.

Her reaction was worse than I had expected. She looked horrified after she read the truth in my eyes. There was no mistaking the sympathy in my eyes for her. The little hope I had held on to seemed to dwindle and I was left with the hard truth: I was going to lose her. It left me struggling to breathe as panic set in.

"I'm sorry," I managed in a whisper. My hand reached for her. I wanted to touch her one last time but she wrenched away from me. The sound of her first sob tore through me like a ragged-edged knife.

"Don't touch me." She put her hand up to keep me away.

Any guilt I had felt before was nothing compared to how shitty I was feeling at the look of betrayal in her eyes. She had every right to feel that way and there was little I could say to take it away.

"How much do you know?" she whispered, looking so fragile like she was about to fall apart.

I wanted to lie to lessen the blow but I knew it would just make things worse in the long run. I had to be honest, even if it killed me.

"Everything."

She began to unravel right in front of my eyes. She pressed her hands to her mouth to smother the horror. And there was nothing I could do to take it back.

"I'm sorry," I whispered again. I tried to step closer but she moved out of my reach and I dropped my hand to my side.

"Stay away from me," she told me.

I kept fighting the instinct in me to gather her up and hold her. Seeing her in so much pain and being the cause of it made me feel sick to my stomach.

"Get out," she said. Her voice was steady but her actions gave her away. She wrapped her arms around her waist like she was still trying to hold herself together.

"Don't do this, Tay," I told her. My instinct overcame my determination and I reached for her again, hoping that if I could at least touch her it might sway her but she refused to let me.

"I didn't want you to know but that didn't stop you." She paused for a moment, closing her eyes for a few moments.

All I could say was, "I'm sorry."

"Get out!" she shouted.

Her big blue eyes watered and I felt like something had sucker-punched me in the stomach. I deserved to feel the pain and the guilt weighing down on me. I deserved it all.

Then to make matters worse the door to her bedroom crashed open and Matthew filled the doorway. He looked at Taylor, who had tears running down her cheeks, and then his tightly controlled features turned to me.

"What happened?" Matthew asked me as he entered the room, looking between the two of us as he tried to read the situation. He seemed to assess her before he faced me, standing protectively before her.

I was already calculating how fast I could get a swing in before he could block me. "This has nothing to do with you." I took a menacing step toward him.

"If it has anything to do with Taylor, then it has something to do with me," he stated firmly, still blocking her from me.

"Just go," Taylor's hoarse voice broke the growing tension between Matthew and me.

She wouldn't even look at me. Her eyes were fixed on the floor. I studied her, trying to figure out what I could say to turn the situation around.

"Tay, just let me explain," I pleaded, trying to get closer to her, but Matthew blocked me.

I clenched my jaw, trying to contain my anger.

"There is nothing you can say." She shook her head.

The broken look she gave me tilted my world and I knew I had lost.

"You need to leave," Matthew instructed fiercely, putting a hand to my chest to stop me from moving any closer.

I glared at him before I looked over his shoulder at Taylor.

"I don't want to upset you more, so I'll leave," I said, finally relenting.

She trembled, clasping her hands together.

"But this isn't over," I warned her softly.

I wasn't going to give up so easily. I would give her time to deal but I was going to be back.

Before I left, I gave Matthew one more look, telling him exactly how close he had come to having a personal meeting with my fists. I slammed the front door when I left.

The heaviness in my chest wouldn't go away. It felt like a weight pressing down on my lungs and it hurt when I inhaled.

I lay on my bed, trying to figure out the exact moment I had realized the confrontation with Taylor had swung against me. The situation hadn't been helped with the interference by Matthew. Just thinking of him made my muscles tense in preparation for a fight.

I spent hours in the garage working out, trying to expel the guilt I was feeling and the anger directed at Matthew. If he hadn't been there I could have talked her around but his interference had stopped that.

He didn't understand how much was at stake. I swallowed.

Slater peered in and asked me what had happened but I couldn't even admit out loud to him what I had done. In a world where we were trying to forget our pasts, I didn't think he would understand my reasons for snooping into Taylor's against her wishes.

And I didn't need another person to look at me with the judgment that I had made a big mistake.

Even I struggled to explain what had pushed me to do something so wrong. I cared for her. There was no doubt about that. So the question still remained, why had I dug into a past she didn't want anyone to know about?

I couldn't pin the blame purely on Connor. He had pushed me but I was the one who had crossed the line into her privacy. I flung my arm across my eyes, trying to block out the pained look in Taylor's eyes when she realized what I had done. Even the memory had the ability to make me feel as bad as I had when I'd been standing in front of her and watching her reaction.

It had been more than just curiosity. Was it a need to be able to understand her better? Every so often when she let her guard down I could see the glimmer of sadness. And I'd wanted to know what had happened to put it there.

Now I knew. I understood her so much more but I had lost her in the process.

Before, I had felt some hope, but now I was wrestling with the fact that this was something she could not forgive. The thought brought an ache to my chest. I put my hand there to soothe the pain as I sat up.

I also understood her brother's protectiveness. I would have locked her up to keep her safe. Even now her fragility pulled at the protectiveness I felt for her.

My somber mood was matched by Slater's. There was something going on with him, he was quieter than usual, but I wasn't in a place to try and figure him out when I was dealing with so much myself.

Walking over to the window, I looked out at the early morning darkness, wondering what Taylor was doing. Thinking about her reminded me of the irritating presence of Matthew. Why was he in her life? I didn't recognize him. Was he a friend? An old acquaintance? Whoever he was I disliked him.

While I searched the starry night for an answer, I had a thought. I touched my tongue to my lip ring as I considered the only way I could even things between us. It wouldn't completely wipe my betrayal but it may lessen the blow.

I hadn't completely opened up to her about my past. Maybe giving her all the rotten details would show her that I wanted her to see all of me and not just the side I showed the world.

But I remembered parts from the news articles that spread fear through me. If I told her the complete truth it might have the adverse effect and send her further away. No, I decided right then and there I couldn't chance it.

Unable to sleep, I went downstairs. The light from the living room told me that I wasn't the only one. I wasn't surprised to see Slater sitting in the chair. He was drinking a beer and set it down when I entered.

"Can't sleep?" he asked.

"No," I said with a sigh as I slumped down beside him on the sofa.

A few moments of silence fell between us.

"You want to tell me what happened?" he asked.

Now that I'd had the chance to work through some of my guilt and pain, I could open up to him. I wasn't going to tell him the details about Taylor's past. He didn't need to know that and I respected her enough not to share them with him.

"I did something I wasn't supposed to."

Slater watched me, with his arms resting on his legs. "What did you do?"

I rubbed my hands over my face, feeling the rising frustration. I let out a deep breath before I answered.

"I did a search on Taylor."

He didn't say anything even though I knew it was something he wouldn't agree with.

"The other night when we went out...I told her some things about my past." I didn't miss the flicker of surprise he sent me. We didn't tell anyone about our childhoods. It was our way of putting them firmly behind us. If we didn't talk about it, it didn't exist. "And when she wouldn't open up about her background I got angry with her."

I paused for a moment, feeling slightly guilty under the intense gaze of my best friend. Was he thinking of his own past that he kept firmly under wraps?

"But I never thought about looking into her background until her brother warned me to stay away. He said something bad happened to her and that she had a very protected upbringing. He told me she wasn't like other girls and she wouldn't be able to recover when I walked away."

"He said that to you?" He looked a little taken aback.

"Yeah." I straightened up and linked my hands, feeling more agitated. "After he left I went upstairs and did a search on the internet."

"How did you know there would be something to find?" he asked. Most people's bad experiences couldn't be found on the web that was open for the public to see.

"Remember the night she got attacked? When she mentioned her name to the cop, he seemed to think he had heard it before."

"Really?" he asked, enthralled in my story.

I nodded. Feeling uncomfortable, I rubbed the back of my neck.

"It wasn't like I was trying to break her trust." I was trying to find the right words to describe the motivation behind my actions. "I thought if I knew, I would understand why she was so naive and understand her better. Maybe even understand why she was so hesitant to report the stuff that was happening to her."

I looked at my friend.

"Why do you care?" he asked, taking me by surprise. "I know you've been fucking her but you're acting like this is something more permanent."

"It's the same way you've been acting with Jordan," I shot back, not liking how he had said out loud what I'd already been wrestling with.

He looked uncomfortable. He hadn't been expecting my remark either.

"It wasn't permanent," he said. "She was just some girl I spent some time with but it's over."

So he'd been strong enough to cut her loose. I wasn't strong enough to do the same with Taylor.

"You know what happens if we let them in." The seriousness in his eyes reminded me of all we had overcome. His eyes transported me back to the first time I'd seen him next door looking so lost and sad.

I looked down, unable to look my friend straight in the eye. "It's already too late."

Despite warning myself, I had done it anyway and now I had to deal with it.

The silence that followed made me look up. I expected to see judgment in his expression but there was only sympathy.

"Then you fight for her."

Chapter Nineteen

Back at college, I kept a low profile. I told myself I was giving her space to work through her anger before I spoke to her again, but the truth was I was unsure of myself for the first time in a long time and I had no idea how to fix what I had screwed up.

The thing was I was so good at cutting girls loose, I didn't know how to keep the one I wanted. What did I say to her? I wasn't ready to share my feelings about her, not just yet. First I needed to get her to realize that I hadn't meant to hurt her. Going behind her back had been wrong and there was no disputing that.

I didn't know the first thing about being with someone. Remembering how much I hurt her made me feel shitty and I wanted to get us back to where we had been before it had happened.

Slater was trying his best to be supportive in the situation but he had as much experience as I had with permanency and girls. We were both clueless.

"Just tell her you're sorry," Slater suggested from where he sat on the sofa with his feet propped against the table. "It's what you're supposed to say when you do something wrong."

I was pacing up and down, trying to decide on what to say.

"That just sounds lame." My tongue pushed against my lip ring.

We had been at this for an hour already but I was no closer to figuring out what I was going to say to her.

I had to do and say something. I didn't want to lose her. And that was something I didn't even want to contemplate. Just thinking about it turned the rawness inside me to an ache that made it more difficult to draw breath.

I considered giving her more details about my past with a few omissions to make it up to her. But I wasn't sure it would be enough. What if there was nothing I could do to make her forgive me?

Feeling defeated, I slumped down on the seat beside Slater.

"What if nothing works?" I looked at my best friend.

He shrugged his shoulders. "Then at least you tried."

In our world it was a lot.

The door opened. I knew it would be Eric. Instead of looking at who was entering the house, I looked at Slater. The last thing I wanted was someone else around when I was in such turmoil.

"I'll get him out," Slater assured me in a hushed tone as he stood. "I'll take him out for a couple of hours."

"Thanks."

As much as I had done for Slater, I didn't know how I would have survived without him. He was the person who got me and understood me like no one else.

"Hi, guys," Eric greeted when he entered.

"I'm going to play pool. You wanna play?" Slater asked in Eric's direction.

He was always eager to hang out with us so Slater knew he wouldn't turn down the opportunity to go out with him. I wished he were more like Tucker. He paid his rent but you rarely saw him. I bet it was because he spent his nights sleeping elsewhere with girls.

Most guys preferred to stay over at the girl's place because when you were done you could leave, minimizing any unwanted uncomfortable situations.

"That sounds great."

The appearance of Eric reminded me of his interaction with Taylor in the kitchen. It had annoyed me at the time and I had been meaning to speak to him about it. And now was as good a time as any.

"Before you leave I want a word with Eric," I said to Slater. He gave me a questioning look but I shook my head. Eric nodded.

I walked into the kitchen and turned to lean against the counter as Eric entered. There was something about this guy that just put my back up immediately.

"What's up?" he asked, looking slightly nervous. I had a way of intimidating people. I didn't know if it was my presence, the tattoos or piercings.

"I would prefer if you didn't speak to Taylor about my sleeping habits." I crossed my arms as I pinned him with a determined look. I stopped myself short of telling him not to go anywhere near her.

I didn't want anyone saying something to her that would remind her about the countless girls before her.

"Sure thing." He lifted his shoulders and let them drop. "I was just trying to make conversation."

His explanation sounded innocent but it didn't sit right with me.

"Don't."

Taylor was off-limits to him. I could tell his interest went deeper than just friendly conversation and I didn't want to spell it out to him that she was mine. That message went without saying.

"Okay." He nodded.

I stared at him for a few moments to ensure he had received the message and once I was happy he had heeded my warning, I pushed off the counter.

"You ready?" Slater asked Eric when he exited the kitchen behind me.

"Yeah." Slater's eyes met mine.

I would explain it to him later.

They left and I was left alone with only my thoughts.

Why don't you just call her? And say what? It was the same problem I had been wrestling with.

An hour later I still hadn't come up with anything but I knew I was running out of time. I had to let her know that I was still around and I hadn't backed off. She had to know that I was staying.

I held my phone in my hands, agonizing over what to say. Eventually, feeling frustrated, I keyed a message and sent it before I could stop myself.

A simple message that said, *I'm sorry.*

I set it down on the coffee table and stared at it. I don't know what I was expecting but I waited and waited. With each minute that passed I felt more agitated. I stood up and started to pace again. I had never wanted to hear the slight ping of a message coming through on my phone so badly before, but there was only a deafening silence.

After ten minutes I was convinced that it hadn't been enough but I didn't know what else to say. Did I send her another one? I rubbed the back of my neck, trying to ease the tension that was building. There were plenty of reasons she was taking so long to respond.

Maybe she was out. Then my mind went into a frenzy of who she could be with if she wasn't at home. My jaw tightened when I thought of Matthew. I didn't want to imagine her going out with him. This time I recognized the searing feeling for what it was—jealousy.

She might have gone out with Jordan. But that thought didn't make me feel any better. Jordan was probably nursing a broken heart after Slater had ended things so she would probably be on the prowl for another guy. I didn't want Taylor out looking for someone to replace me. Then I remembered Matthew again. Was he going to take my place?

The knock at the door was unexpected and I felt irritated by the interruption. I opened the door and anything I was going to say was stuck in my throat when I saw Taylor standing in front of me.

She was dressed in a simple shirt and jeans. Not a stitch of makeup, but she had never looked more beautiful. I was blown away.

My eyes met hers. I felt the effect of her presence immediately in the way my heart sped up. The anger and anguish that had been in her eyes the last time I had seen her was gone. Now it was replaced with apprehension and determination, which I took as a good sign. I smiled at her.

Then I noticed she hadn't come alone. Matthew stood just behind her. Why was he here? My walls that had been weakened by the sight of Taylor were hardened by him. My smile waned.

Any momentary relief vanished. If she had shown up alone it would have been a good sign but it only spelled the opposite that she had come to see me and she had brought him with her. Was she here to tell me that whatever had been going on between us was really finished and she was moving on to him?

Still reeling, I glared at the person to blame even though I knew I shouldered most of that responsibility. I pressed my lips into a tight line.

"What the fuck is he doing here?" I asked before I could rein in my temper. Now my anger was directed at her.

"Calm down. Don't jump to conclusions," she told me, holding up her hands to me. "Just let us in and I'll explain everything."

I could at least give her the opportunity to explain but it was difficult to keep a lid on my anger. I stepped back and allowed them in. Her explanation had better be good, otherwise this was not going to go well.

The fact that Matthew walked in looking relaxed and unfazed by my anger made me want to pummel him with my fists. He was so confident and here I was so unsure of what was going to happen.

"I need to talk to him alone," she said to him and he nodded. I frowned. Why the hell did she need his permission to talk to me? I crossed my arms to stop myself from doing something stupid. I needed the full picture before I allowed myself to respond.

"I'll stay here," he said, taking a seat on the sofa without even looking in my direction.

When her attention moved back to me, I dropped my arms and walked upstairs, trying to get as far away from Matthew as possible. Inside my room, I waited for her to enter before I closed the door and leaned against it.

"Where's everyone else?" she asked. Was she worried someone would interrupt us?

"They're out." My tone was abrupt.

She quieted.

"So are you going to explain the tag-a-long?" I asked, crossing my arms as I held her gaze. I wanted answers.

"You've met my overprotective brother," she said and I

nodded. I had a few added descriptions that weren't good but I kept my mouth shut.

"Well, that overprotective brother hired a bodyguard," she said with a sigh like she wasn't totally on board with the idea.

A bodyguard. It explained why he was always around her. I should have known better. Her brother was very protective of her and with the money available he would choose an option that would not leave her at risk. She clasped her hands together as she waited for my response. My anger evaporated and I felt relieved she wasn't trying to replace me.

"And I thought that overprotective brother of yours was stupid." I dropped my defensive stand. She didn't look too happy about it but I was glad she was being watched.

Then I realized why I it had never occurred to me.

"He doesn't look like a typical bodyguard." I cocked my head to the side. Bodyguards were supposed to be big, bulky and intimidating. The guy downstairs was just annoying.

"I know, it's probably why he is so good at his job," she said, shrugging dismissively.

Now that we had clarification on that issue it was time to move on to the next. The most important one.

"And here I thought he was my replacement," I admitted my fear that I might have pushed her too far. Feeling unsettled, I straightened up.

When her eyes met mine, I saw she still cared even though I had hurt her. I'd made mistakes and so had she but I wanted to find a way back to where we had been before. But even though I could read her feelings for me in her eyes, she was hesitant. I had hurt her multiple times but I was done denying that this wasn't more than just sex.

It was still difficult to look at her without remembering what I had read and I even fought the sympathy I felt for her. There was no hiding it and I saw the moment she stiffened slightly.

"I'm sorry for shutting you out," she said softly. She bowed her head slightly. I could hear the emotion in her voice and I wanted to touch her to bring her back to the present where she had nothing to fear. She wasn't alone; I was with her.

"I'm sorry too. I shouldn't have taken things into my own hands. You didn't want me to know, but I went searching anyway," I said as she looked up. I rubbed my hands over my face and into my hair. "But no matter how mad you are and how sorry I am, it doesn't change the fact that I know."

I dropped my hands. She continued to stare at me.

"I was upset after I'd told you stuff about me and you refused to open up. I was angry so I tried to shut you out. Then your brother came to see me." I raked a hand through my hair. She rolled her eyes at the mention of her brother. "He told me to stay away from you. He said that you wouldn't recover if I hurt you."

Looking back I could understand his concern and the motivation behind his underhanded actions. But at some point he had to realize he couldn't keep her locked up. This was her life and she had every right to live it with her own choices. On paper I was the worst possible choice, and even I knew that.

Seeing the fragility in her eyes, it was difficult not to think about the little girl who had witnessed something that should never have happened.

"I know that you didn't want to tell me about your past, but after your brother came to see me I couldn't stop myself," I said, my voice was soft and soothing. She bit down on her lip and I knew she was fighting the renewal of the memory. "There were so many things about you that just simply didn't add up. Your naivety and lack of knowledge. Then your brother came to see me and told me to stay away from you. That just pushed me over the edge and I had to know. I tried asking your brother, but he wouldn't tell me so I did the only thing I could think of, I googled your name."

I was tired of talking. Staying away from her wasn't an option. I needed to touch her so I stepped closer.

"I've been through some rough shit, but I don't know how you survived what happened to you," I murmured softly.

She fought for control over her emotions. I didn't like to see her like this. I moved closer and she gazed up at me. The raw emotions flooding through her tore at me.

"I don't like it," I told her hoarsely, wanting to be able to take it away.

"What?" she asked.

"I don't like seeing you upset." I wanted to see her smile and see the light filter through her eyes like a ray of sunshine. I didn't want to see the darkness that scarred her childhood and her young adult life.

"You don't have to talk about it." I wanted her to know that I didn't need her to open up about it. My hand lifted to caress her cheek. Her skin was as soft as I remembered.

"I've been trying to forget that day for as long as I can remember," she breathed, looking like she had the weight of the world on her small shoulders.

It might have happened a long time ago but it was something that she would never get over. It would stay with her until the day she took her last breath.

Wanting to give her my strength, I reached out and took her smaller hand into mine. I held it in my hand like I could remind her that despite the terrible memory, she was here with me. She had survived.

"I was nine." She swallowed while she struggled to continue. "It was a Friday night and Connor went out to a party. He was eighteen at the time and he'd planned on sleeping over at his friend's house."

I had read all the details. I knew how this story ended but listening to her talk about it made it so much more real and heartbreaking.

Chapter Twenty

I didn't want to hear her talk about that night but I stayed quiet and listened, seeing the ghosts from her past fill her big blue eyes. The newspaper articles had been extensive on their coverage so there would be nothing gained from taking her back to a moment that had marred her life.

"I spent the evening watching a movie with my mom and dad. They liked to do that with me so I wouldn't miss Connor too much when he was out." She smiled as she started her story. The love she felt for them was evident in her eyes as she fondly remembered her parents.

Before that moment she'd had the perfect type of childhood with a family who loved her. It had only taken one night for the actions of others to take that away from her, leaving her broken.

She trembled and I told her to sit down as I pushed her down onto the bed. She rubbed her forehead like she was trying to collect her thoughts. I lowered myself beside her with her hand still in mine. I needed to touch her and link myself to her while she walked back through the horrific events of that night.

She didn't have to reopen the wound. I was about to tell her that she didn't have to do this.

"I'm not sure what time they tucked me into bed and read me a story. My mom gave me a kiss on the forehead and told me to have sweet dreams. My father came to kiss me goodnight and told me he loved me. It was our usual routine for bedtime."

But the truth was she was giving me a closer look into why she was the way she was and I wouldn't give that up for anything. I wanted to know it all. Even if it hurt to hear it. I gave her hand a reassuring squeeze and she gave me a slight smile.

"I'd been going through a stage of having nightmares and that night I woke up scared. I held my favorite teddy, Mr. Cuddles, tightly in my hands and went to my parents' bedroom to ask my mom if I could sleep in the bed. Still half asleep, my mom opened her covers and I climbed into the bed bedside her." She paused to take an emotional breath. "I was jolted awake by my mom. She was scared and shaking. My dad wasn't in the room. She'd told me to remain calm and to hide in the closet. Confused and still half asleep, I asked her what was wrong. She whispered to me that there was someone in the house and told me I needed to be quiet. I didn't understand what was happening, but I did what she told me. Once I was safe inside the closet she closed the doors. There was enough of a gap to be able to see my mother walk to the door."

There was a faraway look in her eyes, like she had been transported back in time. She looked at the floor. I didn't want to see her like this.

"You don't have to." I took her other hand in mine. Her

eyes lifted to mine. I wanted to be able to go back into her memories and stop what was going to happen.

"You know everything, but I need you to understand why it was something that was so hard to carry around with me. What you read would have given you all the grim details, but I want you to understand why I am the way I am," she explained hoarsely. "There was some noise inside the house and I heard my father shout. My mom looked frantic and scared. I'll never forget that fear that I saw on her face. She hurried back to the closet and got me out and then she led me to the window. She opened it up as quietly as she could. I wanted to stay with her, but she begged me to be a good girl and to climb through the window."

My chest tightened when I saw the first signs of tears filling her eyes. They fell and she pulled a hand free to brush them away.

"I whimpered as I climbed through the window. She told me to go and hide in the back yard. I had no idea what was happening, but it was the desperation in her voice that made me run through the darkness to the back of the house. Our property was quite large with a tall boundary wall so I ran as fast as I could still holding onto my teddy bear. I tripped a couple of times... I don't know if it was the adrenaline that kept me from feeling the pain."

More tears spilled down her face and she swept them away with her hand. It was hard to watch her try and keep herself together when her world had been falling apart. I lifted my hands and brushed the wetness from her cheeks.

"I don't like it when you cry," I told her softly. It was tearing me up inside.

"I hid in some thick bushes against the wall. I huddled holding Mr. Cuddles, too scared to move. It was only when the sun came up that I came out of hiding. In the daytime, everything seemed less scary. The house was quiet and the front door was wide open. The house had been ransacked and I crept as quietly as I could. I was scared that the intruders were still in the house. The first place I went to was my parents' bedroom."

It became too much and she closed her eyes for a few moments. I squeezed her hands and held them.

"While I'd been hiding in the dark, I'd imagined all sorts of scenarios, but nothing prepared me for what I found. There was so much blood. My father was lying on his stomach with a knife sticking out of his back. I rushed over to him, but he didn't respond. I'd never seen death before, but I saw it in his eyes. I heard a slight noise and realized my mom was still alive." A sob tore from her and she pulled her hands free from mine to put them to her mouth. She was shaking. "Crying... and becoming more hysterical, I rushed over to her. She was lying in a pool of her own blood. She had a couple of stab wounds...honestly, I don't know how she'd survived that long. I wanted to go and get help, but my mom held my wrist and...told me to stay with her."

She took a moment to try and regroup so she could continue.

"She knew she wouldn't make it and she didn't want to die alone. I held my mother's hand as she struggled to breathe. I told her I loved her just before her chest stopped moving and I couldn't hear her breathe anymore. It was the hardest thing I've ever had to do."

The lump in my throat made it hard to swallow.

"I'm so sorry," I murmured, letting go of her hands to hug her. She leaned her head against my chest. I consoled her for a few minutes before she abruptly broke away from me and stood.

"I kind of shut down after that. It was like I was in a bubble. I knew exactly what was going on around me, but I couldn't interact. I lost track of time. The next thing I remember was when Connor came home and discovered what happened. It's hard to remember exactly what happened after that because I had some sort of breakdown. I just couldn't cope with everything."

At such a young age I couldn't imagine what it would have been like to go through something like that. Her eyes meshed with mine.

"I wasn't crazy." I would have lost my shit had that happened to me.

"You weren't crazy, you just lost your parents and you couldn't cope. It's understandable." I stood up, closing the distance between us.

I was well aware of the stories of her mental breakdown after the murder of her parents. It had been covered along with the trial.

"You look at me the same way they did," she said in an accusing tone. She stepped back.

I felt empathy for the little girl who'd had to grow up practically overnight to deal with a situation she should never have been exposed to. She wasn't crazy.

"That's not how I see you," I argued, refusing to allow her to keep me at a distance.

She was so brave and she didn't even see the inner strength I saw in her. To overcome what she had took a strength not a lot of people possessed.

"How do you see me?" she asked softly. The vulnerability in her eyes unraveled a warm feeling in my chest.

I moved closer.

"When I look at you, I see someone who is strong and fearless," I whispered. "There aren't many girls who see what they want and go for it."

When I remembered how she'd come after me, I smiled.

"No one has ever asked me to take advantage of them like you did." My grin widened. She broke her gaze from mine and looked down at the floor like she was trying to hide something from me but I wasn't having any of that. I lifted her eyes back up to mine with a finger underneath her chin.

"I see a beautiful girl who is just as beautiful on the inside. Finding out about your past has made me understand you better, but it hasn't changed the fact that I wanted you then and I still want you now." My tone was serious so there was no doubting the sincerity of my words.

Her eyes softened and my heart warmed. Physically I still wanted her as much as I had the first moment we had met. I wasn't sure I would ever tire of her. Whatever I felt for her went much deeper than the chemistry we shared.

For a moment I dropped my eyes to her lips and I wanted to kiss her.

"Show me," she whispered nervously. It lit a fire inside me and when she wet her lips with her tongue I felt the surge of heat that pumped through my veins. She was the only one who could ease the burning ache inside me and any control I had previously exerted disappeared.

I couldn't resist her. I leaned closer. My breath fanned against her cheek as I lined up my lips with hers. Her eyes closed and I stilled. When I didn't kiss her right away she opened her eyes again. I rested my hands on her hips and she held her breath.

"You are so beautiful," I told her before I gently kissed her. Taking into account her emotional state, my kiss was gentle. Her hands gripped my arms like she was anchoring herself to me.

Then her hands loosened their hold to move up my arms and link around my neck. I moved my lips against the softness of hers. I swept my tongue against her bottom lip and she groaned. It was the most erotic thing to hear.

I wanted to feel the same loss of control I felt when she was near. I gathered her in my arms and allowed myself to kiss her more deeply to show her just how much I wanted her. Her mouth opened and my tongue slipped into her mouth. I caressed her tongue gently with mine and her arms tightened around my neck in response.

I needed her in that moment more than I needed air in my lungs or blood in my veins. The realization scared me. I drew in a deep breath and pushed through it.

I moved her closer to the bed. When I felt the slight resistance as she came into contact with the bed, I laid her down, breaking my lips from hers. The sight of her on my bed, looking up at me with her slightly red, thoroughly kissed lips, caused warmth to spread inside my chest. I swore that I wouldn't fuck this up.

She reached for me as I joined her on the bed. My body shifted above hers. Our lips met again and her legs wrapped around my waist. Pressing down against her, I showed her how much I needed her with my body instead of words I couldn't say. She kissed me as I rocked against her.

Feeling like I was about to explode, I moved away to pull my shirt off. I knelt beside her to help her remove her top. She sat up and I helped her out of it. I threw the piece of clothing in the same direction I had dropped my shirt.

I shifted off the bed to rid myself of my jeans, which I kicked free. Her eyes feasted over me, heating my skin just before I moved to her jeans to unzip them and tug them down. She lifted her hips to help me and then she lay only in her underwear while looking at me with the same need I had for her.

There was no time to waste. I covered her body with the warmth of mine. Her skin was soft against mine. Her hands went to my face as I settled my body against hers. It felt so right, like we had been made for each other. It was overwhelming to think that only she had the power to make me feel this way and I had nearly lost her. I stopped myself.

What was in the past I couldn't change, all I could do was ensure I never again gave her a reason to walk away.

Even though I had done this more times than I could remember, it felt like there had only been her. Our eyes held. The power and intensity of it took my breath away. Then she lifted her lips to mine and kissed me softly. Pressing against her, all I wanted was to bury myself as deep inside her as possible.

We still had too much clothing on and it was time to rectify that. I broke away to pull off her underwear and then I leaned forward to unclasp her bra. She lay back down and I allowed my gaze to sweep over her, caressing every naked inch of her. The possessiveness I had been wrestling with came out in full force. I got rid of my boxers.

I bruised her lips with the next kiss. The only sound was our intermingled deep breathing when I allowed my mouth to close over one of her nipples as my fingers gently worked the other. She took me by surprise when she pushed me down onto my back. She was more confident and it thrilled me.

There was nothing sexier than a woman who knew what she wanted, and I allowed her to take control. I held my breath as her mouth trailed kisses down my body. The warmth of her mouth branded my skin. To keep myself from reaching for her, I put my hands underneath my head.

The first flick of her tongue made me tense. God, it felt so good. I moved a hand to thread through her hair as she took me into her mouth. I gritted my teeth to stop myself from unloading right then and there in her mouth.

"I can't take much more," I managed to get out as I moved to push her down on the bed.

I reached for the protection in my side table and tore it open with my teeth. As quickly as I could I rolled it on before I moved between her legs.

My hand guided her leg around my waist. I kissed her

just as I pushed into her in one smooth stroke. Her hand gripped my shoulder as she allowed me to enter her. She gripped me tightly as I moved in and out of her with only one goal in mind. I increased the tempo and covered her mouth as she gasped.

I could tell the moment she began to tense that she was about to climax. I pushed in deeper and she trembled. It only took a couple of thrusts to follow her over the edge. My breathing was hard and my heart was racing like it was about to break free from my chest. Then I leaned my forehead against hers. There was a faint sheen of sweat on her face that made her glow. I kissed her before I moved off the bed to get rid of the protection.

Not only was I physically satisfied when I joined her in the bed again, but our physical connection had appeased the fear inside of me. I just wanted to hold her close.

What if my path had never crossed with hers? Would I still be moving from one girl to another with no idea how it felt to really care?

She laid her head against my chest as I held her in my arms. I dropped a kiss on her forehead to reassure her that she was safe with me.

"What are you thinking about?" I asked.

"Not much." I wondered if she had any idea what was going on in my head.

I squeezed her before I lay facing her. I liked the way she looked at me. It was something I couldn't explain.

"Thank you for telling me your story." I touched her cheek gently with my fingertips.

Chapter Twenty-One

"I needed you to understand why I didn't want anyone to find out about it," she explained. "It was bad enough going through what I did but doing it under the watchful eye of the press was traumatic. It didn't just affect me. I put Connor through hell. Not only did he lose both of our parents, he lost me for a while and he fought hard to get me back. My parents had left us some money, but my brother worked hard to make sure he had the money to send me to the best shrinks and get me the best help money could buy. When most people had given up, my brother refused to. And then one day about a year after it happened, I started to improve a little. It took a long time, but I recovered."

Knowing about her past allowed me to understand her better. It even helped me understand the overprotectiveness of her brother. But he had to realize that although at times she looked so fragile and vulnerable, I saw a steely strength in her. She was stronger than she looked.

"Now I understand why your brother is so protective of you."

I fell silent for a few minutes.

"But at least they caught the guys who murdered your parents," I told her.

It would have been so much worse if she still had to contend with the threat that the people responsible hadn't been brought to justice and were still free to come back after her. It must have been some sort of relief to know that the guys who had so thoughtlessly taken the lives of her parents were paying for their crimes.

But nothing would undo what had been done and there was no way to bring her parents back.

"Yeah, they both got life sentences without the chance of parole even though they'd argued they'd been high on drugs," she told me.

I swallowed, not liking how her words reminded me of some mistakes I was still trying to forgive myself for. *She will never have to know*, I told myself. The more I cared for her the more the fear that I would lose her intensified.

I kissed her forehead and held her tighter as I rode the emotion.

Only a few minutes later she moved away and I let her go. She got up and started to gather up her clothes. I frowned.

"Where are you going?" I asked, feeling the fear that no matter how much I tried I wasn't going to be enough for her to stay.

I could link the feelings of inadequacy to my parents. I hadn't been enough for either of them.

"I have to go." She pulled up her panties. "Matthew is still waiting downstairs."

"Ah, Matthew. I forgot about him." I had totally forgotten about the bodyguard still in my living room. She smiled and it lifted my heart before she put on her top.

Despite her outward body language, I could tell there was something on her mind. Was she still lingering on what she had told me or was there something else she was thinking about? My gut feeling was confirmed when she smiled at me again. This time it didn't reach her eyes. I slipped out of bed. I reached for my jeans and put them on before shoving my feet into my shoes.

"I'll walk you out." I opened my bedroom door for her.

She approached me and the opportunity to ask her what was wrong was over when she hurried past me. I followed her downstairs.

Matthew was casually watching TV when he turned to see Taylor descend the last few steps. He picked up the remote and switched the TV off as he stood up.

Taylor blushed lightly when Matthew took in my half-dressed state. I didn't care. I wanted him as well as every other guy to know she was mine. I eyed him but he remained unaffected, where other guys would have felt intimidated.

Then I moved my concentration back to Taylor.

"At least I know you'll be safe." I walked her to the door and Matthew opened it. He left us alone as he walked to the car.

"Yes, he is the best my brother could find," she assured me as she lingered.

"He'd better be." Thinking that something could happen to her wasn't something I wanted to consider. I'd just found her and I couldn't lose her.

To ease the fear, I leaned forward and pressed my lips briefly to her cheek to reassure myself that she was here with me and safe.

"I need to go," she mumbled.

I didn't want her to go but I also needed space to work through the emotions I had no idea how to handle.

"Bye, Tay," I said, watching as she walked to join Matthew by the car.

He opened the door and she got in. I remained outside, watching them leave.

I shoved my hands into my jeans as I contemplated how my feelings for her were going to change everything. I couldn't even look at another girl. There was no attraction for anyone but her.

Even though we had managed to sort things through, there were so many things that could go wrong. She was in so much danger. She had already been attacked.

For the moment she's safe, I reminded myself.

If her brother had bothered to take the time to warn me to protect his sister, I knew he would do everything possible to keep her safe. I bet he was spending a small fortune for Matthew to keep her from harm. Short of keeping my eyes on her twenty-four seven, I couldn't do much more.

Even with all that logical reasoning I couldn't smother the foreboding feeling I felt in the pit of my stomach. Was it because of my childhood? That I had been let down so many times that I expected it to happen? It wasn't a matter of if but when.

You can't think like that, I told myself. But nothing gave me the surety I needed.

Back inside the sanctuary of my room I lay back on the bed, enjoying the comforting scent of her still on my sheets. It gave me some solace from the thoughts going around in my head.

There wasn't just the threat against her that was on my mind.

Now that I knew more about the events from her childhood, a new fear had developed. A chill raced up my spine at the thought that she would discover what I had done. *There is no way she can find out. It's not like she's going to go digging in your background,* I assured myself but it did nothing to dampen the fear.

Maybe later once I'd had the time to strengthen our fragile connection it would be able to withstand the information from my past. But if she found out before then, it would be too much for her and she would walk away from me.

The physical ache in my chest reminded me how much it would hurt if she couldn't see past the mistake I had been forced to make. I'd had nothing to lose before, but things were different now.

I got my phone out and typed a text. I wanted her to know I was thinking of her.

My message was simple. *Sweet dreams Tay.*

A minute later my phone pinged with a message. It was from Taylor.

Night Sin. It read.

I brushed my fingers over the message.

I knew she cared for me but I didn't want to analyze how I felt about her. It didn't matter if she discovered the secret from my past that could change everything. It hadn't been a decision I had made alone. Slater made the same decision. We'd done it together. But would she be able to understand? I couldn't fully embrace the fact that despite my underhanded decision to snoop into her background, it hadn't broken us.

It was late when there was a knock on my bedroom door.

"Come in." There was only one person who would invade the privacy of my room.

The door opened slightly and Slater poked his head in.

I sat up as he entered my room and closed the door.

"You sort things with Taylor?" He came to a stop at the end of my bed.

"Yeah," I admitted, still surprised that it had all worked out even if I wasn't convinced it would last. "Who knew that saying sorry would work."

He gave me a ghost of a smile. "Good to know."

"You never know, you might need to use it one day." I don't know why I said it but the words were out before I even thought about it.

His smile dropped and he shook his head. "I won't be needing it."

There was the familiar haunted look in his eyes that had chased him for most of our childhood. That night I didn't sleep well.

I smiled when I spotted Taylor walking to class with Matthew following closely beside her. I'd just seen her last night, but it had felt longer.

She'd surprised me when she'd finally opened up and told me about her past. It didn't matter that I'd already read all of it off the web. Hearing it in her own words had made it more real and more heart-breaking. She'd forgiven me for finding out about her past, but I still felt a pang of guilt when I thought about it.

It had been my concern for her safety that had pushed me to search her name on the Internet. Just thinking about what happened to her made me sad and angry at the same time. It was different having parents who couldn't give a shit. I couldn't miss something I'd never had. I couldn't imagine losing the unconditional love from a parent after experiencing it.

Something was off. Matthew was watching his surroundings like a hawk. It wasn't like he was being obvious, I think the only reason I picked up on it was because I knew he was a bodyguard. Taylor seemed a little jumpy and nervous. It wasn't like her. I frowned as I reached her.

Matthew swung his gaze at me and his features seemed to relax when he recognized me. Taylor gave me a weak smile.

"You okay?" I asked, letting my gaze move between the two of them.

"Everything's fine," she tried to reassure me with a weak smile but I could see past the front she was trying to put on.

I gave Matthew a questioning look.

"The stalker left a note on the door of the apartment," he told me. Taylor glared at him for revealing the information.

"What did it say?"

My question was directed at Taylor, but she hesitated. My unease grew.

" 'I know where you live, whore. You can't hide from me. You're my whore not his,' " Matthew told me and something in my gut twisted.

You're my whore not his echoed through my mind. I stepped closer to Taylor and scanned her features. It explained her nervousness and I took her hand in mine. The thought that the crazy guy who had tried to attack her was stalking her made me angry. After everything else, she didn't deserve this. She bit on her lip nervously as she held my gaze. I wanted to make her feel better and I wanted her to know I wasn't going to let this guy get anywhere near her. I leaned closer and kissed her. I pulled back in time to see her lip tremble and I hugged her for a moment. I forgot about Matthew as I held her.

"I'm okay," she assured me as she pulled away, but I knew she wasn't okay.

"Are you sure?" I asked, watching her carefully. She nodded her head at me, but I could still see the fear in her eyes.

"It's okay if you're not," I tried to tell her. No one expected her to be brave in the situation she was in.

"I'm fine," she insisted with determination.

In that moment, I glimpsed the part of Taylor who had survived the horrific deaths of her parents and the downward mental spiral afterward. It was the part of her that wouldn't just lie down and let it consume her. I understood that part of her. My life hadn't been good and I also had that same part in me that part that fought for survival. We were different people with different circumstances, but we both had that survival part that had kept us going through the tougher times.

"Are the cops any closer to catching the guy?" I asked Matthew.

He shook his head. "No," he revealed.

I looked to Taylor again and felt a pang of something in my chest. I didn't want anything to happen to her.

"Why did you come to school? Don't you think it would be safer to stay at home?" I asked softly.

She shook her head.

"I tried to tell her that it might be a good idea to stay at the apartment today," Matthew added.

"I won't allow this to make me too scared to do the things that I want to," she told me.

I understood that she didn't want what was happening to dictate her life so I tried to keep myself from bundling her up and taking her home. She'd fought to lead the normal life she was and I could see it was difficult to give that up because some crazy guy had a fixation on her.

"Come on, I'll walk you to class," I offered as I took her hand in mine. She smiled at me as we walked to her class with Matthew still watching the surrounding crowd.

At the doorway of her classroom, I gave her a brief kiss and watched as she entered the classroom with Matthew. There were no clues and the cops had no suspects. My eyes scanned the room, lingering for a moment on each guy in her class. I couldn't help wonder if it was someone sitting in her classroom. My eyes went to Matthew who was sitting beside her. I didn't trust a lot of people and it was difficult to trust Matthew to keep her safe. Taylor had told me that he was the best that her brother could find who was young enough to pass off as a college student, but that didn't make it any easier to walk away from her classroom.

I noticed Caleb, the preppy boy that she'd briefly dated and my eyes narrowed. He was sitting at the desk beside her on the opposite side to Matthew. I would be late for my class, but I couldn't pull myself away. Caleb leaned over to say something to Taylor and I felt a pull of possessiveness inside of me. Fisting my hands, I stopped myself from walking over to him and beating the crap out of him. She was mine. The brightening in his eyes as he talked to her told me volumes. Despite Taylor telling him she only wanted to be friends, I could see he felt more.

I wondered if he could be the stalker.

You're my whore not his.

It sounded like something that someone would say because they were jealous. Was it Caleb, who clearly still had a thing for her? Was he jealous of the fact that she'd been spending time with me?

It wasn't like we were dating or anything like that. As much as I wanted to stay there to watch Caleb around Taylor, I turned and walked away from the classroom before I did something I would regret. I rubbed my hands over my face, trying to get my thoughts together. There had to be another way to see if my suspicions for Caleb were correct. I pulled my phone out of the front pocket of my jeans. It didn't take me long to find the contact I was looking for. I dialed the number and waited for him to answer.

"What's up?" Jeff asked as soon as he picked up.

"I need you to do something for me," I said.

I didn't question why I had such a need to protect

Taylor. Maybe it was because I was scared to face the reason why I felt the way I did. I wanted to believe it stemmed from the fact that she'd had a hard life and I wanted to make sure nothing bad happened to her again. She'd fought hard to overcome her mental breakdown and it worried me that if something horrible happened she wouldn't be able to recover from it.

But the truth was, even if I didn't want to admit it, I cared about her. More than I should. She'd been the first girl that I'd screwed more than once. Usually if there was any sight of any drama, I'd have been the first one to walk away, but despite Taylor's past and the whole stalker thing, I was still around. I didn't want to analyze why; instead, I was going to make it my mission to keep her safe.

Chapter Twenty-Two

My mind was elsewhere. I tapped my pencil against the table, counting down the minutes that felt like hours.

The girl who sat beside me had given up flirting with me. My lack of response had been a clear message I wasn't into it. The only girl I wanted to take to bed was Taylor and I couldn't get her off my mind. But it wasn't just desire or want, it was more.

I was worried. I'd hoped that Taylor reporting the attack would scare the guy off but hadn't happened. It indicated to me that the person wasn't going to stop until he was either caught, or worse, he got Taylor.

A sense of dread covered me like a darkness, making it more difficult to focus or breathe. What if Matthew wasn't enough to keep her safe? *Stop it*, I admonished myself. *Taylor is safe and the expensive bodyguard won't let anything happen to her.*

I was preoccupied when I finally left my last class, only to

208

be irritated when the girl who had been flirting with me stepped in beside me. She would have been my type before but the only one who raced my heart now was a pretty blonde with big blue eyes.

"You have plans this weekend?" she asked sweetly, which only got more on my nerves. Even the flowery smell of her perfume was suffocating. She flipped her long blond hair.

"Yeah," I said in a dismissive tone. My previous attempts of sending the message hadn't worked. Maybe she was someone who needed it spelled out.

"Really?" she said, sounding surprised.

I stopped and set my determined look on her. "I'm not interested," I told her as nicely as possible. "I already have plans with someone this weekend."

And I planned to spend the rest of my foreseeable weekends with her.

She looked surprised by my admission. "Are you dating someone?"

Bad boy, Sin Carter, dating? I could see the disbelief in her wide brown eyes.

I didn't date, but what I had with Taylor was more than just an arrangement of sex. I couldn't bring myself to admit it was dating even though we were exclusive. That was enough to break me out in a cold sweat.

"There is someone." I gave her a one-shoulder shrug, trying not to make a big deal out of it. I wasn't ready yet for the world to know how special she was to me. I needed time to get my head around it before it became public knowledge.

"She's a lucky girl," she said with a wistful smile before walking off.

Her words echoed in my mind as I watched her retreating figure. *A lucky girl.* She deserved much better than me but I wasn't going to admit that to anyone.

That thought stayed with me until I knocked on the door

of Taylor's apartment later. Matthew opened it.

"It's for you," he yelled.

Taylor peered down the hallway to see me. Her eyes lit up and my heart inflated like it was going to break free from my chest. She walked to where I was still waiting for her. It still astounded me that she could make me feel like this with only the slightest look.

I matched the smile she gave me. "Hi."

She stepped aside to let me in before closing the door behind us.

"Hi," she said.

Matthew was seated in front of the TV again, flicking through the channels before he turned to watch us. It was like having a third wheel. Taylor took my hand and led me to her room. We heard Matthew laugh as she closed the door.

"Sorry about that—the disadvantages to having a bodyguard," she told me.

"The advantages are he won't let anything happen to you," I said, reminding her why he was an important fixture in her life at the moment.

Her eyes held mine and I felt the chemistry between us. It sizzled in the air, pulling us together like magnets. The slight curve of her lips caught my attention and I really wanted to kiss her. I couldn't fight it even if I wanted to. It was something bigger than the two of us drawing us together. Her eyes followed my slow, deliberate movement of my lips touching hers. Her hands went up against my chest just as our mouths fused together.

It only took a gentle touch of my tongue against her lips to open her mouth. Her arms snaked around my neck, locking me into place as my tongue caressed hers. My hands pulled her body flush against mine as the kiss intensified.

The feel of her against me sent my mind racing. *Lucky girl.* The thought popped into my mind. Dating and commitment were the words that followed and I felt my body shake slightly at the fear. I stopped kissing her, fighting the strength of her hold on me. But there was no winning. I wanted her and I wasn't going to walk away.

Her fingers touched her slightly red lips, evidence of how hard I had kissed her. And then I gave in and pushed her up against the wall. I gave in to the wild need to possess her, to get as close as two people could. My mouth covered hers, needing and bruising.

I pulled her top off and kissed her again. I wanted to groan in agony when I realized she was only wearing a skirt. The rush of blood that pounded through my ears made it impossible to form a coherent thought. My hand reached for the side of her panties and pulled them down. She stepped out of them.

I got a condom out of my jeans. My hard-on strained against my jeans and I unbuttoned them, freeing myself. I put on the protection as I kissed her again. The heat and softness of her mouth under mine reminded me of how it felt to be inside her. I was losing control. The only thing that mattered was sealing our bodies together as quickly as I could.

Roughly I turned her around and she braced herself with her hands against the wall. I didn't know how much longer I would last and I wanted to come inside her. Buried as deep as I could get. The strength of my physical reaction to her scared me but I couldn't slow myself down or be gentle.

I pulled her breasts free from her bra and pushed the annoying clothing down. I lined myself up with her warmth and pushed into her as my one hand flicked her nipple, bringing my body tightly against her back. She moaned when I began to fuck her. There was no foreplay or sweet caresses, there was just a need to have her as quickly as possible.

She steadied herself against the wall as I thrust into her over and over again. I had no control as I held her hips, angling her against me to penetrate her deeper. She gasped as I pounded her. She fit me like a glove and I bit down on my lip to hold on long enough for her to come before I sought my own.

My body began to tremble and I bit gently into her shoulder, running the sharp edges of my teeth into her soft skin. I was about to reach my release but I stopped myself. My hand reached to the front of her and I stroked her, knowing exactly the pressure she needed. She tensed for a long moment and then she shook as she came.

I followed only seconds later, groaning against her neck.

I couldn't move for a while after. My breath was still hard and it felt like my heart was still racing. Only as the haze of sexual need started to dissipate did I begin to realize how roughly I had taken her up against the wall. It reiterated my already low confidence that I wasn't good enough for her. Something shifted in my chest and I felt regret for not being able to control myself.

It was like the need had taken control, making anything else inconsequential. I got dressed and disposed of the condom while she got dressed and arranged her clothes.

She was smoothing her hair when she noticed I was watching her. She swallowed when she looked at me with the vulnerability that made me feel even worse.

"I'm sorry if I was a little rough." I ran a hand through my hair, feeling agitated, and I wasn't sure what else to say.

"You weren't." She shrugged.

She sat down on her bed and I joined her. I took her hand gently in mine. The blood was still pounding in my head and then I realized I was starting to get a headache. It was like my mind was working overtime with my thoughts and it was leaving me drained. We started talking about school and anything else that didn't involve the stalker or what had just happened between us. My headache got progressively worse.

We both ended up lying on her bed, not touching. I lay with my hands under my head while she lay with her arms straight on either side. After a few minutes she got up and went to the bathroom.

"Have you got any headache tablets?" I asked, eventually realizing it wasn't going to go away. I sat up on her bed.

"Yeah, in the drawer by my bed," she answered through the door.

I wasn't comfortable going through her personal stuff but the headache I was wrestling with was getting worse. I opened the drawer. There was no mistaking the thick folder. My curiosity got the better of me and I looked inside.

It was unreal. Inside was a photo of me that I'd never seen before. My eyes swept over it, picking up the details of my past all printed nicely one line beneath the other in chronological order.

My gut twisted when I realized what I was holding and what it meant. Betrayal was my first emotion closely followed at the outrage of what it meant. I wanted to throw the folder but I wasn't going to lose control until I'd had a chance to confront Taylor.

The sound of a door opening brought my attention back to the present but I refused to look at her. Instead I paged through the rest of the folder. My whole life was bare to see in the folder, from my time in the gang and short time in juvie. Even the part of my life I had been trying to hide from her was in it.

"I can explain," she said nervously as I closed the folder and stood.

I couldn't look at her. I was disgusted that she had gone behind my back and investigated my past. *You did the same to her.* But there was no arguing with my reasoning. My jaw tightened as I held on to my temper. The anger I felt was beyond words at the moment.

The one thing that could tear our fragile togetherness was inside the offending folder that I still held tightly in my hands. Even though logically I knew if she had read it then we wouldn't be standing here. She would have already walked away. But the cloud of anger refused to allow me to look at anything in this with any logical reasoning. I was angry and hurt, which was all that counted.

"I don't think you can explain this," I told her in a tightly controlled voice. "I think it speaks for itself, doesn't it?"

Then my eyes lifted to hers. I gave her a look to reflect the anger and pain I felt. Her eyes pleaded with mine. My look hardened and I took a step away, putting more distance between us. I couldn't. The hurt that ached inside me was too painful to hide.

"You need to let me explain," she pleaded, standing between me and the door.

I shook my head at her. I didn't want to hear any of it. Nothing she could say would ease the pain and anger I was experiencing. Right at this exact moment I wasn't sure there was anything she could say to explain away why she had a folder of my background.

"I don't have to do anything for you," I told her firmly, refusing to allow the hopeless look she gave me to weaken the intensity of my anger.

I swallowed, hating how I felt like the scared little boy who had felt so lost in the world. I'd promised when I got my life together I would never feel that way again and up to now I had been able to keep myself protected. But now I wasn't. I had let her in and she had betrayed me.

She looked panicky as I refused to be dissuaded by her pleading.

"I didn't read it." She tried another angle but it didn't

matter. Even though I knew she hadn't read all of it, I couldn't be sure she hadn't read at least some of it. But that didn't matter. She was in possession of it and that was bad enough.

"Connor gave it to me, but I never read it."

It made sense that her meddling brother would do everything possible to ensure she had every reason to walk away from me. I took a measured breath, feeling the depth of my anger skyrocket. In that moment I hated both of them. The brother who couldn't allow his sister to live her own life, and Taylor, who wasn't strong enough to tell her brother to stay out of her business.

"Why?" I asked.

"I told you he was overprotective. This is him taking the over protectiveness a step too far." Her eyes held my dark, brooding gaze.

"Yeah, I get it. One look at me and he knew I was no good," I finally said out loud what I had been thinking from the moment I had met her.

"You are good—"

"I trusted you," I said, feeling the tightness in my throat.

You broke your rules and this is what happens when you let someone in. I had worked so hard to keep people at a distance and the first person I had let in had effectively ripped my heart out of my chest and stomped on it.

I looked down at the floor to keep myself together. "I opened up to you and told you things I don't tell many people."

She closed the distance between us but I wasn't going to let her near me. I moved away from her. She gave me another pleading look before the hopelessness filled her big blue eyes when she realized she couldn't say anything to fix the damage that had been done.

The hatred I directed at her made her close her arms

around her waist protectively but I told myself I didn't care. I wanted her to hurt like I was hurting.

"If you wanted to know so badly, all you had to do was ask. If you'd asked...I would have told you." My voice broke slightly.

She teared up and bit down on her lip. My heart tightened at the sight but I hardened myself against her.

"There are a lot of things I've done that I'm not proud of." I raked a hand through my hair, feeling like the earth beneath my feet was being yanked away. "I did them for survival."

She of all people knew what it was like hiding a childhood that she didn't want anyone to know about.

"After I found out about your past, I didn't want you to find out about some of the stuff from my past. I was scared about how you would handle it," I whispered, feeling the control I was exerting was about to snap and I was going to break in front of her.

My anger was replaced by a desolate feeling of sadness that there was no going back to a place where we could be together. I had just discovered a happiness I had thought was not possible and it was being torn from me. The pain was indescribable.

"But it doesn't matter anymore." The finality in my voice made her eyes mirror the heartache I was feeling.

There was no hope and I had to ensure she knew it. I could still see the glimmer of hope in the depth of her eyes. I couldn't allow her to hold on to that, not when I was sure I wouldn't be able to put myself in this situation again.

I had a set of rules that had kept my heart safe and the only way to survive would be to ensure I never broke them again, not for anyone.

"We're done," I stated tightly.

'Sorry' wasn't going to fix this.

Even though she hadn't read it, it didn't matter. She had it. Why had she kept it if she had no intention of reading it?

I looked at her one last time before I made the decision to leave. I had said everything I needed to, there was nothing left to say.

She stood unmoving as I walked past her and opened the door. I left with only one thought—to get away as far as I could. The tightness in my chest kept my breathing shallow as I slammed the front door closed. It echoed down the hallway as I left.

Chapter Twenty-Three

My anger was still going strong when I got home. I didn't even greet Slater when I entered the house. I went straight up to my bedroom, slamming the door behind me.

Why had she allowed her brother to interfere? I sat down on my bed, trying to deal with the suffocating emotions that were making me feel like my chest was being split open. The rawness confirmed I was damaged. I raked my hands through my hair before slightly pulling some clumps of hair in my hands to direct my emotional pain to a physical one.

I couldn't stop myself from ruing the moment I had given in and made the decision to take Taylor's virginity. What the hell had I been thinking? I had allowed her to push me into a corner. The idea of someone else doing it had pushed me into action. I wouldn't allow that to ever happen again, I swore to myself.

If I hadn't broken my rules I wouldn't be feeling like the weight of the world was on my shoulders. So I shouldered some of the blame. It wasn't entirely her fault.

I rubbed my forehead as I tried to figure out what to do next. I couldn't stand to even look at her at the moment.

For the rest of the day I stayed in my room, unable to face anyone while the feeling of betrayal was still fixed in the middle of my chest like a metal chain. Even when Slater had knocked a few hours later, I had told him to go away.

He was worried. I had never acted like this before but I couldn't even bring myself to lie and tell him I was fine, because I wasn't. There was no use denying what anyone could see for themselves.

The thought of going back to college and possibly running into her held no appeal at all. I only got a raised eyebrow from Slater when I missed the first day of classes.

"You ready to talk about what's been bugging you?" he asked when I didn't bother to go the next day either.

"No." My answer was tight.

He waited a few moments for me to say something more but when I didn't he moved on to the next subject.

"You talk to Taylor?" he asked.

I'd been a nightmare to be around. I had been moody and uncharacteristically withdrawn.

I shook my head. "There is nothing left to say." I was being stubborn. Even though I had done almost the exact same thing, I didn't know if I could find a way to forgive her.

My past was firmly in my present, wreaking havoc, and I had no idea how to put it away again. But I didn't want to be crippled by a past I couldn't change. Like my issues with my mother, I had plenty of issues with my father.

Even in my mind it felt like an alien statement. Father.

I didn't even know what he looked like. I had never seen a picture of him. In my mind he was a dark form of an evil man that my mother had built up with her bitterness. He was human, with flesh and blood. He wasn't an all-consuming presence that plagued my mind.

When I thought back to what my father had done, my mother had every right to feel betrayed. But it didn't give her justification in blaming me and holding on to that excuse to stay locked in her heartbreak. She'd never allowed any guy close enough to hurt her again.

I tried to keep my mind off Taylor and the horrible feeling that spread in my chest when I remembered back to our last encounter. The throbbing pain in the middle of my chest felt just as raw as it had when I had discovered the folder.

It was getting late but when there was a knock on the door, I gave Slater a questioning gaze.

"You need something to distract you," he said, heading to the door. "And I have the perfect solution."

I wasn't in the mood for company. I crossed my arms as I waited for him to spit it out. "And that is?"

"Poker night," he announced as he opened the door. In walked Traye and Dominique holding a six-pack of beer.

They were football players and were usually the life of the party. Dominique was built, with wide shoulders. He wasn't your typical pretty boy, having a slight reddish tint to his blond hair, but the girls loved him. Traye was leaner, with dark brown hair and eyes to match. He was a few inches shorter.

We came from such different backgrounds but here and now it didn't seem to matter.

I shook my head at them but Slater wasn't going to let me sit this one out.

"Come on," he said, throwing an arm around me and leading me to the sofa. "It's time to have some fun."

"You just want me to take your money." I frowned but sat down on the sofa. "Why don't you save yourself the trouble and just hand it over now?"

"One of these days I will beat you," Dominique swore and I smiled, loving the challenge.

"You can keep trying."

I had a knack for poker. I don't know if I had the best poker face or just the best luck, but I had only lost a handful of times.

"No more smack talk. Shuffle the cards." I caught the beer Traye threw at me.

Two hours later, Dominique and Traye had left with their pockets empty. And I felt a little more relaxed than I had in a while. It could also be the result of the couple of beers I had drunk already.

"How do you do it?" Slater asked, taking a swig of beer as he propped his feet up on the coffee table.

I shrugged. "It's a gift."

My one hand rested on my leg that was propped against the table and my other was tightened around the neck of my bottle of beer. It was empty but I continued to hold it.

"You and Jordan sorted yourselves out yet?" I found myself asking.

He wouldn't look me in the eyes and his easy-going features tightened.

"No."

"It looked like there was something going on." I sat up and set down my empty beer bottle.

"It doesn't matter what it looks like." He cradled his beer in his hands, his attention focused on the bottle. "After everything that's happened, I can't let anyone else in."

I leaned back as I studied him.

He looked like he had been transported back in time to when I had first met him. He had been so badly traumatized that he had barely spoken a word for the first couple of days. All he had done was give me this intense look before walking away.

It had taken a few weeks before he had come out to play. Slowly but surely we had become friends and the foundation to our long-lasting friendship had been lain.

When he had told me about his past it had left me reeling. That was when I realized that although my upbringing had been difficult there were kids out in the world with worse.

"You let me in," I murmured. There had been no reason for him to trust me but he had.

His eyes met mine. "You were my lifeline. If it hadn't been for you, I'm not so sure I would still be here."

I didn't like to get emotional but hearing the sadness in his voice that matched the despair in his eyes made it impossible to sit there without thinking about the weight of guilt on his shoulders.

"It wasn't your fault." I had told him that countless times but it wasn't enough.

"I don't want to talk about it." He shook his head before taking a gulp of his beer.

I had been unable to release him from the guilt that haunted him and there was nothing anyone could do. Some things couldn't be forgiven or changed.

I didn't know what to do to get rid of the pain inside. It was like a physical pain that constantly brought attention back to what I had lost. I closed my eyes and pinched the bridge of my nose.

The next morning Slater cornered me again in the kitchen. I don't know why he was so worried about me sorting myself out. *Maybe it's because when you're upset you're an asshole*, I reminded myself.

I looked down into my mug, wishing I was anywhere but

here.

"They say talking about it helps."

I looked up to glare at him. "No amount of talking about it is going to erase what happened."

He shrugged. "You have to try something."

He leaned back against the kitchen counter and crossed his arms as he studied me a little closer. "It's Taylor." He knew who it was about but he had no idea what had happened.

I looked away from him, not wanting him to see what I didn't want to say. I didn't want to admit out loud that I had been an idiot to trust her and that now I was dealing with the consequences of that betrayal.

"What happened?" he asked when I didn't respond.

I leaned against the counter opposite from where Slater stood and set my mug down on the counter. Feeling my agitation rise at the prying question into what was going on only angered me more.

"I let her in," I told him, looking him in the eye. "You warned me." I rubbed my chest when the pain sharpened and it felt like a knife had cut through me.

"I don't think it was ever a choice." He gave me a haunted look. His words didn't make me feel any better. I had always believed that I was in charge of my own life and that I could control what happened. It was my decision to take her virginity, the reasons were inconsequential. But the rest had happened without me being aware of it. And when it was too late, I knew how much she meant to me.

My phone rang and I pulled it out of my pocket. I was half expecting it to be Taylor but it was my mom. I watched it ring for few more seconds before I answered it.

"Mom," I said more sharply than I had intended.

Slater left me alone in the kitchen to talk to her. Sometimes I wondered if my mother reminded him of parents he was trying to forget. Or it could be the fact that she rarely left me in a good mood after a phone call.

"Hi," she responded in a soft voice, which just made me feel guiltier for speaking to her so harshly.

This time she hadn't been the cause of my anger and I had to remind myself of that fact.

"How are you?" I asked, pushing off the counter just as I dragged my hand through my hair.

"Good."

There was an uncomfortable silence while I debated what to say next.

"You sound preoccupied."

"It's nothing," I said, brushing it off. I didn't want to open up to her about what was going on.

"If something is bugging you, you can talk to me."

I rubbed the back of my neck before lifting my gaze to the ceiling. I didn't want to talk, I just wanted the hurt I was feeling to disappear so I could go back to my old life that didn't include a complicated blue-eyed beauty.

"Thanks, Mom," I said, not wanting to hurt her feelings.

I began to pace.

"Why don't you come and visit?" she invited.

I paused. Before, I would have made up some excuse as to why I couldn't. The need to pack my stuff up and leave for good was gripping more tightly. Going to visit my mother would give me the space I needed.

"Sure."

She seemed momentarily stunned that I had agreed to it.

"I'll be there later today," I added.

"That's great." There was no mistaking the happiness in her voice. I held the phone tighter as it loosened something in my chest. "I'll see you then."

I went upstairs to finish some assignments before I left for my mom's. It took me hours to complete my work. My concentration was shot. I rubbed my hands over my tired features.

I stuffed some clothes into a duffel bag, not sure how long I was going to go for. The folder that held all the details of my dark past lay beside my bed. I put that in as well. The loose plan was for me to go and stay with my mom until I felt I had the strength to be able to face Taylor again. It was inevitable.

With my mind fixed on my plan, I put it into action.

"Where are you going?" Slater asked when he saw me walking down the stairs with my bag.

I didn't want to tell him I was going to my mom's. It rehashed memories for him that I knew he would rather forget.

"I need space." I wanted to run and never look back.

He didn't push me further for any more information.

"You can get hold of me on my phone if anything crops up." He nodded.

I left, throwing my bag in the back of my car and headed to my mom's.

It was late by the time I arrived. I knocked. There was some noise inside before the door opened. My mother was already dressed in her pajamas and a dressing gown.

"You're here." Her eyes lit up when she saw me and it was difficult not to be affected by it. She was more than happy to see me. And for once, the rest of my life was worse than any guilt or memories I held for my mom.

"Where's Sally?" I asked when she ushered me into the house and closed the door behind her.

"I gave her the night off," she explained before she followed me into the living room where I put my bag down beside the sofa.

"Are you hungry?" she asked.

I don't think I had eaten all day. "Yeah."

She hurried into the kitchen.

"I can make you grilled cheese sandwiches," she said as she began to open the cupboards. For a moment I saw a glimpse of the part of my mother that had only come out very rarely to do something for me, like make supper or put me to bed.

I swallowed. "Yeah...that sounds good."

Watching her make me supper made me feel sorry for all the times she hadn't been there to make me something to eat or care about what was happening to me.

"Here," she announced, sliding the plate with the sandwich over to me.

"It smells good." I took a bite and ate. She sat down beside me and watched me eat.

My stomach grumbled as I finished the last of my food.

"You're too skinny," my mother said before she got up and put my plate in the sink.

"I'm fine, Mom."

She stopped. Her eyes were on me, her easy-going look she had just worn moments before was gone. Her features looked more serious than before.

"What's going on?"

Opening up to my mother wasn't something that came easily.

"It's a girl." Her guess was spot on.

How did she know that? Did I have some message on my forehead that said I had been stupid enough to allow myself to care for a girl who would hurt me? I couldn't bring myself to confirm it.

"I know that look." She came back to sit down beside me. The light that she had held before was gone. In just a few minutes she looked much older, and tired. "It's that look when your heart no longer beats in your own chest."

I frowned.

"It belongs to someone else."

My frown deepened. I cared for Taylor but love was something much more than I had ever contemplated.

"And they've broken it."

She was reading too close to actual events and it made me shift slightly in my seat.

"What happened?" she asked softly, searching my features.

"It's not like that," I said, brushing off her concern.

She gave me a sad smile. "I can tell. It happened to me."

I only had a rough outline of what had happened between the man who had fathered me and the mother who had only been able to cope with the help of alcohol to numb the pain.

"I know the story." I wasn't sure I wanted a walk down that memory again.

"Loving someone makes you feel like you can do anything, but on the reverse, heartbreak can slowly kill any will to live." She looked down at her clasped hands. "I thought I had found the type of love that would last."

I pulled my hands from the table.

"The reality was it only lasted until I got pregnant with you."

"I was a reminder of that," I snapped, feeling angry.

Chapter Twenty-Four

Her eyes watered and I felt shitty for making her cry. Her hand reached out and touched my arm. I tightened my other hand to stop myself from covering her hand with mine.

"You look so much like him," she whispered as her eyes caressed my features. But she wasn't seeing me, she was seeing the man who had broken her heart and left her pregnant. I hated it when she did that. I hadn't done anything wrong, yet I felt the weight of the guilt of actions I had no hand in.

"I was working as a waitress. The first time he walked in I noticed him straightaway. He was tall and handsome." The daydream look gave her a brief break from the pain. "When he noticed me, he gave me a smile that made my knees go weak. And that was it."

Knowing then what she did now, I always wondered if she would make the same mistake all over again, and the look in her eyes told me she would. My father had used her and when confronted with an unwanted pregnancy, he had discarded her.

It still didn't fit with the man who had left me all his money. I would probably never know why. Had he been trying to make it up to me in some way?

"We saw each other every spare moment we could. I knew he was married but I believed him when he told me that he was going to leave her for me." She gave a dry laugh. "I should have known better but I was naive. Love is blind."

My jaw tensed while I listened to my mother relive her heartache.

Her hand trembled slightly as she brushed her hair out of her face. That inner part of me that didn't want to care began to crumble. On the outside I was stiff and unmoving but inside it felt like I was being shaken to the core.

"When I first discovered I was pregnant I was elated."

She pressed her lips together. Her emotions bubbled to the surface and a tear streamed down her face.

"I was so excited... I couldn't wait to tell him." She let out a heavy breath. "He came by the restaurant I was working at. I couldn't wait until he could get another night away from his wife. I took a break and went outside to speak to him. I expected him to be happy but he wasn't."

She dropped her gaze to her hand. "He just left."

She let out a deep emotional breath. "And that was the end. He stopped taking my phone calls. It was like it hadn't happened and it had been a part of my imagination." Her eyes met mine. "But the morning sickness reminded me daily that I was still very much pregnant with you. I was so scared and alone. I had no one."

She had been my age when she had gotten pregnant with me. I couldn't imagine dealing with such a life-changing event with no one to help. Her home life hadn't been desirable and she had moved out of her parents' home when she had turned eighteen. With a pregnancy and no boyfriend, it would have been too much for my grandparents to accept. No matter what life threw at me, at least I had Slater and Jeff.

"You're strong," she said out of the blue. There had been plenty of times in my life when I hadn't felt strong. "You won't fall apart like I did."

It made me feel sorry for her. I don't know if it was the bare truth of what my father had done to her or something in my DNA that connected us together that made me soften toward her.

"I'm not pregnant," I shot back, trying to break the heaviness of the atmosphere.

She laughed with her eyes still watering as another tear escaped. She wiped her face and this time she smiled at me.

"Love is a strong emotion but you're stronger. I wasn't."

For once I felt the need to defend her actions. "You were young and alone."

Our eyes held. I don't know what I was waiting for but I kept quiet.

"I'm sorry," she murmured softly. I felt the pain that had slightly ebbed began to throb with renewed life.

"I know."

"At least we still have time," she said, the sadness disappearing, and she gave me a weak smile. "I can be the mother you always deserved."

The lump in my throat made it difficult to reply and I nodded. There had been nights when I was younger that I had bent down on my knees, clasping my hands together, praying that she would wake up the next morning and be the loving mother I had needed.

Usually when things got this deep I was looking for an exit or a way to extract myself from it but this time was different. This time I didn't feel the need to escape.

My father was gone so there was no confronting him on why he had acted the way he had or why he had left all of his fortune to me. But my mother was still alive and we had a chance to try and make new memories to take the place of the old ones. They could never be completely forgotten but maybe I just needed to give her a chance to give me some good new ones I could remember when she wasn't with me anymore.

Her time was limited. Drinking had taken its toll on her body, especially her liver. She was fragile and although I had no exact time, I knew I couldn't count on any of the time we still had.

"We have time."

With that I allowed her back in with the chance to be there again as the mother who loved me.

Her bottom lip trembled as she gazed up at me like I had opened the gateway to Heaven for her. She put her arms around me and hugged me. I loosely put my arms around her and held her close.

"I love you," she whispered hoarsely.

I love you too. I thought what I couldn't say aloud just yet. Baby steps, and when the time was right I would be able to tell her everything she needed.

She released me and gazed up at me. Her hand fondly caressed my cheek. "Whoever this girl is she must be very special to you."

Her words reminded me of Taylor. I frowned as my mood darkened. I didn't want to think about her or what she had done.

"She was," I admitted, making it clear that what we had was in the past. "But she did something behind my back."

My mother studied me for a several moments.

"Can you forgive her?" she asked quietly.

I considered what she said. I had done the exact same thing to her and she had been able to forgive me. Why couldn't I forgive her?

The memory of what I was hiding replayed in my mind. The difference was she nearly found something that would tear us apart and nothing would be able to put us back together again.

"I don't know."

If I forgave her and she discovered my secret, then it wouldn't matter. My forgiveness would only give us a temporary reprieve before the real issue would break us. Was there any point?

This gave me a whole lot more complicated questions I hadn't even considered. Should I have just come clean and allowed the cards to fall where they may?

No, the control freak in me couldn't allow me to do something like that without knowing the odds were in my favor. It was probably the reason why I was so good at poker. I could calculate the odds and play the game. But Taylor wasn't a game and I had only one chance.

I was frustrated and angry. Physically putting distance between Taylor and I should have fixed the problem, but it hadn't. She was all I could think about. I dropped my head into my hands and rubbed them over my face. It didn't help that every time I closed my eyes I saw her smiling at me and I felt guilty for leaving abruptly the way I had. Granted, I'd been clear that things between us were over, but packing up and leaving had been going a bit overboard.

When I'd packed my stuff, I'd had no intention of ever going back. Now, sitting in the house I'd bought for my mom, I knew that I had to go back. I couldn't run away from the problem. The only way to deal with it was to face it head on. I eyed the offending folder that still lay on the coffee table. I hadn't been able to open it up and look at what it held, but I had a pretty good idea since I'd lived through all of it—stuff I wasn't proud of.

Feeling agitated, I stood up and began to pace the room.

She'd told me that she hadn't read the folder and I believed her because, if she had, I was pretty sure she wouldn't have wanted anything to do with me. I wouldn't have had a chance to tell her that we were over; she would have told me to leave if she knew. I'd never wanted to erase my past as badly as I'd wanted to when I'd first found out about the murder of Taylor's parents. It was only a matter of time before she found out. I thought about coming clean with her, but I wasn't sure she would want to ever see me again after that.

My phone began to ring and I pulled it out of my jeans pocket. I'd expected it to be Taylor, but it was Slater.

"Hi," I said as I answered the call.

"You need to get your ass back here," he instructed forcefully. He sounded upset and it wasn't like him.

"What's wrong, man?" I asked, knowing my best friend well enough to know that something was going on.

"Look, there's no good way to say this..." he said and I felt a sinking feeling in my stomach.

"It's Taylor," he admitted.

My heart stopped beating for a split second as I felt the fear crash over me like a wave.

"What happened?" I said tightly, already having every worst-case scenario cycling through my mind.

"She's gone," he revealed, and I felt my legs weaken and I slumped down in the chair.

"What do you mean she's gone?" I asked, my voice already thickening with the emotion I felt. I'd asked the question, but I wasn't sure I wanted the answer.

"She's missing," he said softly.

"How long?" I asked, my mind already jumping to the

next action I needed to perform.

"A day," he answered. It was already too long.

"I just found out from Jordan," he added.

"I'll call you back," I told him, trying to ignore the fear I felt. I disconnected the call, not giving him a chance to say another word. I searched through my contacts on my phone and dialed a number.

"Yeah," Jeff answered.

"You still tailing the guy I asked you to?" I asked urgently as I ran a hand through my hair.

"Yeah," he answered.

"Does he have a girl with him?" I asked, and I held my breath.

"No," he said and I felt my world begin to disintegrate around me.

Caleb didn't have Taylor; he wasn't the stalker. I'd put my guy on the wrong guy.

Fuck!

"You need me to find someone for you?" Jeff asked on the other side of the call.

"Yes," I answered, hoping that it wasn't going to be too late. I gave him Taylor's name. He was good—he wouldn't need any more details than that to be able to gather the information he needed.

"How long has she been gone?" he asked.

"A day," I answered.

I heard him sigh on the other side of the phone. Twenty-four hours was too long already.

"You know the odds are she is dead already," he said aloud, which is what I was already thinking.

"I don't fucking care, I want you to find her!" I yelled, not wanting to believe for a second that she might not be alive.

"Sure, boss, I'll find her," he assured me before

disconnecting the call.

I began to pace. My shock and fear turned to anger. I called Slater back.

"What happened?" I asked, trying to mentally prepare myself for what I was about to find out.

I didn't understand how she could be gone with a bodyguard glued to her side. How on earth had the guy gotten to her with Matthew around? He was the best that money could buy—I'd checked. It had been the only reason I hadn't hired a bodyguard myself.

"She was with Matthew," he began to explain. "He was driving them to the movies."

I held my breath.

"A car hit them from behind and knocked Matthew out. By the time the ambulances arrived, he was conscious but Taylor was gone, as well as the car that hit them," he finished explaining.

It was unbelievable that the guy had gone to those lengths to get her. I didn't want to think about what he would do to her if he was capable of that.

"Was she hurt?" I asked, feeling the fear clog my throat.

"We don't know," he replied. "Her blood wasn't in the car, but that doesn't mean there weren't any internal injuries."

I began to pace again, not knowing what to do next. She could be seriously injured and in the hands of some crazed stalker.

"I'm on my way back," I informed Slater. I had to get back.

"Sin," Slater said, stopping me, "it wasn't your fault."

He knew me too well. I pressed my lips together, trying to stop myself from arguing about it. It was my fault. If I hadn't left, I probably would have been with her and I might have been able to stop him from getting her.

Twenty-four hours. I closed my eyes for a moment, trying to push away the voice in the back of my mind that told me she was probably dead already. I would never forgive myself for abandoning her.

"I'll see you soon," I told him before I ended the call.

"You leaving already?" my mom said as she walked into the room. Her face was pale and she looked tired.

"Yeah, I have to go," I said as I walked down the hall to the room I'd been using.

I got my duffel bag and just started shoving stuff into it. My mind was trying to process everything I'd just found out while trying to concentrate on getting my stuff together so I could get back and find out what was happening.

Did the cops have any leads? Had anyone witnessed the accident? Did they have a description of the car?

I got my leather jacket and put it on. If I hurried, I could be back in an hour. When I reentered the living room, my mom was sitting in the chair.

"I have to go," I told her as I walked to her and dropped a kiss on her cheek.

"Okay, baby," she said, giving me a weak smile. It was still hard to link the person she was now with the mother she'd been to me growing up.

I found my mom's nurse in the kitchen.

"I've got to leave. Keep an eye on her," I said to her. She gave me a brief nod.

"You don't have to worry, Mr. Carter," she assured me kindly. "I'll look after your mom."

"Thanks," I replied before I left. I hurried to my car and as soon as I got into the driver's side, I shoved the duffel bag onto the passenger seat.

I started up the car and prayed that Taylor was still safe. I broke nearly every speed limit, and within forty minutes I was pulling up outside Taylor's apartment.

I felt a nervous fear engulf me as I got to the door of the apartment and knocked.

Matthew opened the door and looked surprised to see me. A large surgical pad covered his forehead.

"Have you found her yet?" I asked as I stepped inside. The look in his eyes made my chest hurt. It felt like a steel grip around my heart.

"No," he said, shaking his head. He dropped his gaze to the floor.

I took a couple more steps before I saw Connor sitting in one of the sofas with his head in his hands and Jordan sat beside him, trying to comfort him.

Jordan looked like she'd been crying.

I didn't want to be around them. It was like they were convinced she was dead already and I wasn't going to give up that easily, not until I saw it for myself.

Chapter Twenty-Five

Time lost all relativity as each minute passed without any news about Taylor. I wanted to go out and troll the streets to find her but logically I knew it was a waste of time. I couldn't eat or sleep. Every single thought was focused purely on her and how to find her. I would stay up all night looking out the window trying to go through my mind with a fine-tooth comb through my memories to make sure I didn't miss something that could lead me to her.

The person who had spiked her drink had attended the party at my house but there was no one who stood out as suspicious. I regretted not taking it more seriously at the time. But even if we had reported it there would have been very little evidence.

I rubbed my hands over my face.

I hadn't even noticed anyone around her acting strangely. Whoever was responsible for kidnapping her had planned it well.

I should have been relieved that the accident he had caused hadn't killed her. But after seeing pictures of the crash, I couldn't believe she had escaped it without injury. There wasn't any blood but that didn't mean she hadn't been injured.

It was a nightmare I couldn't wake up from.

Jeff was doing his best to track her down. He wasn't convinced we would find her alive but I wouldn't accept any other outcome.

It was the reason I had kept away from Connor, Matthew and Jordan. I couldn't stand to watch them mourn for her like she wasn't here anymore. I needed all my strength to keep myself focused on the fact that she was going to be found alive.

Slater hadn't left my side since I had returned. He didn't know how to help me so he sat across from me when I was quiet and subdued. He listened when I ranted and raved, unable to deal with the anger that someone had taken her. And he was there to tell me that it wasn't my fault even though his words fell on deaf ears.

I blamed myself. If I hadn't taken off then I could have stopped it from happening. If I hadn't gotten so angry with her and shut her out, she would have been safe with me. Not out with Matthew on the way to the movies.

I stood up and began to pace again.

"You need to get some sleep," Slater said, his voice pulling me out of my dark thoughts. It was early evening and we were in the living room.

Other than a few hours here or there I hadn't been able to enter a deep sleep. The worry and guilt was eating me alive. I was struggling to function.

"I can't." I shook my head. I knew I couldn't carry on like this much longer but I didn't know how to handle the reality that I had no control in Taylor's situation. It was out of my hands and I could only wait it out.

When I was alone the thoughts that plagued me were so horrifying I sometimes couldn't bear to close my eyes for a few minutes. Images of her scared and alone, hurt in a dark environment at the mercy of some sick guy who was doing God knows what to her. The pain that swept over me was suffocating and relentless.

No. I stopped myself, forcing myself to keep the panic at bay, and my lungs opened up again. I couldn't think about what might be happening to her. I rubbed my forehead again, trying to stop the dark thoughts from taking over.

I had to believe she was still okay.

No experience in my life was worse than what I was going through while waiting for Jeff to find her. *What if he doesn't?* I closed my eyes briefly when the pain of losing her assaulted me again. I had never felt so helpless.

My mind was so tired I kept going around in circles. My thoughts were muddled and confused. I was struggling to concentrate. I rubbed the back of my neck to ease the tiredness of my aching muscles.

"What's taking Jeff so long?" I muttered, redirecting the little energy I had at the only person who had any hope in finding her.

"You want coffee?" Slater asked, standing.

I nodded, feeling the tiredness grip me and I slumped down on the sofa. I closed my eyes briefly and tilted my head up to the ceiling.

I'd never believed in a higher power, not since I had been a small child praying that my mother would stop drinking. When my mom had continued her downward spiral, I had convinced myself that no one was listening. But now I prayed. It was all I had. *Please let her be okay and let her find her way back to me.*

I promised if I ever got the chance to hold her again I

would never let anything happen to her. When something as serious as this happened, the betrayal seemed inconsequential —especially when I had done the same. Anything that had kept us apart before didn't matter anymore. The only thing that counted was her safe return to me.

But what if it doesn't happen?

It only took a quick look back to the newspaper articles I had read about Taylor's parents' murders to show that bad things happened to good people all the time. There was no guarantee that Taylor would survive this ordeal.

My instinct told me to prepare for the worst-case scenario, that she wouldn't be coming out of this alive. But I couldn't. It was something I wasn't in any state to face. I doubted it would ever be something I could handle.

Feeling agitated and hyped from the energy drink I'd had earlier, I sat up and interlinked my hands loosely.

It didn't matter how much Slater told me her disappearance wasn't my fault, I couldn't see it that way. I even held some resentment toward Matthew for not being able to stop the deranged kidnapper from taking her. It didn't matter that he had been unconscious.

But I blamed myself more.

Slater walked out of the kitchen carrying a hot mug of coffee. He set it down in front of me on the coffee table. "Here."

"Thanks," I said, taking a gulp. I needed the caffeine to keep going. The hot liquid burned my tongue slightly. The pain was welcome, it momentarily took my attention from the internal mess I was.

The seat next to me dipped as Slater dropped down beside me.

"She came by, looking for you." I looked at my friend.

"When?" I felt shaken.

"After you left."

An overwhelming feeling of guilt pressed down on me and I tried to allow it to pass but it weighed down heavily on me. I deserved to feel like the asshole I was.

"You have to at least consider that this might end badly," he whispered. He had grown fond of Taylor so I knew he was worried too. I put my coffee down and glanced at him. He was staring at the wall across from us. We were both overtired and running on empty.

"I'm afraid of what I might do if..." I couldn't complete the sentence. He turned his head and our eyes connected.

"You were there for me when I didn't know how I was going to carry on."

I nodded and swallowed hard. I remembered our positions being switched and I had been the one telling him that it hadn't been his fault.

"And I'll be there to make sure you do get through this," he assured me with somber determination.

I looked away as I let out an emotional breath, feeling like all my emotions were trying to break at the same time.

The cops didn't have a lot of evidence and I didn't have a lot of confidence in them to find her. There had been no witnesses. It would take them time to try and get a match on the car that had caused the accident. Time Taylor didn't have.

Every incident replayed in my mind as I tried to figure out the motives behind her kidnapping. Would knowing help deal with what the outcome would be? If I could figure out why she had been taken and the intent behind it, I could tell myself that he didn't intend to hurt her.

But remembering the words 'Whore' written on her missing underwear made my stomach drop. I had been her first and only lover. The thought of someone taking her against her will made me sick to my stomach. I tightened my fists when a red-hot burning anger flowed through me like a volcano ready to explode.

We had to find her. And quickly.

I got my phone out of my pocket and called Jeff. I'd already spoken to him a few hours earlier so I doubted he had any more news but it gave me some comfort calling him, like I wasn't sitting around doing nothing.

Connor had a massive team already trying to find Taylor. He had the best money could buy. But Jeff was still out looking for her too.

"Anything yet?" I asked. My bad mood had only worsened with the lack of sleep and worry.

"Nothing concrete. I have a lead. I'm on my way to investigate it now," Jeff answered. It sounded like he was driving.

"What lead?" I asked, feeling my heart race with nervous curiosity.

"It could be nothing."

I looked down at the floor so as not to react to his words. It was like riding a rollercoaster, up one second and then down the next.

"Okay," I breathed. He couldn't do his job if I kept him glued to the phone.

"I'll call you as soon as I have anything," he assured me.

I disconnected the phone and held it in my hand.

"What'd he say?"

"He is following up on a lead." I felt a glimmer of real hope that he would be able to find her but I had to remember it could be nothing.

My hand tightened over my phone. I paced the room as the minutes ticked by.

Slater ran his hands through his hair as he tried to refocus his eyes. Our bodies craved the sleep our minds couldn't slow down enough to give us.

Over an hour later my phone started to ring. It was Jeff. I

had been staring at it, hoping Jeff would call me to tell me if his lead had led to anything. I answered it.

"And?" I whispered, not sure I could handle whatever he was going to tell me.

"I found her."

My world tilted and it felt like someone had spun my insides. My next question was on the tip of my tongue but I couldn't ask it. Instead I held my breath, trying to prepare for whatever he was going to say next.

"She's alive."

I bent over, trying to breathe as I felt the relief overwhelm me. I couldn't talk. Barely keeping myself upright, I held the phone so tight against my ear my hand ached.

The touch of a hand on my shoulder reminded me I wasn't alone.

"She's in bad shape."

I let out a hiss of pain. In that moment I wanted to kill whoever had harmed her.

"She's being admitted."

"Which hospital?" I finally managed so ask, straightening up. Slater dropped his hand from my shoulder.

The only thing that mattered was getting to her as fast as I could. It was something I couldn't explain. He gave me the name of the hospital and I disconnected the call.

I jolted into action. Where the hell were my car keys? I patted my jeans down but they weren't in my pockets. I needed my jacket. My mind was still reeling from the news that Taylor had been found.

"What did Jeff say?"

I began to look around the living room for my jacket. I was sure I had dropped it over the back of the chair closest to the door.

"We need to go," I mumbled, angry with myself that I wasn't more organized.

But there was no way to know that she would be found. I stopped. My lungs hurt and my head began to throb.

"Where do we need to go?" Slater asked, stepping in front of me to get my attention.

"She's at the hospital." I couldn't repeat what Jeff had said about her being in bad shape. But the mention of the fact that she was in the hospital would tell him what I couldn't.

He gave me a slight nod.

I nodded back. I found my jacket and shrugged it on just as I looked up to see Slater with my cars keys dandling from his fingers. "I'll drive."

I wasn't going to argue, I was in no state to drive. I was too wired to be able to concentrate enough to get us to the hospital in one piece.

There was only a moment's hesitation in the doorway. *She needs you to be strong for her,* I told myself before I followed Slater to the car.

I don't even remember if I closed the front door. Nothing mattered other than getting to Taylor. Slater drove as fast as he could while still staying within the speed limit. Feeling frustrated that it was taking longer than I wanted to get to her, I wrestled with my annoyance. I was barely keeping the fear of what she had been through at bay.

Bad shape. The words echoed in my mind with images of her bloodied and afraid.

I tightened my fist to keep my anger from taking over. *Keep calm. She needs you to keep it together.*

Keeping that thought repeating in my mind was the only way I held it together. Slater dropped me off at the front entrance so he could park the car.

As I rushed into the hospital, I called Jeff. He answered on the first ring.

"Where are you?" I asked in a hurried voice.

He told me and I ended the call. While I raced to the

room Taylor was in, I felt my heart hammering inside of my chest. As I entered the unit, I saw Jeff standing outside a door. His entire focus was on the door in front of him.

I jogged to him and at the sound of my approach he turned to face me.

"The doctor is checking her over," he told me solemnly.

I rubbed my forehead. There were so many questions flitting through my mind it was almost impossible to focus on one. There was no more delaying. I needed to know how bad it was.

"How bad?" I asked hoarsely and held my breath. I noticed the blood stains on his shirt. It was Taylor's blood.

"She took quite a beating."

I closed my eyes briefly, trying to fight the internal struggle going on inside of me. *There will be time for revenge but you need to focus on her now.*

Slater arrived at that moment.

"The cops are looking for him," Jeff said.

Feeling a swell of anger, I turned around and ran my hands through my hair. I wanted the guy responsible to suffer like she had. No, worse. I wanted him to feel pain for every second he had held her against her will.

Slater stood beside me. "Focus on Taylor. She needs you."

His words pulled me back from the murderous rage that was taking root in me.

I promised myself that I would find a way to ensure the guy responsible for this would pay in some way. I looked at Jeff, who was standing on the other side of me.

"Who was it?"

He hesitated for a moment.

"Eric."

At first the name didn't register but when it sank in, I looked at him incredulously. "My roommate, Eric?"

He nodded.

I was floored. Wimpy Eric, who had constantly played on my last nerve? It was like telling me Tinkerbell's true identity was the Hulk. It made no sense. My mind struggled to place the guy I knew with the monster who had hurt Taylor.

Slater's stunned expression matched mine.

Then the guilt of not being there to protect her was only intensified with the knowledge that someone we knew had been responsible. But why? I remembered the brief encounter I had eavesdropped on when he had spoken to Taylor in the kitchen after I had slept on the sofa.

I walked to the wall and leaned against it, still trying to catch up with the idea that Eric had kidnapped her.

"How did you figure it was him?" I directed my question to Jeff, who was watching with his arms crossed as I grappled with the truth.

"He was renting two places. It didn't make any sense so I thought I would check it out."

"I still can't believe it was him." Slater had echoed my exact thoughts out loud.

"What happened?"

Jeff, who was usually very controlled, let out a heavy breath as his arms dropped to his sides. "I found her in the road around the corner from the rented address."

She had escaped. My heart inflated with pride that she had managed to get away.

"I recognized her when I went to help her. She was in shock and badly injured."

She was so small and delicate I couldn't believe someone would intentionally hurt her but Eric had. The familiar anger I had been wrestling with reasserted itself. I wanted to hurt Eric so bad. And I knew if he was in front of me now the only way he would leave was in a body bag.

But he was out of my reach and I could only breathe through the urge to end his life.

Chapter Twenty-Six

"She was only dressed in her underwear." The way he said it and the way he looked at me, I knew immediately what he suspected.

"No." I shook my head. I couldn't accept it.

"We won't know anything until the doctor is finished with her," Jeff said.

Slater put a hand to my shoulder and I looked at him, struggling with the anguish inside.

"Let's wait to see what the doctor says."

I wanted to believe that we were just jumping the gun in our thoughts and that Taylor hadn't been tarnished by Eric. The thought that he would have forced himself on her sickened me. My heart squeezed like it was stuck in a vise. I drew in a sharp breath.

"Tell me everything," I instructed Jeff. Whether I wanted to or not I needed to know everything. I had to know exactly what happened. Even if it hurt more than anything I had ever experienced before.

Jeff shared with me all the details he knew. From the moment he had spotted her form bent over on her hands and knees in the road to when he had brought her into the hospital, yelling for help when she had passed out.

"I need to call Connor."

I walked away as I found Taylor's brother's contact information on my phone and called him.

"Sin," he answered. He sounded as tired as I felt.

"We found her." I swallowed while I gave him a few moments to take in my words.

"Where is she?" he asked tersely.

"At the hospital." I gave him the name. "The doctor is in with her checking over her injuries."

"Injuries?" he whispered. In that moment nothing divided us. He was going through the exact same fears I had when I had first found out.

"She was beaten but they don't think it's life threatening." It was our only consolation at the moment, until we got to see her.

"I'll be there in ten minutes."

I pocketed my phone and returned to my waiting spot just outside the door to her hospital room.

I would have given all the money I had to be able to go in to see her but they wouldn't let me in. It was only prolonging my torture. I just wanted to see her. I knew what to expect so I had prepared myself for it. She was safe in a hospital but until I could see her for myself, my mind didn't fully comprehend it.

So I waited, leaning against the wall with my arms crossed, my leg bent to rest my foot against the wall.

My muscles ached from the stress and tiredness from the last two days but I had to hold on a little longer. Once I had a chance to see her, I could go home and get a little sleep. I was no good to her if I couldn't function.

Jeff left briefly and I was waiting with Slater when Connor arrived. I pushed off the wall when I spotted Matthew and Jordan following behind him.

Slater tensed slightly beside me and I knew the reason why. The sight of Jordan was where his eyes were. But now wasn't the time to concentrate on that.

"They won't let me in to see her," I said when he stopped in front of me. My shoulders slumped in defeat.

"They didn't tell me much over the phone. Is the doctor still assessing her?" Connor said, looking to the door that led to her room. He looked like he hadn't gotten any sleep since I had last see him.

Had he called the hospital to get more details? It shouldn't have surprised me. He was a guy who always seemed to be in control of any situation. And his protectiveness over his sister would have sent him into overdrive.

I nodded. "He has been in there for a while."

Jordan and Matthew mirrored my concern.

"How did you know she was here? How did she get away? How did she get here?" Connor began to ask while he raked a hand through his hair, leaving his usually neat hair in disarray.

"Jeff—a guy who works for me—managed to find her," I explained. I lifted my hand to my forehead to rub my temple. The lack of sleep and worry had left me with a headache. "He was on his way to check out Eric's house when he found her in the street."

"Eric?" Jordan asked, sounding just as surprised as Slater and I had been. No one had seen this coming.

"He was the one who took her." I nodded at her.

"She was badly beaten and..." I told them. My eyes met Matthew's. His guilt was evident in his features but even I couldn't hold him responsible. He had done everything he could.

"And what?" Connor snapped.

I wanted to save them from the pain but they needed to know.

"She was found in her underwear."

Jordan put her hands to her mouth to stifle her shock and Matthew put an arm around her to console her. The grim look in his features told me he was holding on to his control by a thread.

I couldn't imagine anyone feeling worse than I was but I was pretty sure Matthew was. He had been with her when she had been taken and it had been his responsibility to keep her safe.

No one blamed him, but I doubted that made much difference to him. The same way Slater had told me that I had no reasons to feel responsible but that hadn't reduced the guilt I harbored.

"He wrapped her up in his jacket and brought her here. He said she stayed awake the whole journey like she was too scared to let go until she knew she was going to be...safe." My voice broke slightly on the last word when I thought about how scared she must have been. Anyone who didn't know Jeff would be intimidated by his shaved head and array of tattoos. But she had been desperate enough to trust that he would help her. Matthew tightened his arm around Jordan, who had paled. She pressed her hand to her mouth.

"Did Eric...?" Connor tried to ask but couldn't bear to say the word out loud.

I felt the same. I couldn't say it, because it felt like I was giving it a hold on our reality.

Feeling myself tremble inside, I closed my eyes for a moment and rubbed my head when I whispered, "I don't know."

I opened my eyes in time to see the horrified look in Connor's eyes.

"We won't know anything until the doctor finishes examining her," I offered him.

A few seconds passed in silence as everyone digested it.

"How did Jeff know where she was?" Connor asked with narrowed eyes.

"I asked him to find her so he started his investigation by looking at the people closest to us." I rubbed the back of my neck, feeling my muscles tense. "He discovered Eric had rented another house. It was suspicious, so he decided to check it out."

"She's okay," Matthew murmured under his breath to Jordan.

Slater was quietly watching her from beside me. No matter what he said I knew he still felt strongly for her. He seemed to tense when Jordan looked up at Matthew for reassurance.

When her gaze shifted to Slater, I saw the look she shared with my best friend, only confirming what I had already suspected. Whatever was going on between them wasn't over.

She looked away, unable to hold his bold stare.

My attention was pulled back to the white walls of the hospital and why we were all together, waiting patiently outside a hospital room. For the second time I prayed that Taylor had managed to fight Eric off before he'd had a chance to force himself on her.

Physical injuries would heal quickly. It was the emotional ones that would take much longer.

I remembered Jeff's words. *She is strong.*

That inner strength that I had seen in her reminded me that she had survived the murder of her parents and she would survive this.

And I would be there, every step of the way, with her.

There was no more running, or misunderstandings.

We all stood outside the door and waited for the doctor to come out. Jordan stood off to the side with Matthew beside her.

Slater stood on one side of me and Connor on the other. I looked at Slater to see him watching Jordan and Matthew. Was there something going on there that none of us knew about? By the way Slater studied them, he wasn't ready to let her go. Even if he couldn't admit it to himself.

His eyes narrowed when Jordan rested her hand on Matthew's arm.

The sound of the door opening pulled my attention to the subdued doctor closing it behind him.

Connor stepped into his path. "I'm Connor Price, Taylor's brother," he said. "How's she?"

I was scared. In that moment I felt an overwhelming fear that there could be something more serious than any of us had suspected. I shoved my hands into the front pockets of my jeans to stop them from shaking.

The doctor's features were unreadable.

"She's been beaten quite badly. It will heal, and I don't believe there will be any scars."

The word 'beaten' sounded so different coming from the doctor. It felt like someone had punched me in the stomach. I hung my head, unable to pretend I was okay.

But it wasn't over yet.

"She has quite a bad cut on her leg but it doesn't require stitches." The doctor quieted.

"Was there any sign of..." Connor tried to ask but couldn't finish it.

My shoulders tensed as I braced myself for the answer. I focused my attention solely on the doctor.

The doctor shook his head. "There are signs her attacker did try but she must have managed to fight him off."

Thank God, I thought, running a hand through my hair to pull myself together.

"When can we see her?" I asked. I couldn't explain to anyone how badly I needed to see her face, even if it was marred with bruises from her attack. I could handle it. What I couldn't handle was being kept away from her.

"At this stage I'm only allowing family in. She's sleeping at the moment. I've decided to sedate her for now. Let her get some rest and tomorrow you can see her."

I was devastated. Waiting another day to see her would feel like a lifetime.

"I'd like to see her now," her brother insisted.

"Sure." The doctor nodded. "The nurses are just cleaning her up. As soon as they are done you can go and see her. Tomorrow I will allow non-family members to see her. She needs time to come to terms with what has happened to her."

I turned away, unable to look at the doctor who was keeping me from seeing Taylor. I tensed my jaw as I worked through the emotional pain that ached inside me.

"She's okay," Slater said to me. My eyes met his. "You'll get to see her soon."

What he didn't say I read in his eyes. *There will be time to tell her everything you need to.* I nodded, not liking it but I had to deal with it. I shoved my hands into my pockets.

The doctor left. It was torture to watch Connor enter her room. My only consolation was I wasn't the only one waiting outside her room.

Feeling tired, I walked over to where Jordan stood against the wall. I leaned my back against the wall, keeping my eyes on the door so I would see the moment Connor exited the room. The touch of a small hand on my arm brought my attention back to Jordan beside me.

"She's okay," she murmured.

I nodded slightly. They were all trying to remind me to

concentrate on what was most important at the moment. But none of them understood the connection I had with her. I had only realized the strength of it when she had gone missing.

I had never felt so strongly for anyone like this before. I didn't want to call it love. Love had ruined my mother's life and I wouldn't allow it to ruin what I had with Taylor.

What we had would endure.

So much had changed since when I had first met Taylor. Jordan had been the one to warn her against getting involved with me and here we were almost friends, supporting each other in our combined caring for Taylor.

She looked emotional and tired, reminding me that I wasn't the only one who was worried about Taylor. She rubbed her temple slightly. Something familiar I had been doing to gather my thoughts because the lack of sleep had made it more difficult to function.

She dropped her hand from mine. I looked to see Slater watching her. Her eyes met his and for the first time I saw how they felt. It was written in their eyes.

I heard the slight, sharp inhale beside me and saw her look away. When I looked back, Slater's eyes met mine. I could see the pained look like he knew that no matter how hard he fought he wouldn't be able to stop what was happening with Jordan.

It only reminded me of my own struggle with Taylor. From the beginning I'd felt confident that we would be able to keep things physical, and look at what had happened. Now she was the only one who mattered and I would do whatever I had to do to keep us together.

Then Connor came out of the room and I pushed off the wall. He looked solemn, which made me feel a moment of panic. Was it that bad? Feeling uncertain, I flicked my tongue against my lip ring.

"How's she?" I asked, feeling anxious. I tightened my hands into fists. I wanted to make Eric suffer as much—no, more—than Taylor had. The truth was I wanted to wipe him from existence. He had no right to still breathe after what he had done.

"I'm not going to lie," Connor said to me, looking visibly shaken. "It looks...bad."

I couldn't imagine anything other than her flawless porcelain skin with big blue eyes.

I would have to face the physical repercussions of her attack and it would only make the guilt harder to bear. If I had been here it wouldn't have happened. My fists tightened harder as I rode the anger directed at myself.

"Go home and get some sleep," Connor suggested to everyone.

The door at the end of the hallway opened and Jeff walked in. I saw the curious looks of the people who didn't know him. To a stranger his outward appearance would be scary but to people who knew him, we knew he was a good guy. Slater nodded at him.

I shook hands with him when he came to a stop beside me. I owed him so much for finding Taylor.

"They get him?" I asked. He nodded. I should have felt relieved but I would have preferred to teach him a lesson before he had been taken into custody.

Everyone watched Jeff with interest.

"This is Jeff," I said, introducing him to Connor. "He's the one who found Taylor."

"Thank you," Connor murmured as he shook Jeff's hand.

"You're welcome," Jeff responded. "She's strong. She escaped on her own, I only found her."

"She is," Connor confirmed in a murmur.

She had made it out of this alive and that was all the counted.

Jordan yawned.

"Let me take you back to the apartment," Matthew said to her.

"I don't want to leave her," she said, looking up at him.

I gave Slater a side glance to see how he was coping and his attention was firmly on the two of them.

"You won't be able to see her until tomorrow. You'll need sleep so you can be strong for her when she wakes up."

"Okay," she agreed.

They walked up to Connor. She refused to look at Slater but her body language toward my best friend spoke volumes. Matthew told Connor he was going to take Jordan home.

"That's fine, I'll come back later to shower and change," Connor said.

Her eyes drifted back to Slater. They were both fighting a losing battle but they had to figure it out for themselves.

I would have my hands full with looking after Taylor. I planned to spend every moment I could with her to help her get back to her life before the attack.

Besides, I still had no idea how to be with a girl. I wanted to be with Taylor but I was worried that, despite my strong feelings for her, I still couldn't make it work.

"Thank you for finding her," I said to Jeff. I had been a crazy asshole since I had discovered she was missing and I had taken my frustration out on the closest to me, which included Jeff.

"I really didn't believe she would still be alive."

I hadn't allowed myself to consider any other option.

Chapter Twenty-Seven

Slater tried to talk me into going back to the house for a shower and a few hours of sleep but I wasn't going anywhere. Even though I couldn't go in to see her just yet I wanted to be close to her. It wasn't something I could explain.

I did drift off for a couple of hours while sitting in one of the chairs in the waiting room nearby her room. The chairs were so uncomfortable but it didn't matter.

Slater had left to go back to the house to shower before he returned. I told him he didn't have to stay but he had refused to leave me. Connor also spent the night.

Slater went to get us some coffee when Connor came out of her room.

"She's awake."

I felt a tremble of excitement.

"She wants a mirror."

I closed my eyes briefly. I hadn't seen her but I knew her injuries looked pretty bad. He walked to the nearby nursing station and got a compact from one of the nurses.

I paced when he went back in. Would it be too much for her to cope? I released an emotional breath. I wanted to be inside the room, making sure she understood that any outward injury that marred her would heal. She was beautiful anyway. Her beauty went beyond her appearance. It was the way her eyes lit up and the way she smiled.

I continued to pace until Slater arrived with two cups of coffee.

"She's awake," I told him. He handed me a cup of steaming liquid.

"How's she coping?" he asked.

"She wanted a mirror so she can see the damage."

His eyes held mine. "She will get through this."

I nodded. We drank our coffee and waited.

Matthew arrived with Jordan and I could feel the tension from my best friend coming off him in waves. He was being pushed to his limit.

Jordan tried to comfort me but there was nothing anyone could say that would make me feel any less responsible for what had happened to Taylor.

Connor looked emotionally drained when he came out of her room a little while later. He was tired but I couldn't imagine it was easy seeing his little sister dealing with this.

I was dying to see her but Connor suggested Matthew and Jordan go in first.

"She is feeling emotionally fragile," Connor warned them before they went in.

"I want to see her," I told her brother after Matthew and Jordan disappeared into her room.

"You can see her next."

It felt like I had waited an eternity for this moment. I felt more nervous with every second, hoping I would be able to keep my shit together. I couldn't allow myself to react badly to her injuries. Her emotional state was my top priority.

When Jordan and Matthew exited after a while, they were struggling to contain their reaction to seeing Taylor. Jordan caught Slater's gaze, then she told Matthew she was going to the bathroom and she hurried off down the hallway.

Matthew looked like he wanted to hit something.

"Your turn," Connor said to me. "I don't want her upset."

I nodded. That was the last thing I wanted to do. I took a moment to prepare myself before I opened the door.

My heart contracted at the sight of the bruise on her face. I didn't understand how a guy could do that to a woman. We were physically stronger and in my book that meant it was never okay to raise a hand to a woman, no matter what she did.

It took everything I had not to react. I worked my jaw tensely when I took in her injuries. She looked so fragile, like the slightest shake would break her. To stop myself from showing my anger, I shoved my hands into my jean pockets.

My eyes met hers. My heart stuttered for a split second.

All I wanted to do was put my arms around her and hold her close. To allow myself to breathe in her hair and assure myself that despite all my fears and nightmares she was okay. I took a step closer.

The last time I had seen her, I hadn't exactly left on good terms. I had been hurt and angry. She watched me with a reserved look that didn't make me feel very confident. Was she still upset over how things had ended the last time we had spoken? She had every right to be. I had been preparing for this moment since Jeff had found her but I had to admit her cool eyes weren't what I had been expecting.

"Hi," she said. I could tell she was trying to sound like her usual self but she wasn't the same person she had been before. Her ordeal had changed her. The light in her eyes had dimmed. The want for life and experience was now changed to fear and uncertainty.

He hadn't just hurt her physically, he had damaged her emotionally as well. I swore to myself that if I ever had the chance to get him alone I would make him pay dearly for what he had done.

"Hi," I said, stepping closer. I was trying my hardest to be as normal as possible but I felt so nervous and unsure. So much had changed since we had last talked.

"Tay..."

"It's okay," she reassured me. "I'll be fine."

Who was she trying to kid? She wasn't fine, even I could see that. It would take time for her to come to terms with what had happened. And even then there would still be something that would stay with her for the rest of her life.

She shrugged and dropped her gaze to her hands.

"The doctors say everything will heal," she stated, lifting her eyes to meet mine.

I wasn't sure how to handle her. Feeling nervous, I ran a hand through my hair. It didn't help that I was so tired it was difficult to think everything through before it came out of my mouth to ensure it wouldn't upset her.

"I should never have left," I admitted, closing the distance between us with another step.

Her hand twitched and I had an urge to cover it with mine.

"I know why you're here," she stated.

I didn't have a good feeling in the pit of my stomach. I swallowed.

"Really?" I asked, unable to hide my nervousness at how this would play out.

"Yes." She nodded. "It's guilt."

I was feeling guilty but that was not why I was here. The foreboding feeling intensified. I frowned and touched my lip ring with my tongue.

"Guilt?" I questioned.

"Yes. You feel guilty because you left and then something bad happened. You probably think that you could've stopped it, but you wouldn't have been able to. Eric was determined, so determined that he would have left a trail of dead bodies to get me."

She was partly right. I did feel guilty for not being around but that wasn't the reason I was here in her hospital room. I shook my head.

"You probably also feel guilty it was someone you knew. But it doesn't matter."

I remained silent.

"I'm going to tell you what I told everyone else. What happened to me rests solely on the shoulders of the crazy...who did this to me," she stated firmly. She was trying very hard to ease the burden of guilt I carried. Her voice broke slightly and I knew she was struggling to hold it together.

Why was she trying to be so brave? She didn't need to be with me.

"You're right, I do feel guilty. I shouldn't have left and Eric shouldn't have laid one finger on you," I admitted. It was hard to keep the anger from seeping to the surface.

"But that isn't why I'm here," I argued. I took the last step to her and reached for her hand.

Holding her hand in mine sent a swell of emotion through me. There had been so many moments I had feared that I wouldn't see or touch her again. I lifted her hand to drop a gentle kiss on it.

"When I first heard you were gone, I was so terrified..." I closed my eyes briefly to deal with the memory. "We had no idea if you were injured from the accident."

Her free hand went to her chest like she was reliving the

moment she had been taken.

"We had no idea where you were," I continued.

She released an emotional breath. While we had all been worrying and frantically trying to find her, she had been going through such an ordeal at the hands of Eric.

"I didn't just come back because I felt guilty," I stated, brushing my thumb over her hand. "I came back because I made a mistake walking away. A mistake I won't ever make again."

There was no more denying how I felt about her. I was manning up and taking control.

She shook her head at me. This wasn't how this was supposed to go. In my head I had already played this out and this was not the way it had gone down.

"I know what you think you feel. But if you really felt that way, you wouldn't have let go of me so easily."

Her words tore at me like a knife straight to my heart. What was she doing?

"You know what I learned from this whole ordeal?" she asked softly, pulling her hand free from mine. I was still reeling from her words so I let go.

"What?" I asked. I watched her, still struggling to hear what she was saying.

"I learned that I'm stronger than I ever thought I was." There was a strength in her that I had seen from the beginning and it shone from her now.

"You were always strong," I said softy. "You just didn't realize it."

She looked a little taken aback but she recovered quickly. "It also made me realize that I need more than you will ever be willing to give," she revealed.

If I was hurt before, it felt like someone was ripping at my heart now. It was one of the things I had struggled with since I had met her. I had never felt good enough for her.

Did she really believe that I wouldn't give her everything I had? Her eyes watered and I hated that she was upset. I didn't want her to cry but I couldn't allow her to keep thinking that she was only a girl I wanted to have sex with. She didn't know she had crept in and taken over my heart. It now belonged to her.

"Don't put words in my mouth," I told her, feeling more determined to fight for her. I wasn't going to let her go. "You have no idea what I'm willing to do to keep you."

She drew in a shaky breath and another tear slid down her face as she looked away from me like it hurt her to look at me. That winded me. Had I made such a terrible mistake that she wouldn't be able to forgive? It was something I had never even considered.

"Leaving town was a mistake and I admit that. I need you to understand why I did what I did."

She refused to look at me as she began to quietly cry. I felt like the biggest asshole on earth that she was crying because of me. I had screwed up more than a few things but this time it really hurt to watch her pulling away from me.

I could see it in her body language and the way she refused to look at me that I may have already lost her.

"Sex with you is...so good—more than good—but I need more than a physical relationship," she said, this time looking at me.

Couldn't she see that she meant so much more than just that?

"What if I want to give you what you want?" I was laying myself out in the open, feeling unsettled like the first time I had met her. She had that way of making me feel so nervous, it left me feeling so damn unsure.

"You've never dated anyone." She said it like my past predicted my future, like it wasn't possible for me to change, but I had. She had made me want so much more. What had made me content in my past wasn't enough now.

"But what if I want that with you?"

I wasn't used to opening up to anyone but I had to be honest with her if I wanted a shot at keeping her.

Another tear escaped down her face. I brushed it away. I didn't want her to cry anymore. This was supposed to be a happy moment. I was supposed to tell her how much I cared for her and she was supposed to be happy that I had finally realized how deeply I felt about her. But that wasn't how this was going down and I had no idea how to fix it.

"No, it won't work." She shook her head gently.

Why wouldn't she give me a chance to try and make her happy? I didn't know how to date someone but I was willing to learn with her. Didn't she know how much I was out of my depth?

"Why are you being so stubborn?" I finally shot back angrily. "I want to give you what you want, and I don't understand why you won't let me."

"Because you left me!" she yelled at me. It felt like she had struck me across the face and I took a step back as I reeled from her accusation.

She was struggling to contain her anger as she took a deep breath. Her eyes found mine and I saw the pain I had caused her. For a moment it shook my confidence in what I was asking her for. Was I being selfish wanting her when I had no idea if I could make her happy?

She took a deep breath to calm herself. I didn't want to upset her more so I kept quiet.

"How am I supposed to believe that you want that when, before the attack, you left me? You didn't give me a chance to explain—you just left. If you cared for me, you would have listened to what I had to say, but you didn't. You only came back because of what happened to me." I shook my head because it wasn't true. She had no idea what had really made me leave.

"Honestly, I don't think you would have come back if Eric hadn't attacked me, and that hurts," she added and to watch her eyes water made me feel horrible.

I knew in my heart that it wasn't true but the way she viewed me hurt.

She was so hurt and she was struggling to keep it under control. I remembered Connor's warning not to upset her but I was fighting for a future with her. If after I told her all the facts she still decided she wasn't willing to be with me, I would have no choice but to accept it and set her free. But she had to know everything first.

"I need to explain to you why I left," I said softly. My eyes pleaded with hers. "And you owe me a chance to explain."

She looked up at me with a look in her eyes that told me that I had said the wrong thing and there was no taking it back. I was making a mess of this.

"No, I don't," she stated calmly.

Her words were crushing. It was difficult to hold on to the hope that I would be able to change her mind. And I knew there was a good chance that even if she forgave me, she might not be able to forgive me for my past. I wasn't convinced she would but I had to try. I couldn't just give her up.

"Don't do this, Tay," I warned softly, knowing that she was too upset to listen to reason.

"I think you should leave," she told me, her eyes holding mine.

I contemplated refusing but I knew it would just get her more upset and that was the last thing I wanted. She had been through enough and it was selfish of me to push her too much now.

My jaw clenched as I fought against my instinct to stay

and fight for her. This wasn't about me. This was about doing the best thing for her. And if she wanted me to leave I would.

She continued to stare at me, waiting for my response.

"I'll leave," I relented, "but I'm not giving up."

I gave her one last look before I turned and left, closing the door behind me.

Chapter Twenty-Eight

The hardest thing I ever had to do was leave my heart behind with Taylor when I left the hospital. I couldn't even tell anyone what she had said. Slater had given me a concerned look when I had left her hospital room. I had walked away without saying anything, needing to regroup and give her some time before I approached her again.

Even replaying what had happened with Slater had been difficult.

"She isn't thinking straight," he told me. "In a few days she'll see things much clearer."

I wasn't convinced.

"I saw how disappointed she was when she came to see you and you had taken off. She cares for you and that doesn't just go away overnight."

His words gave me some hope that she was just too upset at the moment and once she had some time she would let me back in.

When I got home I was agitated and angry. I headed for the room Eric stayed in and opened the door. I don't know what I was expecting but it looked like a normal college student's room. There was nothing that screamed 'crazy stalking kidnapper.'

I wanted to throw his stuff out but I didn't want to get rid of anything that might help put him away. Surveying the room, I stepped inside. The closet caught my attention. I opened the door and stood back. Inside the door were pictures of Taylor. They ranged from when she was younger to more recent pictures of her.

I closed my eyes briefly. It had been right under my nose and I had been clueless.

The next day I felt more confident she would relent and see me but Connor had shaken his head at me. "She doesn't want to see you. And I can't go against her wishes."

I had bent my head slightly, trying to figure out what to do next. The waiting around was slowly killing me and I didn't know how much longer I could stand it.

"Give her some time and she will come around," he had assured me.

Her brother's view of me had changed dramatically since our first encounter when he had tried to interfere with me seeing his sister. I don't know exactly what had changed his view on me. Maybe it was my reaction to his missing sister and the fact that Jeff, who worked for me, had found her.

"I'll keep you updated on how she's doing," he suggested. I nodded and left, feeling more desperate with every day that passed. Even though I felt the way I did, there was no way to fix what had gone wrong between us and change Taylor's mind.

I kept in touch with Connor and got regular updates on her.

"She is doing as well as can be expected." His words reminded me that she hadn't come out of this emotionally unscathed. Her wounds would heal with time but it was the wounds that no one could see that worried me more.

Then she was discharged from the hospital but when I didn't see her around campus, I called Connor.

"She won't leave her room," he told me in a tired voice.

It was only natural that she would feel fearful of what had happened but she couldn't spend the rest of her life holed up in her room.

I considered going around to talk to her but Connor wasn't convinced it would be a good idea. And I conceded that my presence might hinder her progress. I was putting her welfare above my own.

"Give her time," he told me, trying to reassure me that she would let me back in. "She is struggling at the moment and she needs time to get back to her life."

Staying away from her was killing me inside. I felt like only half a person. Slater tried his best to help but the only thing that would help was Taylor. I missed her.

I held on to the memories we had shared. Lying in bed with her in my arms, the feel of her body against mine. The sparkle in her eyes when she laughed. The way she made me feel. I clung to it like a lifeline until I could get her back.

It hurt that she didn't want me around.

I tried to reach her but she never returned my calls. And all of my text messages went unanswered. I wanted her to know that although I was keeping my distance from her, I wasn't giving up. I was just giving her the space she needed to work through her ordeal and when she was more settled I would give her all the facts so she would be able to make a decision that affected both of us.

The details from my past gnawed at me, festering with every moment. There were a few things from my past I wasn't proud of but this one thing had the power to derail anything that I had with Taylor.

Every day that I went to classes, my eyes scanned the crowds for her, hoping to get a glimpse, but the first week after she got back there was no sign of her.

By that weekend I had to get away. I was falling apart. So I went to see my mother again. She was so happy to see me but when she took in my tired face and the heaviness in my features, she frowned.

"What's wrong?" she asked softly as she led me into the house.

Sally, her nurse, gave me a slight nod before she left us alone in the living room.

"Sit down," my mom said, steering me to the sofa, where I dropped down into the seat.

She sat down beside me as I rubbed my hands over my face, trying to figure out where to start.

"I fucked up," I admitted, unable to look at her when I said it.

"Tell me what happened," she suggested. She touched my arm and I looked at her.

I told her everything. From the first time I'd met Taylor to when I had left the hospital with her refusing to see me. I told her about Taylor's past I had discovered and the folder with my background that I had found in her bedside table.

I looked to her for answers and she gave me a thoughtful look.

"She is dealing with a lot," she said and nodded, understanding. "She just needs time. Let her work herself through her ordeal and then she might feel differently."

I wanted to believe her but I was scared that even if she did, the one thing from my past would end it.

I stood while my mom remained seated, watching me. I raked a hand through my hair.

"What happens when she finds out what I did?" I asked my mom, scared at what she would say.

She gave me a sympathetic look tinged with her own guilt. "If she truly loves you, she will understand."

I let out a deep breath. Would she be able to see past the act to the reason why I had done it? There was so much riding on this.

Even though none of this had gone as planned, I couldn't wish that it hadn't happened. Caring about her had given me meaning in a life I had been wasting on nameless girls and endless parties. She had shown me there was so much more to life than the shallow one I had led.

But the chance I was going to lose her scared me.

"I'm sorry," my mother said, sounding hoarse. I looked at her with my hands resting on my hips.

"Why are you sorry?" I asked her softly.

"It's my fault," she said as her eyes began to fill up with tears. "If I hadn't been drinking my way into an early grave, you wouldn't have been forced into it."

Her words were true but I didn't blame her. Not anymore. There was no point in hanging on to all those old feelings because it would only hinder any relationship we could have now.

I sat down beside her and put an arm around her. She trembled as I hugged her.

"We've all made mistakes," I said gently. "I don't blame you anymore."

She pulled away and looked up at me with tear-soaked cheeks. "You should."

I smiled and shook my head. "What counts is what you do now."

She nodded and brushed her tears from her face.

"You've really grown up into a good young man," she said softly, looking at me proudly. I one-arm hugged her gently in response.

"You might be a little biased," I teased, wanting to lighten the emotional moment, and my mother laughed.

It wasn't a sound I heard often. It made me hold her a little tighter. The emotions I felt for her swept through me.

It also gave me hope. If I could mend things with my mom then it gave me the confidence that I could fix things with Taylor.

I hoped that when Taylor found out the truth she would be able to understand why I had done what I had. I wasn't a bad person, but I had been forced into doing some things I wasn't proud of because of circumstances beyond my control.

I couldn't erase what I had done but I couldn't allow it to ruin the future I wanted, with Taylor.

Every day without her dragged on. And the hope that she would eventually get into a space where she would at least let me talk to her died a slow death.

She was sticking to her guns by refusing any contact with me. Waiting her out wasn't working; I had to come up with another way.

I called Matthew.

"Hi, Sin," he greeted suspiciously.

"Matthew," I said, "I need your help."

There were a few moments of silence. I knew he hadn't been a fan in the beginning but I was hoping his view of me had changed. Otherwise getting to Taylor was going to be much more difficult.

"What do you want?'

"I need to see Taylor."

He was quiet for a moment. "She isn't ready to see you."

"Come on, Matthew. This is killing me." I paused as I tried to find the right words to reach him. "All I need is a chance to speak to her and if after that she still doesn't want to see me then I will back off."

"You're not going to upset her, are you?"

"No. I just want to talk to her."

He let out a deep breath. "Come over in an hour."

"Thanks," I said, feeling relieved I was going to get my chance.

"I'm doing this for her."

He ended the call. I took a breath to ease the tightness in my chest. Was she as much a mess as I was? Was that why he was going to help me see her? It didn't really matter what his reasons were, all that mattered was I was going to see her. It gave me hope that I would accomplish what I had to.

I got ready. As I pulled a new shirt on, I spotted the folder. I didn't want her to know what I had done in my past but I knew it might be the only way forward. Reluctantly I took the folder with me when I went over to the apartment.

The moment I felt nervous was when I was standing outside the door, waiting for someone to answer my knock.

My hand tightened its hold on the folder just before the door opened. Matthew greeted me and let me inside. He pointed to Taylor's bedroom door.

I gave him a nod before I walked to her room. The door was open. For a split second I took her in, sprawled on her bed and working on an assignment. My heart began to race.

"Tay."

Her eyes widened at my unexpected presence. She hurried off her bed. She kept her distance from me and crossed her arms.

"What are you doing here?" she asked. I took the fact that she looked unsettled and not angry as a good sign.

I studied her face, taking in her fine features. Just looking at her was enough to take my breath away. She didn't have any reminders marring her face anymore. The bruises had healed but she still wore the fear of her ordeal. I had seen it momentarily in her eyes when I'd surprised her just a few moments ago.

"I had to do something. You won't answer my calls or return my texts," I said.

She frowned like she was figuring something out.

"This isn't fair," she told me, sounding a little angry.

This I had been prepared for but I was ready to fight for her.

"Who said I had to play by the rules?" I shot back fiercely. "And I'm not leaving until you hear me out."

I was determined. I had done enough waiting for a lifetime.

"Fine," she said in a short tone before she sat down on her bed with her arms still crossed.

Her eyes went to the folder I held in my hands. She knew what it contained. I closed the door and turned to face her.

"How did you get Matthew to let you in?" she asked, not looking happy about it.

"I called him. He gave me a chance to tell him why I needed to speak to you and, well, here I am," I explained, looking around her room.

"I'm listening," she said. She looked resentful of my presence in her room.

"You have it in your head that I just came back because I was concerned and because I felt guilty," I started, taking a step closer.

My eyes softened as they caressed her face. I wanted to reach out and touch her cheek but I stopped myself. First I had to win her back. She pressed her lips into a tight, determined line.

"What I feel is so much more than that," I admitted.

Now was the time for the truth, no more games or hiding how I felt. I had to lay it all out in front of her to win her back.

I looked down at the folder.

"I know you didn't read the folder," I admitted softly.

"Why do you suddenly believe me now?" she asked. My reaction to the folder had been an all-consuming anger and betrayal. It had been impossible to listen to reason. "I don't understand."

She dropped her arms to her sides. Her body language was not as defensive as before. I took that as a sign that I was reaching her.

"I want to explain everything to you, but I think you need to read it for yourself," I said, holding out the folder to her. I was taking the biggest risk of my life but I couldn't win her back with this between us. She looked at the folder I was holding out to her.

"Take it."

She reluctantly took it from me and held it with both hands.

"I want you to read it." Even if I lost her, she had to know it all. I couldn't hide this and risk losing her all over again.

She studied the folder briefly before raising her eyes to meet mine. I felt nervous that this could backfire and this would be the end of us. My tongue touched my lip ring.

"I don't need to know about your past," she stated with a sigh. "It doesn't matter to me."

My heart inflated with her words but I couldn't take the chance that her curiosity might get the better of her further down the line.

"I know," I said. I resigned myself to the fact that there was no going back and what would happen was going to happen.

"I'm not sure why you want me to read it now." She gave me a questioning look.

"I never wanted you to know any of it," I told her truthfully. I raked a hand through my hair, feeling more agitated. "But you've left me no choice. It's the only way for you to understand why I didn't think I was good enough for you and that was the reason why I left. I didn't leave because I didn't care about you."

The silence between us was strained. She swallowed. She studied me as she sat, still holding the folder. There was no hiding my true emotions from her. She had to see how much was riding on this.

"Why are you nervous?" she asked.

I couldn't keep the sadness at bay when I thought of the worst-case scenario playing out when she read the truth.

"There is a chance I will lose you anyway," I said, feeling scared and defeated at the same time.

Her beautiful blue eyes held mine.

"Promise me you will read it," I said, hoping she wouldn't refuse.

She nodded. "I'll read it."

I could tell from her expression that she didn't believe anything that the folder held would change anything. But she hadn't read it yet and once she had she would be able to decide if it was something she could forgive me for.

I didn't want what we had to be tainted with deception.

"You know where to find me when you're done," I said. I turned to leave and then stopped. "I'll see you soon. Even if it's just to tell me you never want to see me again."

With my part done I left her room. Matthew wasn't in sight when I left the apartment and I was glad I had no one to witness the rawness I felt.

You did the right thing, I told myself even though the ache in my chest throbbed.

Chapter Twenty-Nine

Slater was home when I got back. He was sitting quietly, drinking a beer on the sofa.

"How did it go?" he asked as I sat dropped into the seat beside him.

I looked at him with the heavy heart.

"It looks like you need one of these." He handed me the beer he had been holding.

I took a gulp but it wasn't going to help the burning feeling inside. I had no idea how long it would take for her to read the folder. I could only hope that it would be soon. Whatever the outcome, I had to know.

"Did you see her?" he asked, watching me take another gulp of the beer.

I pressed my lips together as I studied the beer bottle I held in my hand as the alcohol slid down my throat.

"Yeah."

"And?" he asked, I could feel him watching me.

"I gave her the folder to read," I said, giving him a side glance.

He frowned like he was struggling to understand why I would do such a thing. "Why?"

I shrugged like it wasn't the most important choice in my life. "She has to know everything so she can make the right choice."

"And what if that isn't you?"

His words reminded me of what could go wrong. I gave him another shrug. "Then I will have to live with it."

My words were braver than the reality of being without her but I had to believe she could choose me anyway. I had never felt good enough for her and even now I didn't fully believe I was the best choice for her but I wanted her anyway.

I would never allow anything to happen to her again. She had been through enough and she deserved to live the rest of her life free of any more violence. Even if she didn't want me to be a part of her life I would still keep an eye on her.

I rubbed the back of my neck, feeling emotionally exhausted as well as physically. I hadn't had a proper night's sleep since I had discovered the folder but I knew until I had my answer from Taylor I wouldn't.

There was a knock at the door. Slater got up to answer it.

"Sin," he said in a tense voice, which made me look over my shoulder sharply to see a couple of cops in the doorway.

We had been on the other side of the law before, where the sight of cops would have sent us fleeing in the opposite direction, but we had changed our lives. We were law-abiding citizens now, with nothing to fear, but it was still difficult for Slater to be at ease with cops around.

I stood up and took over from Slater as he stood back with his arms crossed, keeping his eyes fixed on the guys watching us with interest from my doorway.

"Officers," I greeted.

"We're here to process Eric Watson's room." He handed me a piece of paper.

I scanned it briefly and handed it back to him. I nodded and opened the door farther for them.

Slater frowned as he watched them enter the house.

The sooner I could get rid of Eric's stuff the better. I showed them to his room and left them to it.

"Is that really necessary?" Slater said, still looking as tense as when they had arrived.

"They need to get everything to make sure he doesn't get away with it."

"He will probably confess," he added. "It's not like they don't have enough evidence to put him away."

That ticked my mind over to the next possibility. What if Eric refused to confess and it had to go to trial? I couldn't imagine how detrimental it would be to Taylor to have to relive the horror of her kidnapping and attack.

I rubbed my forehead, trying to figure out if there was anything I could do to ensure that didn't happen. But I didn't have access to him so it wasn't like I could even threaten him.

I called Jeff.

"Boss," he answered. "What do you need?"

"We need to find a way to make sure Eric confesses so it won't go to trial." I wasn't going to leave it open to a possibility.

"I'll look into a couple of options," he replied.

I had been on the straight and narrow since I had inherited the money from my father but this stepping across the line was a necessity I didn't even feel guilty for. He was lucky he wasn't on a feeding tube or worse, dead.

It took the cops a few hours to go through Eric's room and then they left.

"What are we going to do with his stuff?" Slater said,

surveying what had been left behind.

"Throw it out." I leaned against the doorway. I wanted his stuff out of my house. I didn't want Taylor around anything that could remind her of him.

But he had lived in this house so I considered that I might have to sell it to be able to escape any possible memories for Taylor. And I also didn't want to be reminded of him in any way.

Slater opened the bedroom door and looked inside the slightly open closet and saw some photos still stuck on the inside of the door that hadn't been removed.

"He was really some sick crazy," he said with a distasteful look when he saw the younger photos of Taylor.

We had discovered the reason why he had gone for Taylor. His fascination had begun with her when she had only been nine and was struggling with the loss of both of her parents in a horrific murder.

Slater left the room and returned with trash bags. He began to shove Eric's clothes into one. I picked up the other bag and started to do the same.

I tried to keep myself busy so I didn't have time to watch the clock but there was no taking my mind off Taylor. I was tired of going around and around in circles trying to predict what she would do. There was no way to know if she was going to stay or walk away.

The next morning even with the knowledge that I was missing classes I couldn't drag myself to campus. There was no point in trying to concentrate when I wasn't in any state to listen.

It had taken Slater and me a few hours to clear out Eric's room. Afterward we had sat and had a beer. Getting rid of his stuff had helped me work through some of the guilt I felt for having had him in my home.

I was sitting on the sofa with my head leaning back, rubbing my forehead. The lack of decent sleep was catching up with me. Slater had gone to classes only after I had assured him I was okay.

There was a knock at the door. I felt my stomach twist with nervousness when I stood up. Even though I was tired of waiting, I wasn't sure I was ready for what her decision would be.

With my hand on the door handle, I hesitated only for a moment before I opened it. I knew it would be her, I hadn't been expecting anyone else, but it didn't stop my heart from racing at the sight of her. Her eyes meshed with mine and I felt alive again, like she was the light in the dark tunnel of my life.

Was I ready for what she was going to say?

"Tay," I said her name and stood back, inviting her inside with the sweep of my hand.

She hesitated slightly, her gaze going on beyond me. Was she looking for reminders of the roommate who had terrorized her? I would have to sell this house because I couldn't stand the fear that haunted her eyes when she came in.

I wanted to hold her hand to remind her that she wasn't alone and that I wouldn't allow anyone to hurt her. But I stopped myself. I still didn't have any right to touch her.

"Don't be nervous," I told her, studying her face. "I got rid of my other roommate. Only Slater and I live here now."

I had told Tucker I was going to sell the house and he had found somewhere else to rent. I had felt bad for the short notice but I didn't want guys around that would make Taylor nervous. Besides, it wasn't like he had actually spent time in the house. He just needed a place to store his stuff.

"Would you rather talk upstairs in my room?" I asked when my assurance didn't seem to ease her anxiety.

"Yes," she whispered.

I led the way up the stairs and she followed behind me to my room. The nervousness I had seen in her before melted away as she faced me. I closed the door. In this room I had taken her virginity. It seemed fitting that if it had to end it would be in the same place it had started.

"You read the file." I watched for any reaction to my words but it was difficult to tell what she felt. Her usual open features were closed off from me.

She bit her lip and nodded. She wasn't angry but I wasn't sure that was enough to convince me I still had a chance.

"There wasn't a lot in that file that my imagination hadn't already conjured up. I know which part you were scared I would find out about."

The truth was out in the open for judgment.

"Dealing drugs," I said out loud, feeling resigned to the fact that no matter what I did, it would always be a black mark against me.

To most people it would be forgivable but to someone whose parents had been murdered by two guys who had been high on drugs might be a struggle to forgive and forget.

She nodded. Then she studied me.

"Why?" she asked.

Would the reasons behind my decision to sell drugs make it easier to forgive me? Even if it didn't, she deserved the whole truth and not just parts of it she had read in a background file on me.

Not feeling proud, I dropped my gaze to the floor.

"I've told you about some of my crappy childhood," I said, lifting my eyes back to hers.

I hated looking back or talking about what had happened but I had to do it. If I wanted to be with her, she had to understand why.

"While my mom was drowning her sorrows with an endless supply of alcohol, I was left to fend for myself." She frowned, like she couldn't fit the type of mother I'd had with the mother she had lost so early in life.

In the luck of the draw I had lost. But in the long run Taylor had lost more. She had grown up without the mother who loved her.

"Slater was pretty much in the same situation I was. His father was a drug addict and his mom could barely make ends meet. Whatever money his mom made went to pay for the drugs his father needed."

She watched me with sad eyes, reminding me of how different our childhoods had been.

"We got involved with a gang."

I quieted for a moment. To open up about things I had kept so close wasn't easy. It was going against everything I had promised myself. I'd thought if I was a good guy now, my past wouldn't matter. But I had been naive and now I was getting a dose of reality that it would haunt my future no matter what.

"There were no options. We did what we had to, to survive," I added.

"I'm sorry you had to grow up like that," she said softly.

"I'm sorry too." I held her gaze while my tongue flicked against the circular metal embedded in my lip. It was a small, nervous act that gave me some comfort.

"We didn't enjoy doing any of the things that were expected of us," I explained, needing her to know that if there had been another option or if we hadn't been in a hopeless situation it wouldn't have happened. "But there was no walking away from it—we needed the money."

"Are you still working for this gang?" she asked, surprising me.

I couldn't help wondering if she had asked that question because of Jeff.

"No." I shook my head and she looked relieved. That was a good sign. I was starting to feel hopeful.

Maybe, just maybe, she would choose me.

"Connor said Jeff worked for you?" Her question confirmed my initial assumption.

She yawned. I wasn't the only one who had been missing out on sleep.

"You're tired. Why don't you sit down?"

She sat down on the bottom of my bed. I pulled the nearby chair that I used by my desk to sit down in front of her.

"Yes, Jeff works for me," I answered.

I watched her mind tick over the information I had given her.

"I don't understand."

It was time to tell her everything. I let out a deep breath and ran my hand through my hair.

"I told you about my father." She nodded.

"While he was alive I'd never met him or had any contact with him, but when he died I inherited everything he had," I revealed. Her forehead creased, like she was having trouble piecing everything together. "His lawyer called me up out of the blue one day and told me about my inheritance."

"But what about his wife and kids?" she asked.

I had asked the same question when the lawyer had contacted me. For someone who hadn't wanted anything to do with me, it made no sense that he would leave everything he had to me.

"His wife died before him and they never had any kids. In his will he left me everything." There was no way to get the answers from a dead guy. I shrugged.

"Wow," she breathed.

"I didn't want to take the money, but I didn't have a choice. Slater and I were getting deeper into the gang and it was becoming more serious. We'd gone from petty crime to dealing drugs and we knew it was going to get worse. It was the only way to get us out before we got in... too deep."

She shot me a questioning look.

"I don't want to talk about it," I said, refusing to elaborate. "That part of my life is over. The money gave me the freedom to give myself a new life and I could help the people I cared about. Slater and I left the gang. Jeff—the guy who found you—left with us. Whenever I need something done, he is the guy I call."

"I'm not judging," she was quick to say and she covered the hand I was resting on my leg with hers. It strengthened the sense she was going to forgive me.

"I never wanted to be seen as a trust-fund baby. I wanted people to care for me, not for the money I had." I tried to explain why I hadn't mentioned it before. Money changed people and for most girls it would have been an incentive. But I knew it didn't matter to her.

The warmth of her hand on mine brought my attention back to her affectionate gesture and I covered hers, cocooning it within mine before I looked back to her.

"My mom had started to get sick. The years of alcohol abuse took its toll on her body. I've set her up with the best medical care money can buy. I try to visit her often, but it's hard trying to care for someone who never gave a shit about me until she sobered up. I want you to know that I never wanted to deal drugs. It wasn't something I was proud of," I told her.

She remained quiet and thoughtful.

"I know it's a lot to take in," I said as I stood up, unable to sit still because I was feeling so anxious. She stood up in front of me.

"It was hard to read your file," she said and I held my breath. "Seeing what you had to do to survive was difficult to comprehend."

It had been even harder to live. I nodded, understanding that the details of my past would be hard to stomach for most.

"I understand why you got so upset when you saw the folder and I understand why you ran," she said. Was her understanding enough to forgive me?

There was so much on the line and I could feel the tension in my shoulders. I dropped my gaze, feeling a momentary fear that I would lose her. I looked at the floor.

"Look at me," she instructed softly. I followed her command and met her gaze. The intensity of the look in her eyes was hypnotizing.

Was the knowledge that I had dealt drugs going to derail the future we could have?

Chapter Thirty

She lifted herself onto her tiptoes and kissed me, taking me by surprise. I was still trying to recover when she stopped and looked up at me. I was still so unsure of what was happening. Did that mean she was going to forgive me?

I was too scared to allow myself to rush to a conclusion, the devastation of being wrong would be too difficult to cope with, so I stayed still.

"I love you," she breathed those three little words that instantly washed over me, making my heart inflate with the emotion I felt for her.

I had spent most of my life not getting what I wanted and the realization I was going to get the girl I wanted more than any other was difficult to accept. I hesitated.

"You don't think you're good enough for me," she said, studying me carefully. I kept my features free from what was going on inside my head but somehow she could tell. Had I been that obvious?

"I know I'm not good enough for you," I said, meaning every word. If I were a good guy I would let her find someone who knew how to love her but I was too selfish. I wanted her for myself.

"Yes, my parents were murdered by two young guys that were high on drugs at the time. Did the drugs put the gun in their hands and pull the trigger? No. Not every person who gets high on drugs murders someone. It wasn't the drugs that ended my parents' lives." She paused. Anytime she spoke of the incident it was emotional for her. "You had a tough childhood and I can't imagine what it was like. It physically hurts to think of what you had to go through. I understand why you did the things you did and I would never judge you." She took my hand into hers.

I could see how much she cared, it shone from her eyes as she gazed up at me. I swallowed.

"You are good enough for me," she whispered, assuring me that my insecurities were unfounded.

And with her words it broke all the emotions I had been trying to suppress. I took her into my arms and hugged her tight. The feel of her body against mine was indescribable and I swallowed the lump in my throat. She lay her head against my chest and I breathed her in, allowing it to reassure me I wasn't dreaming. She was really here with me.

When she tried to break away I couldn't let her go. I wasn't ready. Not yet. I just needed a few more moments.

"Give me a minute," I breathed into her hair.

She allowed me to hold her for as long as I needed. I held her tightly, assuring myself that I wasn't going to lose her. Then I pulled away and gazed down at her.

"I was so scared I was going to lose you," I said, admitting out loud my inner fear.

"I'm not going anywhere," she stated confidently, staring at me.

She was mine. The feeling in the middle of my chest made me bend down to kiss her. She put her arms around my neck. The real thing was better than any memory of kissing her before.

The intensity of it left me breathless when I stopped and I leaned my forehead lightly against hers.

"I've never done this before," I admitted softly.

"What exactly are we doing?" she asked lightly but I could tell it was important to her. Was she scared that I only wanted what we'd shared before?

"This is going to be more than one night," I assured her, feeling lighter. I gave her a playful smile. I hadn't felt like this in a long time. "No hooking up with other people."

She looked at me and she couldn't hide the look of disappointment that passed over her features momentarily before she had a chance to hide it.

"We get titles as well," I teased.

"Titles?" She gave me a questioning look.

"Yeah." My smile widened. "Girlfriend."

This time when I kissed her, she clung to me. Now she knew how serious I was about her.

"Does that mean I get to call you my boyfriend?" she asked playfully when I ended the kiss.

I nodded. "I never thought I'd ever want more, but I do with you."

'It scares me," she admitted.

I had an awful track record with women but I knew that whatever we had was what I wanted. Even though I didn't know all the ins and outs of being with just one girl, I was willing to try and that was more than I had ever given anyone else.

"Don't be scared," I told her. "The way I feel about you is nothing like I've ever felt before."

She looked less hesitant at my assurance.

"When I heard that you'd been taken, it felt like someone had ripped my heart out of my chest," I admitted. "I've never been so scared in my life."

I let out a deep breath, holding her gaze. I wanted her to see how much it had affected me.

"I never want to feel that again," I said, pressing a kiss to her forehead to assure the resurge in fear from the memory that she was safe with me. "I felt so guilty that I'd left you and then you went missing."

"There was nothing you could've done to stop Eric."

I wasn't convinced of that. "Maybe...maybe not."

Still feeling unsure of how to date, I wanted her to know that I was committed to this.

"I won't lie—I have no idea how to do this, but I promise to try to do everything I can to make you happy," I promised, hugging her.

I had fought so hard for this moment.

"When I first saw you, I never imagined we would end up where we are now."

I'd tried to convince myself that she was only going to be a temporary arrangement that would run its course, but from the first moment she'd affected me differently than any other girl.

I released her.

"From the first time I saw you, I knew there was something different about you," I told her, cupping her face.

"Really?" She stared at me.

"Yes. And then you came to see me, wanting me to 'take advantage' of you."

She looked mortified and I smirked. She was so different and I had seen it in her from the start.

"But why did you turn me down?"

"You were so innocent." I trailed my knuckles down her face, still in awe of her. "And I wasn't. You deserved so much better than me."

She shook her head

"I'm so glad you were my first," she breathed softly.

I didn't want to think what I would have missed out on if I hadn't agreed to taking her virginity. It was something I didn't want to even consider.

"I tried to do the right thing—I really did—but I couldn't stop thinking about you. And then I saw you drinking with Slater and I couldn't handle seeing you with someone else."

"You were jealous?" I smiled and nodded.

"I think I was and then I knew that, even though you deserved better, I couldn't let you go. I couldn't stand the thought of you being with someone else. I knew I would have to step up and give you what you wanted or I would lose you."

Opening up wasn't something I usually did but with her it was so easy. It was also my way of allowing her to see I was serious about her.

"And then after our night together?" she asked.

"One night with you was never going to be enough," I admitted. "I was always going to want more."

"But I saw you with hat girl," she reminded me.

Nothing had happened with that girl.

"I didn't like the way you made me feel. I felt vulnerable and I hated feeling like that. I tried to move on, I really did, but there was no getting over you."

"Did you sleep with that girl?" She blurted out the question.

"No, I couldn't do it."

She let out the breath she had been holding.

"I haven't slept with anyone else since our first night together." She hadn't been expecting that. Her eyes widened in shock. "Really?"

"Yes."

I had been convinced at first that she'd had something going on with Caleb.

"When I saw you with Caleb, I was so angry." She looked a little guilty.

"And you thought I needed a rich, preppy boy?" she asked, remembering what I had said when she had stopped me from taking her in the bathroom.

"I tried to convince myself that was the reason why you were with him. It would've hurt more to know that you were with him because you liked him." Even saying it aloud, it still had the power to make me feel raw inside.

"I was trying to fill the hole that you left in my heart and I shouldn't have used someone else to do that."

"There were more than a few times after you went missing that I thought I would never be able to hold you again." There was no disguising the fear I had felt.

"You don't have to think about that anymore." She took my hand into hers. "I'm okay now."

It was still too soon to be able to look back at the experience and not feel all the emotions it had entailed.

"Everyone was getting more and more scared that you weren't coming back, but it wasn't something I could accept. I called Jeff as soon as I found out you were missing. I told him to find you."

Giving up on her had never been an option.

"I was so scared when he found me in the street," There was a dark fear in her eyes like she was reliving the moment.

"If the cops hadn't gotten to Eric first, I'm not sure I could've let him live for what he did to you." Controlling my anger when it came to Eric was nearly impossible.

"Then I'm glad the cops got him first."

I didn't agree. "If I hadn't killed him, I definitely would've made him wish he'd never touched you."

"And you would have been up for assault. With your previous criminal record they wouldn't have been lenient," she reminded me.

It still would have been worth it, especially after what he had done.

"It's finished," she said with fierce determination.

"But I'm so thankful that you are here with me now." I held her.

"Me too."

But being so close to her, I could feel our attraction shift the mood from talking to something else entirely. I wanted her. I put my hands on her hips and leaned closer before my mouth covered hers. My tongue trailed against her bottom lip and she gasped, opening her mouth. I swept my tongue inside and deepened the kiss. Her hands gripped around my neck tightly, telling me that she wanted me too.

When the kiss ended we were both breathing hard.

"Do you want to meet me at my apartment and we can spend the day together?" she asked with an inviting smile.

"Yes." I didn't want to be anywhere else. I walked her out of the house and back to the car where Matthew was waiting for her.

"Hey," he greeted.

I looked at Taylor. She was smiling and I liked that I was the reason why.

"I see you guys have sorted things out," he observed.

I gave him a nod. "Thanks."

If he hadn't allowed me to see her, I wasn't sure we could have sorted things out.

"You're welcome."

"I'll see you soon," I told her and she left with Matthew.

Half an hour later I was knocking on the door of her apartment. Matthew let me in and Taylor took my hand to lead me to her room.

I closed the door and leaned against it, taking in the sight of the way she was looking at me. I was sure I was looking at her the same way.

"I think you have way too many clothes on." I moved closer and she gave me a seductive smile that made my heart stutter.

"Really?" she teased. "What if I'm cold?"

"Then I'll keep you warm." I pulled her to me.

I kissed her softly, wanting to savor what I was feeling. I was hot for her but it wasn't just a physical thing. I could recognize that now.

"I've missed you," I felt compelled to tell her while staring into her glittery blue eyes.

"I missed you too. I can't help feeling that if I'd just let you explain, we would've been able to sort things out sooner."

I didn't want to spend time on something that we couldn't change. It was just wasting energy.

"Let's not think about that. All that matters is that we have sorted everything out now and we're together." I kissed her, hoping to make it impossible for her to think about that.

To kiss her, feel her and know that it was where I belonged was a feeling I was becoming addicted to.

We undressed slowly, taking our time. It was like I was seeing her for the first time and I didn't want to rush it.

As she lay on the edge of the bed, I worked her up, wanting to hear her moan and gasp as my tongue flicked against her. Her hands tugged at my hair as I made her shatter.

She was still riding the wave of pleasure when I reached for a condom. I wanted to be inside of her so badly. She reached for me when I aligned my body with hers. She was more than ready when I entered her.

Sex had always been good but what I shared with Taylor was something so much more. I knew it was because the feelings we felt for each other intensified what we felt physically.

I moved in and out of her, covering her mouth with mine as she gasped. She lifted her hips to meet each thrust and I strained against her. My strokes became faster and deeper, needing only what she could give me.

She gasped when I moved into her faster. I was nearly there, feeling the initial tightening of my body.

"You feel so good," I whispered, barely holding on. And the moment she trembled and gasped with her second orgasm, I allowed myself to seek my own release.

I thrust as deeply as I could, bringing my body flush with hers, and my body tensed when I came. Holding my weight off her by my elbows, I kissed her forehead and then rolled off her so I could get rid of the condom.

When I returned, I slid beside her into the bed.

My body still thrummed from our physical act and my heart filled with emotions that were difficult to decipher. All I knew was she mattered more than anyone. The depth of what I was experiencing took my breath away and scared me a little. But it was only a momentary fear that passed when I looked at her.

"I love you," she said, softly searching my eyes. Was she expecting me to say the same?

It felt like a vise tightening around my insides. My feelings for her were stronger than anything I had ever felt for a girl but I didn't know if it was love.

I remembered how much my mother had 'loved' my father and how much he had 'loved' her until he had found out she was pregnant with me. To me it was a destructive force that ripped people's lives apart. It hadn't been love, it had been lust.

What I felt for Taylor wasn't like that. I knew it was deep and emotional but I didn't know if I loved her. I wasn't even sure if I was capable of it.

I had to be honest with her even if I didn't know how she was going to take it. I turned to face her and let out a sigh, knowing this could hurt her, but I couldn't say something I didn't mean.

"I want to be able to say those words to you and mean them. Most people know what love means because they've experienced it, but I haven't." I paused. "That doesn't mean, though, that you aren't the most important person in my life. I will do everything I can to make you happy and keep you safe."

Holding her gaze, I touched her cheek. She looked a little sad and it made me feel guilty for not being able to say the three little words she wanted me to say to her.

"I'm sorry I can't say it to you," I admitted, not sure what else I could say.

Then I waited for her reaction. She didn't look away or get angry. Instead she said, "You don't have to say the words." She kissed me briefly. "It doesn't change what we have together."

No, it didn't. She was everything I wanted and needed. And I would prove that to her every day we had together.

Chapter Thirty-One

I checked the time. She would be home at any minute. I knew she was safe because Jeff was her shadow when I wasn't with her. I wasn't taking any chances with her safety. There wasn't an active threat; it was more for peace of mind for me. And deep down inside I believed it helped give her the freedom from her fear to live her life.

There were still moments when she hesitated and I could see the debilitating fear in her. And she struggled through it. It was the strength in her that had been born when her parents had been murdered and now it carried her through the difficult times.

Some nights she still suffered from nightmares. I hated that the ordeal had left a lasting fear in her. I could only hope that time would heal the wound.

I was a lucky guy. Having her made me richer than all the money I had in the bank.

I had just finished in the shower and gotten dressed. I felt a thrum of excitement for what the evening would hold.

The front door opened and closed, signaling she was home. I found her sitting on the sofa with her eyes closed. The sight tugged at my heart.

"Rough day?" I asked.

At the sound of my voice she opened her eyes. I leaned down to kiss her.

"Yes. I'm tired," she replied, letting out a heavy sigh.

"You know you don't have to work," I reminded her. We'd had this conversation so many times but she was too stubborn and refused to quit her job.

It was a struggle between my need to care for her and her need to make her own way. Connor had been on my side in that particular argument but that had held no weight with her.

She sighed as I massaged her shoulders to ease the tension from her muscles.

"You know, if you didn't work, we would have more time to spend together," I reminded her.

I had bought a condo not long after we had officially started dating. The house had held too many memories of Eric for me to keep. And Taylor moving in with me had been the next logical step.

With her I found myself embracing the commitment I had dreaded before and I had used every personal rule to avoid it.

"Mmm," she murmured, side-stepping by suggestion. My hands kneaded her tense muscles.

"You're not listening to me, are you?" I asked.

She mumbled a yes.

I lifted my hands from her shoulders, to her vocal disappointment, and sat down beside her.

Her hungry eyes met mine. I knew that look. It told me I could have her right here and now on the sofa. And if it weren't for my other plans I would not have hesitated.

"You like what you see?" I teased with a knowing smirk.

"Yes," she breathed with a touch of a smile.

Our attraction was just as powerful as it had been the first time we had locked eyes. The only difference now was she was confident in what she liked and what she didn't when it came to the bedroom.

"Why did you stop?" she moaned.

"Because you weren't listening to what I was saying," I told her. I reached for her hand and took it into mine.

"It's because I can't think of anything but you when you touch me," she admitted huskily.

"Really," I said with a mischievous grin, contemplating giving in to my need for her as I leaned closer.

"Yes," she whispered, watching me close the distance between us. Then I kissed her. She tasted so damn good I had to remind myself why we couldn't have hot, wild sex right now. Exercising the little self-control I had, I pulled away before it became impossible to stop.

"As much as I want to take you to bed, we have plans for tonight," I said. It was too important to cancel.

She crossed her arms and pouted. I laughed and gave her a brief kiss. There wasn't anything I would deny her but she had no idea what I had planned tonight. She would understand later.

"You're no fun," she said when I stood.

"Come on, I'll start the shower for you," I offered, pulling her to her feet. She looked tired.

We entered the bedroom we shared and I left her to rummage through her closet while I went into the adjoining bathroom to start her shower. I turned the taps and got the water temperature just right before I went back into the room. She was still standing in front of the closet with a frown I wanted to kiss away.

"Your shower is ready," I announced. She gave me a peck on the lips as she passed me on the way to the bathroom.

I lay down on the bed and gazed up at the white ceiling, thinking of how differently my life had veered off course since I had met Taylor.

And now I was making another big decision I had never thought I would. She made me want things I never thought I would. It was as simple as that.

When she finished her shower, my eyes went to the door as she opened it and stepped into the room with a towel wrapped around her body. I let my eyes sweep over her, taking in every beautiful curve—even the ones hidden by the small towel. I had her body memorized in my mind.

How was I supposed to resist her?

She gave me a seductive smile like she knew getting naked would be enough to derail my plans. I had to remind myself why I couldn't give in. *Damn it!*

"Out," she ordered. I let myself look at her for a few moments before I let out a frustrated sigh and got up.

"You're no fun," I repeated the words she had said earlier to me. She shook her head at me like she disagreed.

"I'll be out soon," she assured me just as I left the room, closing the door behind me.

She wasn't one of those girls who took forever to get ready. Just twenty minutes later she walked out.

"You're so hot," I murmured, knowing exactly how I would undress her later as my eyes trailed down her body suggestively.

"Don't look at me like that," she warned me but I couldn't stop the way my eyes drifted over her.

This time I wasn't strong enough to resist. I pulled her to me and held her hips. Just as I leaned closer, she moved her face and my lips landed on her cheek.

"We need to leave now or we'll be late." She stepped

away from me.

She had me wrapped around her finger. I liked how she was more confident in herself and with me. She had come a long way from the naive virgin who had asked me to sleep with her. The memory brought a smile to my face.

I grabbed my keys and headed for the door.

"Is Jeff coming with us tonight?" she asked as she followed me.

"No. I'll be around so we don't need him tonight," I told her.

I opened the door for her and locked it behind us.

She hesitated for just a split second. She was feeling nervous. The only time she wasn't was when we were home. It was the one place she felt totally safe. I took her hand in mine and held it to remind her she had no reason to fear anything. I would keep her from harm.

Slowly I led her to the elevator. She shifted from one foot to another while we waited.

"Relax," I instructed.

"I'm good," she tried to reassure me but I knew her tell-tale signs that she wasn't. She didn't convince me even with the weak smile she gave me.

I put an arm around her and she leaned against me.

I had done everything I could to lessen the stress on her. Even going as far as putting pressure on Eric to do the right thing. Dragging it to trial and making Taylor relive it would only make it harder for her.

It had taken some pulling strings by Jeff to ensure Eric pleaded guilty. If he hadn't I would have done everything I could have to make him regret it. I didn't look at it as underhanded or illegal. To me it was just speeding things up.

It wasn't like Eric was doing 'hard' time. It hadn't taken them long to figure out that he wasn't mentally stable and his fascination for Taylor had started at the trial for her parents' murders. His uncle had been one of the guys who had committed the killings.

"You sure you're okay to go out? If you'd rather stay at home, I'll cancel our plans tonight," I offered her, studying her features because I knew she wouldn't admit how she was feeling inside.

"I'm fine," she assured me and breaking away from me, taking my hand in hers. When Taylor made up her mind there was no changing it so I got into the elevator with her.

I hid a secret smile. I had been planning this night for a while and now that it was about to happen I felt empowered. If anyone had told me I would be doing this before Taylor I would have told them they were crazy.

She had no idea what was going to happen tonight and it gave me a thrill of excitement.

She was quiet while I drove us to the bar where we were meeting our friends. No one except for two people knew what I was planning to do. I gave her a side glance but she was looking thoughtfully out the window. I reached over and placed my hand over hers. She looked at me and gave me a smile that made a warmth spread in my chest.

I hadn't recognized the feeling for what it was before, but now I knew what it was.

When we arrived, everyone was already seated at a table. I led Taylor to the table with a guiding hand on the small of her back. Slater and Jordan were sitting on opposite sides of the table. Now that I had found that special closeness with Taylor, I wanted the same for Slater. But he had to work through his own demons to do that, it wasn't something I could do for him.

For the last few weeks, he'd been going through some major stuff that I still couldn't wrap my mind around.

Then my eyes fell on Matthew, who was seated beside Jordan. It was all coming together. For me it was a decision I had made knowing that it was the right thing and I wanted it. Maybe that's why I didn't feel anxious like some people did when they were about to significantly change their life with one simple question.

"You made it," Jordan said when she stood up to give Taylor a hug.

I shook hands with Slater and then Matthew. Jordan released Taylor, and Slater hugged her.

"Good to see you," Slater murmured to Taylor. She smiled at him before she released him to direct her attention to Matthew.

"I'm so glad you made it," she said excitedly. He hugged her.

It had been a while since she had last seen him. He was working on a new assignment and that kept him pretty busy.

"I'm sorry I've been so busy with work. It's been hard to get time away," he said, releasing her.

"I'm going to get you a drink," I told Taylor. Everyone else already had one. Slater and I headed to the bar.

I gave the orders to the bartender before turning to my best friend. He had been away for five weeks. "How did it go?"

"I thought it would be so much easier but it's not." He let out an emotional breath.

"Is there anything I can do?" I asked, not wanting to see him go through this and knowing there was very little I could do about it.

He shook his head. "She needs time to come around."

He had discovered something recently that had spun his whole world off his axis and he was still trying to come to terms with it.

"How are things with Jordan?" I asked.

"Complicated."

It hadn't been that long since I had been in a similar

position with Taylor but we had sorted our shit out.

Our drinks arrived and we took them to the table. We were still missing one person but I knew he was on his way. I kept my eyes on the door and it wasn't long before I saw Connor step into the bar. He had impeccable timing. He headed straight for us.

"I have a surprise for you," I whispered to Taylor.

"What?" she asked, looking at me with those big blue eyes that made my heart skip a beat.

"Your surprise just walked into the bar," I revealed. She turned to see Connor walking toward us. She looked at him with surprise and confusion. When he reached our table, she got up to hug him.

"What are you doing here?" she asked, still sounding a little stunned.

It was nearly time. The only person missing was my mom but I was planning on taking Taylor to visit her the next day. The first time Taylor had met my mother it had been a tense and uncomfortable meeting. I think it was because Taylor still had some resentment for the woman who had failed me in so many ways. Their second meeting had gone slightly better, giving me hope that one day they would get along.

"You will have to ask your guy that question," Connor revealed, shaking my hand.

There wasn't much traditional about me but I had felt compelled to ask him for his permission to made my relationship with Taylor official.

He had been hesitant but after I had given him a speech about how much she had changed me for the better he had given me his blessing.

Connor sat down as Taylor turned to me for answers.

Now with all the attention on me, I felt a flutter of nervousness. With Taylor looking at me with a questioning gaze I took her hands into mine and squeezed them gently.

All my planning had led up to this moment.

"I have no idea if I'm doing this right or not," I admitted. "From the moment I met you, I knew you were going to change my life. I just had no idea how much."

I swallowed nervously, dropping my eyes to her smaller hands in mine.

"From the word go, I cared for you, but up until now I haven't been able to say the words to express just how much you mean to me." She had assured me it hadn't mattered.

She shook her head. "I don't need you to say the words. You make me feel loved."

I let out a deep breath, building myself up as I lifted my gaze to meet hers. Although we were surrounded by people, it felt like it was just the two of us in that moment.

"I love you." It had just taken me a little longer to realize it.

Her eyes widened slightly and her mouth opened. The familiar warmth that spread through my chest was the love I felt for her. Now I understood that.

"I love you." She wrapped her arms around my neck and pressed her lips to mine.

We kissed for a moment before I stopped. We weren't finished yet.

"There's more."

We weren't done yet. I was taking the biggest gamble of my life. She had no idea what was coming.

"I wanted to make sure our friends shared in the moment." Her eyes questioned mine.

"Realizing just how much you mean to me made the next step so much simpler," I explained, reaching for the small box in the pocket of my jeans. Her eyes followed my action but I could tell she still hadn't figured it out.

I bet she thought the guy who couldn't admit he loved her would never be able to give her more. Despite that, she had been content and happy.

I opened the box to her and her eyes focused on the beautiful ring I had picked out for her. It was simple but beautiful. I watched an array of emotions cross over her features. I saw the exact moment she realized what I was going to do and she gulped.

"I know exactly how I feel about you and I know you are it for me," I said to her as her eyes began to water. "Will you marry me?"

"Yes," she answered, no hesitation.

Feeling complete, like we had everything, I slid the ring onto her finger.

"I love you," she murmured to me when I pulled her close.

"I love you too," I whispered back, feeling freer than I ever had before.

I would make sure I told her every day how much she meant to me.

Then our bubble broke when our friends began to congratulate us. She glowed with happiness and I knew I had made the right decision for the both of us.

We didn't feel compelled to live our lives by the expectations of others. We lived our lives by our own needs and choices.

"I love you," I whispered to her, loving the way it made me feel when her eyes lit up when I said those three little words.

"I love you too."

My heart no longer beat in my chest. It belonged to her. And I wouldn't have it any other way.

About the Author

Regan is a South African who is married to an IT specialist. She is also mom to a daughter and son. She discovered the joy of writing at the tender age of twelve. Her first two novels were teen fiction romance. She then got sidetracked into the world of computer programming and travelled extensively visiting twenty-seven countries.

A few years ago after her son's birth she stayed home and took another trip into the world of writing. After writing nine stories on a free writing website, winning an award and becoming a featured writer the next step was to publish her stories.

If she isn't writing her next novel you will find her reading soppy romance novels, shopping like an adrenaline junkie or watching too much television.

Connect with Regan Ure at www.reganure.com